J. A. BERNSTEIN

RACHEL'S TOMB

a novel

New Issues Poetry & Prose

Western Michigan University
Kalamazoo, Michigan 49008

First American Edition, 2019.

ISBN-13: 978-1-936970-58-2

Library of Congress Cataloging-in-Publication Data:
Bernstein, J. A..
Rachel's Tomb/J. A. Bernstein
Library of Congress Control Number: 2018947278

Editor: Nancy Eimers
Managing Editor: Kimberly Kolbe
Layout Editor: Danielle Isaiah
Copy Editor: Danielle Isaiah
Art Direction: Nick Kuder
Cover Design: Lilee VandeZande
Production Manager: Paul Sizer
The Design Center, Gwen Frostic School of Art
College of Fine Arts
Western Michigan University

This book is the winner of the Association of Writers & Writing
Programs (AWP) Award for the Novel. AWP is a national, nonprofit
organization dedicated to serving American letters, writers, and
programs of writing.

Go to www.awpwriter.org for more information.

J. A. BERNSTEIN

RACHEL'S TOMB

a novel

NEW ISSUES

 WESTERN MICHIGAN UNIVERSITY

לדינה, שרה, נעמי, ואברם

So come, my friends, be not afraid
We are so lightly here
It is in love that we are made
In love we disappear

—Leonard Cohen, "Boogie Street"

PROLOGUE

In December of __, I was among some twenty Americans, all of us Jewish, to varying degrees, who had volunteered to fight for Israel. As I look back, it seems to me that we were fairly unique, the twenty of us, in that there wasn't a real fighter among us. A number had been taunted as kids, or had captained the debate team, and most bore the typical Jewish physique: scrawny build, curly hair, bad skin, etc. Some had worked out at gyms, but it hadn't much changed their temperaments. The irony is that when we found ourselves assigned to an infantry base, where we were to undergo basic training, alongside three hundred drafted Israelis, we were hardly alone in these traits.

Here it was, the vaunted Israeli Defense Forces, and barely anyone could do a dozen pushups, much less fire a gun. For better or for worse, I had endured summer camp as a boy in the northern woods of Wisconsin, where the gentiles taught me to shoot. In the

IDF, I was soon promoted to marksman, and I became as much an object of fascination among the Israelis as I had been among the gentiles at camp, where I had had to explain, however woefully, why I wasn't attending the Sunday morning worship in the lodge.

That December was a cold one, with a seemingly endless rain. We had just completed our training and were awaiting deployment to the line, so for one month we guarded a base in Neve Yaakov, a pine-studded settlement in Jerusalem's east half, which also housed Central Command. Ostensibly a general worked there, though we never saw the man. We simply blew on our hands, perched inside the steel lookouts, shivering away in the gloom. I imagined the conditions in solitary weren't much worse. About the only solace I had was books, which I read in secret beneath the dull glow of my phone. One was *Nine Stories* by Salinger, which I didn't much like, the other a tattered volume of poems by e.e. cummings, including my favorite, "the bigness of cannon":

> *I have seen all the silence*
> *full of vivid noiseless boys*
>
> *at Roupy*
> *i have seen*
> *between barrages,*
>
> *the night utter ripe unspeaking girls.*

War in the trenches was evidently different from this; we had lost one man to suicide already, and several more would be dead soon in Lebanon, but the war as we knew it was itinerant, more or less random, and completely without logic or cause. Men simply guarded, went on arrests, staged patrols or raids, and, as we were soon to discover, got shot in the head late at night, or while walking back from a bathroom, or carrying a carton of food. In Jenin, one man, a guy I disliked, took a mortar in the cheek while losing at *Halo 2*. No one shut the thing off for weeks. They just left it on pause, as if believing that he was frozen within the stalled screen.

Around the third week at Neve Yaakov, some artillerists arrived, and we were given a weekend leave. One of my platoonmates, Scott, a bulky teen from Connecticut, who had recently failed out of Bates, invited me to stay at his apartment in Jerusalem, for which his parents helped pay rent. I took him up on the offer, since I myself lived in an army-subsidized cell on a molding kibbutz thirty miles west of the city. Scott lived with another soldier, Mike, an American stoner who had also volunteered and, like him, was trying to get his life straight.

We were all planning to go out for drinks that evening and pick up some girls, which they seemed somewhat regularly to do. Not being the flirting type, I bowed out around five and headed over to the Kotel—or the Wall, as Americans call it—to try and find a meal. As any freeloading foreigner in Jerusalem knows, dozens of families congregate around the Western Wall after dusk, inviting upstanding youth—mostly dressed in jackets and hats—to join them in their homes for a warm Shabbat meal. Mainly it's a chance to preach to them or bring them into the fold, if they haven't been swayed enough already. Personally, I just missed my mother's warm matzo ball soup.

After making my peace at the Wall—*God, please don't kill me*—I loitered by the fountain, decked out in my service dress uniform and jacket, along with my emerald beret. The first man who approached me wore a typical Old City getup: pressed suit, wide hat, shiny galoshes, and a neatly trimmed beard, which he stroked occasionally while sizing up those he'd invite. He nodded to me and another, a Black Hat, mid-thirtyish, in a double-breasted suit, who might well have been homeless but had certainly dressed for the meal. "Mordechai," said the host, shaking our hands. Then he rushed us back through the dark, along the wet alley-stones, beside the flooding entrails and garbage of the souk. We climbed some winding steps, ascending what looked like a medieval grotto, until we arrived at the warmly lit cave. The door was ajar, and we could smell cumin, or nutmeg.

"Please, come in," he said in Hebrew, though inside, English was being spoken: a woman was screaming at her kids. The apartment was your typical, cramped, two-bedroom affair with slat shutters, cloth couches, and dozens of trays all covered in tin foil and softly ticking on heaters.

We all pressed around the table—twelve of us in total, like Christ at his supper. Mordechai mouthed prayers while his wife kept berating the kids, not all of whom, I gathered, were hers. A few other relatives glared at me. I pretended to nod along.

One girl, who had a striking young countenance, kept watching me from the end. She had a dimple in her chin, and a faint spark in her eyes that marked her as strangely adult. She was the only one who didn't sing—not the *brachot*, nor the hymns. Throughout the salad course, she didn't talk. She just looked at me guardedly, avoiding eye contact, it seemed.

"__—you said your name was __, yes?" Mordechai glanced at me from across the table, one hand hoisting a drumstick, the other pouring out schnapps. "I see you're serving in the Nahal," he said in English.

I nodded.

"The *Stick-Lights*," he said, referring to my glow-stick-colored beret, from which our brigade had acquired its nickname. "How long do you have left?"

"Twenty-two months."

"God-willing, he'll be safe," said his wife, a thick, pallid figure in a snood, who was feeding her youngest.

"You know, Daddy was in the Paratroopers," said the daughter, the first words she'd spoken that night.

"Esther," said the mother, somewhat scornfully, "Daddy doesn't talk about that."

I wasn't sure if she was challenging me with the comment, since the Paratroopers were more prestigious than the Nahal. It was also about the last thing I'd expect of her father, given his frail, business-suited frame.

Mordechai then explained, somewhat hesitantly, that he had come from Brooklyn as a teen, lived on a kibbutz up north, and only become religious after serving in "the war"—Lebanon, I presumed.

"He fought with valor," said the daughter. "He even has a medal—"

"Enough."

Mordechai kept pouring us schnapps while his wife kept feeding us food—mountains of chicken and fish, even the packaged carrot salad, which was soaked in brine and yet somehow tasted delicious. It must have gone well with the schnapps.

"Besides," Mordechai added, "the army was a lot different back then. We didn't evict other Jews." He must have been referring to the recent pullout from Gaza.

Beside him, the homeless man drunkenly grinned.

Before I was finished, Esther and some others excused themselves from the table. As she bounded off, I noticed that her body was changing—especially in the firming of her hips, which clung to her charcoal-gray, ankle-length skirt, and in the stiffening of her posture, which was better than that of most of my platoon at review. She had a certain grace to her, too, as she moved, that was well beyond her years and like something out of old movies.

Later, as Mordechai preached to us, alternately recounting

the *parshah* and explaining how the Gaza retreat was a sin, I watched her from the corner of my eye. She was reading to her sister, then helping her assemble some Legos, and I could see that she too occasionally looked back.

"So what did you do in the States?" Mordechai asked me, nearly interrupting himself.

I explained, with equal hesitancy, that I had been a writer, but growing frustrated with it, had decided to come overseas.

"Well, that's great. What kind of writer?"

"Fiction, I guess. But I shouldn't really call myself a writer. I've only been out of college a few years."

"Did you publish?" he asked me.

"Not much." That was always a sensitive topic.

"*I* write stories," Esther interjected from her place along the floor. "My teacher says they're really good. She says I'm a natural at it."

"Esther, honey," said her mother, gathering plates. "You should put your sister to sleep."

Esther sighed deeply. "She said *mine* were the best in the class."

"Well, I'm delighted to hear that," I said.

"What do you write about?" she asked me.

"Well, that's the problem. I don't really know."

"Maybe you could write about me." She smiled obliquely, through a trenchwork of braces.

"Esther, please put Miriam to bed."

As she did so, Mordechai began reciting more blessings, and the bum fell asleep in his chair.

Afterwards, Mordechai had Esther and his youngest accompany

me down to the Cardo. Grinning, she carried the child on her chest, its nervous legs kicking and flailing away within its snagged linen tights. "Miriam's tired," Esther said. "So tired now, she can't go to sleep. Mom said she needs some fresh air."

I slung my rifle behind me as we snaked through the alleys and down the dank steps to the lighted stone colonnade.

"Why did you come to the army?" she asked.

"You should ask your father that."

"*He* was religious."

"And I'm not?" I was still wearing my yarmulke, a synthetic white loner I had stolen from the box at the Wall.

She smiled. "Maybe you're an idealist. Or maybe you're romantic, like him."

"Romantic?"

"Romantic."

"That's a big word," I said. I guess it wasn't in Hebrew.

"Well, folks say I'm smart for my age."

A throng of fur hats jostled by us, dutifully trailed by their kids.

"I guess I can't shake your hand," I said, preparing to depart.

"No," she said sternly. The baby wheezed on her chest. "Can you—" she trailed off a bit, as if lost in thought. "Never mind."

I hitched my M4 up. "What?"

"This sounds silly, but my friend Devorah, she had a cousin who was in the Nahal, and he sent her a *stick-light* last year. It was really cool, but Rav Moshe took it away. He said it was *yetzer hara*." That means sinful, or lustful. "But I was thinking that maybe if you had one for me—"

"We don't really use those."

"Oh," she said, a bit dejected. The floodlamps outlined her sweater and blouse and brightened her ash-colored hair. I thought she was the most gorgeous child I had seen.

"I'll bring you one," I said.

"And write me a story, too."

Back at Scott's place, his roommate, Mike, was slumped along a couch, nursing a carton of Häagen-Dazs. On the end table beside him stood a carton of Pringles, which had been fashioned into a bong. Clad in sagging Knicks shorts and a *March* '__-emblem hoodie, he was simultaneously eating, picking out pot seeds, and sorting his dust-covered mail.

"You get any?" he mumbled.

"No." I seized a bottle of Mountain Dew from the fridge. "Where's the stud himself?"

"He done well for himself. Up at Hebrew U."

"At least it wasn't a Birthrighter."

"What's wrong with that?" Mike snapped.

"Hey, man, can I ask you a question?"

His eyes shone brilliantly red. "Yeah."

"Why did you come to the army?"

"Well, it sure as shit wasn't for the girls." He stuffed another bowl and offered it to me. "And I can't say I'm much into God. But you know, some things in life..." His words drifted off. "I guess they're like, how do you say it—"

"Ordained?"

"Ordained?"

"It means predetermined."

"Yeah," he said, lighting his bong.

Back on base the next night, I was holding down the two a.m. shift, which was always the most difficult, since it was painfully cold, and you had to stay awake until dawn. A misty rain had passed over, and my toes were burning sharply, the rubber soles of my boots nearly frozen to the serrated steel floor of the lookout. I tried to distract myself with cummings, and my breath hovered over the book:

> the bigness of cannon
> is skilful,
>
> but i have seen
> death's clever enormous voice which hides in a fragility
> of poppies. . . .

Beyond my steel ledge, a quiet moon sliced through a stand of Aleppos, igniting a barbed wire fence. A few car alarms echoed, somewhere far off, and a *jobnik* was blasting his Trance.

At around four, just as the base had finally grown quiet, a yellow light flashed through the pines. Then a Humvee ground up along the mud fence path, shaking the stairs to my booth. My First Sergeant popped out. He mounted the steps and handed me a warm cup of tea. It must have been three-quarters sugar but tasted incredibly good.

Clutching his handheld, his boonie cap beaded with rain, he surveyed the walls, which were strewn with graffiti, and said, "Make sure you stay awake."

It was hard to imagine why at this outpost, unlike others we'd see. Meanwhile, I was still holding the book in my jacket, hoping it wouldn't fall out. Men had been sentenced for less.

"You need anything?" he asked obligatorily.

"Yeah. You wouldn't happen to have a glow-stick, would

you?"

He did a double-take. "What?"

I said it again, this time in English. My accent was never great.

"What the hell for?"

"I said I'd bring one for a friend."

His brows crinkled sharply. "Go to a fucking store."

As he barreled down the steps, two at a time, I heard him whisper—rather loudly, it seemed—"I hope you don't want it to read."

The next morning, when I was woken for my ten o'clock shift, I found, atop my trunk, in the eight-person trailer that comprised our crude barracks, a tiny green glow-stick, sealed in a package, along with a cold cup of tea.

Two weeks later, our company left for the line. We spent a week in Jenin, then toured the central West Bank, mainly in and around Bethlehem. I didn't get back to Jerusalem much, and when I did, I forgot to bring the damn light.

The rest of the story is hard to relate. You remember that guy Mike, the stoner? He was shot in the head at a town called Ayta ash Shab. This was during the Second Lebanon War, where the army was deeply engaged. The Armored Corps got it the worst. They were sitting ducks inside the Mark IV's, which weren't even close to thick enough to take on the Kornets, much less the RPG-29's. You might have seen the videos. I remember thinking each time one of those metal boxes imploded, there were people inside of them, though you couldn't really tell. I saw the clips on the news, though that was weeks later, by which point we had returned.

Mike's company was told to secure the Litani, which was a

stupid idea from the start, since it was swimming with rockets and the air protection was sparse. They couldn't even bring the tanks—because of the mines. And time was running short near the end. Apparently, we had to withdraw. I won't go into the politics of the conflict—whether it was right to invade or not. I will say this, though: it was actually my former First Sergeant—you remember the one who brought me the tea?—who was driving along the border of Shtula one morning—it was about ten o'clock—when a set of prepositioned explosives blew out the front of his Humvee. He didn't feel a thing, I later learned. Two more were kidnapped from the Humvee ahead of his, and that's why the incursion began.

Again, whether it was right or not, I cannot say. As Orwell once put it, talking about his service in Spain, "People forget that a soldier anywhere near the front line is usually too hungry, or frightened, or cold, or, above all, too tired to bother about the political origins of the war."

It's nine-thirty at night at Ben Gurion Airport, twelve miles south of Tel Aviv. It's mid-October; a gauzy sky looms through the glass. Inside the third terminal, beside an abandoned Air France desk and hundreds of unpeopled seats, an Ethiopian woman vacuums, then fixes her snood, then vacuums, and the tile floor glistens in the cool light of dusk. Near the back of this waiting area, bent forward, with his head in his hand, a young man is nervously pinching a cigarette. He has contemplated lighting it but knows he cannot.

He hasn't slept in weeks.

He focuses briefly on the shadows beside him. An incoming plane touches down. Two weeks ago, he realizes, he would have rolled over and covered his ears with his hands. But he doesn't now, grinning, twisting the seal on his Reds.

At his feet sit two hulking green duffel bags, one stolen from the army, the other recently bought. This is the whole of his possessions. He wears ripped jeans, a white t-shirt, and a battalion-marked, green, wrinkled fleece, which he was awarded, along with the rest of his draft group, during his initial tour. He'll wear it proudly in the States, he knows. But in Israel it doesn't mean shit. Then again, he realizes, he'll bury the thing in his bag, house it in his basement, and never look at it again. He tries not to think about Mike. He never really knew the guy—but strange things happen in war. You become attached to those you have lost—more than those you still know.

The soldier, or the former soldier, that is—he was discharged last week—is heading home to Chicago, where he'll try to make a new start. His parents think he's been working on a kibbutz. They know not a thing of his service, nor does anyone else. This was less by choice than decree, since he knew his mother would worry herself endlessly, and if he died, well, he wouldn't have had to deal with her then.

He wrote a farewell letter once, which he sealed in plastic the night before the Lebanon War, and mailed it to Scott and Mike's, since he figured at least one of them would return. The letter said, among other things, *I love you, Mom, I love you, Dad, I'm sorry I didn't tell the truth. But I've never been very good at that, anyways. And I hope you'll understand.*

He knew that they wouldn't have, and they wouldn't now if he tried to explain where he was.

Near the front of the terminal, a bar television glimmers. The bar itself is empty, minus a squeegee or two, and the screen shows some news: the IDF Chief of Staff is under fire. Apparently, the war was waged erroneously. Too many souls were lost. The former pilot looks somewhat defensive, angrily waving his thumb, while the blonde interviewer grills him. Then the news shows old footage of soldiers returning from war, marching over the border with Lebanon. It's late at night, mid-August, and he recognizes the men from his brigade. He can't see his company, but he notices the light-green berets, which their brigadier, a self-seeking leech of a man, insisted they put on. He rises and tries to find himself. Then the news flips to images of exploding Merkava tanks. For the first time, he feels sorry for the men inside of them.

Still stewing over the berets, he recalls the word *stick-light*—a word he hasn't heard in months—and remembers that he probably has one in his bag.

He scours his belongings, dumping his clothes on the floor. The Ethiopian woman watches him warily. She has probably seen worse in this place. Then he searches the second bag, digging through journals, pay stubs, faded IDs, phone bills he's never paid, until he comes up with the glow-stick, which somehow managed to clear security. It has never been used before, and he stowed it inside of a sock—a torn one he meant to discard.

He zips his duffels and sprints along the waxed hall.

During the cab-ride into Jerusalem, between the mountains that straddle Route One, he watches a thin sliver of moon pass through the clouds and light up Givat Shaul Cemetery. Mike is out at Mt. Herzl. He'd visited a few weeks before, and the place looked decrepit: row upon row of shaved limestone, all the same squat, chiseled squares. *Who would want to be buried in a place like this?* he thought. As he stood over the grave, which was heaped up with flowers and shoulder-tags soldiers had left, he tried not to shed any tears. And he didn't really. He thought he just wanted a drink.

Tonight, though, driving past a different cemetery, beneath this thin shell of a moon, watching the mists funnel over the pines of Har Nof and its endless blankets of sage, he starts to sob a bit.

For what he doesn't know. Probably not Mike, he knows.

Outside Zion Gate, he tips the cab driver well, only realizing after that he has twenty-six sheks to his name. He'll have to spend the night at a hostel, maybe one of the religious ones, which are proselytizing but clean. He's already phoned up the airline and changed the flight, despite the enormous fee.

Inside the Old City, he winds through the souk's arching maze, hefting his bags, inhaling the traces of lamb meat and garbage, the thuribles scented with myrrh.

No lights are on in the apartment. It's close to eleven, he sees. He thinks about affixing the stick to the mezuzah, or smearing it over the doorpost, like some alien's blood. Instead he knocks gently. Then hard.

Finally, Mordechai answers the door in his bathrobe, frazzled-looking, angry, it seems. His beard has since grayed. "Who are you?" he asks beneath the locked door-guard.

"You don't remember me, I guess. I was here two years ago. Three, perhaps. Look, I'm sorry to bother you, but I have something for your daughter."

"My daughter? Which one?" Mordechai eyes him appraisingly.

"Esther."

"What do you want with Esther?"

"I just have something for her."

"Esther's away at boarding school." Then he surveys his living room, as if contemplating letting him in. He probably has dozens of such requests every month from people who have dined at his home. "I'm sorry," he says. "I have to go now. I wish you luck in your life."

"Wait," I say, putting on my fleece.

Mordechai eyes the thin emblem of Nahal—the half-sickle and sword—and says, "Oh yeah, you're the writer. I remember you."

I nod gently.

He does as well. "So what the hell do you want?"

I sift through my bags and pull out the glow-stick. "Do you think you could give her this?"

Mordechai eyes me appraisingly again. "A *stick-light*?" he asks me.

"You bet."

That night, I slept outside the Old City in a hostel by Damascus Gate. The place was owned by Arabs, but the price was much cheaper, and for some reason I fell asleep.

Dear Esther,

I doubt you remember me. We met about ten years ago when I dined at your parents' home in Jerusalem. Please excuse me for finding your address—or what I hope is your address. I know it must seem bizarre to hear from someone you only encountered momentarily. But I wanted to tell you that I've finally finished the story I promised to write for you. I'm afraid it's gotten rather long. I make no excuses for that. It's about a platoon of soldiers serving at the Rachel's Tomb Checkpoint, near Bethlehem. That's where I also served, as it were, shortly after I left you. I'm sure this contains numerous falsehoods, like everything else that I write, though most of the characters in it are real and, in some cases, based on people I knew. Forgive me for abridging it in places. It doesn't really have the structure of a novel, nor a group of short stories for that matter. I'm not even sure what to call it—fiction or non— though it's the truest account I could give.

Yours faithfully,

—

P.S. I hope you got the glow-stick I left.

1 SHAUL

Lt. Shaul Braverman had, when I knew him, a somewhat raggedy appearance: stubbly chin, ear-length brown hair—both of which were contra-regulation—and heavy-lidded, icy, blue eyes, which looked out with dismay on the world. His uniform, which barely contained his muscled arms, stood threadbare in places, ash-covered in others. The pockets needed buttons, and the trousers, like him, smelled of smoke. One might have called him good-looking, had he showered the past week.

One evening, a Friday, shortly before dusk, he was standing beside a toilet in an Ottoman home that comprised the south end of his base.

What kind of motherfucker would leave a helmet here, Shaul wondered, as he lowered his hand to the seat. He was debating whether or not he should touch the white bowl or the mesh-covered helmet beside it. Both were looking wet and slightly dank in the light, and someone had missed in the corner. He opted for the helmet, pinching its strap, holding it up with his fingers. Then he lifted the seat with the heel of his boot and examined the base of the helmet. No name was detectable, at least that he saw, though he knew it belonged to his soldiers. There weren't any extras to go around on this base, and someone would have to come claim it. Someone would need it for the mission tonight. He wiped off the seat with its net.

He scrubbed off a chunk of brown crust near the back, smearing it up into the lining. And the mesh lining worked well, replacing the smudge with a shiny white porcelain finish. He wondered which one of them would wear this thing now. He was hoping for one of the Russians.

The light filtered in through the boards on the window, piercing at Shaul's eyelids. He sat down on the bowl and lit up a smoke—a Camel he had stolen from his sergeant. Then he eyed the chipped walls of this seized Arab home. Not a bad site for his throne.

He was sitting in the commanders' bathroom of the Rachel's Tomb Outpost, of which he was commanding officer. This bowl belonged to him and his four NCO's, though he had deigned to share it with soldiers. Why, he didn't know. Perhaps he was nice. Somehow they'd clogged up their own one downstairs. And he shouldn't have let them use this, his Seat of Command, because his soldiers had begun disturbing his privacy. Not to mention his sleep, of which he got little. Maybe four hours a night on a good one.

Shaul looked at his boots and the sparkling mesh, both bathed in a swath of pink sunlight. The name "Boaz," he could see, was markered along the band, and the chinstrap said "Death to all Arabs." Shaul found this telling, because Boaz was an Arab. Or at least he was born to two Moroccans.

"Shaul, you done yet?"

Call me sir, motherfucker, is what Shaul wanted to say to his shiny-booted, nasal-voiced sergeant. Pinchas, or Penis, as they called him, hailed from Efrat, a nearby settlement, where his parents had moved from Johannesburg. He was also astonishingly haughty for a man who'd just been promoted to squad leader. He'd been sent to this base about seven weeks back and introduced himself then as religious. He had stopped wearing skullcaps—they had matched his fatigues—because someone had said they looked gay. But he still had that smirk and that arch tone of voice and that sureness with which he commanded. Shaul envied that about Pinchas, and he wanted that smirk, and he thought about donning a skullcap. "Not yet."

As Shaul sat forward and leaned to his boots, he examined the green bulk of netting. He dipped out his smoke in the puddle beside it and twisted his ash in the lining. There was fur in there and some kind of crud, which he wincingly smelled through the singeing. On the back of the helmet was a painted white box, which denoted an ordinary soldier.

Shaul's had a triangle: an officer in war. And yet he wondered why he didn't have paper. They never did on base, not even at Command. This was how he knew he was in Israel. In the Marines, they had cushions; in China, dead hands; in Israel, they wiped with the pavement. Fortunately, Shaul had planned for this event. Hanging from the sink was his vestpack. In the frontal flap pocket, he kept a bundle of napkins, which he'd stolen one time from a restaurant. They were fine linen things—embroidered in gold—and too good to be used on a seat lid. In fact, he dimly recalled the meal where he'd stolen them. It was about a year back, with his folks.

"I don't understand," Shaul asked his mother. "What the fuck is wrong with shellfish?"

"It's not that there's anything wrong with it," she said. "It's just that you're not allowed to eat it."

"Why?"

"Because it's not kosher."

"Since when do you believe in God?"

"Recently."

They were sitting in a restaurant called J.R.'s. It was the fanciest location in Jerusalem, and they were celebrating his mother's new book deal. She had edited a collection called *Authors for Peace*, promoting "reconciliation and dialogue"—which Shaul found ironic, because the last time he was home on leave, his mother had hit him with a spatula. His father, for his part, was now studying the English menu, unsure of what they meant by "crustacean." It was obvious the place wasn't meant for Israelis, as they were the only ones here. And with the glass chandelier and crowd moldings above, it resembled some seedy French brothel.

"I don't see why we can't get the shrimp," Shaul said, knowing his pleading was useless.

"Because you're a Jew," she said. "Would you eat pork if they brought it?"

"Yeah, I think I would."

Ten minutes later, the shrimp was brought out: six legs sticking up from a metal cup.

"I'm glad they didn't have pork," sighed his father.

"Why not?" she groaned. "You can have it."

Shaul wondered how his parents were going to pay for this meal. His father made his cash picking melons. His mother's parents had money, back in the States, but they refused to send it on to this country. And his mother's new book, which had finally come out—and for which she should thank all the terrorists—was not going to sell. Not in this place. Though she had managed to make rounds on the circuit: the six o'clock news, then the eleven. Last weekend, she'd talked at his high school.

Shaul touched the plate with the spindly pink shrimp and his mother pushed it back with her thumb. "No."

"What do you mean, *no?*"

"It belongs to your father."

"I ordered it."

"No, he did." She smirked beneath a fringe of red hair. "If you want some, you ask his permission."

Shaul had stopped trying to figure out his mother; this latest had to do with possession. She insisted that everything that one owned or might have was considered to be personal property. This, of course, was her revolt against their kibbutz. Recently, the place had gone private. And Shaul's father had supported it. He said he worked hard and would do better if everyone were held accountable—which his mother had protested, or initially ignored. These days she appeared to be mocking him.

"Dad, can I have shrimp?"

"No," he replied. "Apparently your mom will not let you."

Sometimes Shaul wanted to stay in the army. The meat there was warm and abundant. And he could deal with his soldiers— their ceaseless complaints—and close his eyes to their bickering. There, all they'd complain about is which weapons they were assigned or who was being forced to stand guard. And Shaul wouldn't have to explain anything. He'd just tell them: *you do what I say.*

"Shaul, just eat it," his mother exclaimed. "I don't give a shit what you have."

A few tourists were looking from the tables around them, and Shaul acknowledged their glances. He didn't deserve this—not while on leave. For eighteen months, he'd trained in the desert. And his mother didn't even say she was glad when he returned. It was the unchanging part of her rhetoric.

That morning, she had picked him up from the bus with an egg salad sandwich and coffee. After that, they went home and she made him move chairs for the meeting she was hosting at noon. While their apartment was small—two peeling rooms—Ilana could squeeze them all in. The rest of them piled on the terrace outside, like some banjoed, Woodstock encampment.

Now the shrimp legs just sat there, beneath their three glares. Shaul wondered if the shrimp had a family. There looked to be several: two parents, four kids. One took a dip in the tartar.

"And so what are we supposed to do when the waiter comes back? Just tell him we're not gonna eat this?" asked his father.

"He's probably an Arab," said his mother.

"What do you mean, 'he's an Arab?'"

"Look, Shmuel. He's darker than Shuli." His mother was always concerned about his skin, that he was exposing his body to cancer.

"So, what are they gonna do? Toss the shrimp out?"

"No. One of them will probably eat it."

"How do you know?" his father said. "Maybe they won't. Maybe the Arabs keep kosher."

"Actually, they do, in a way. The laws of halal are quite parallel."

She talked for a few minutes about Arabs and shrimp, and Shaul got up for the bathroom. He took out his glass piece and smoked a quick bowl in a stall that had an overhead window. Returning to the sinks, he rinsed out his mouth and noticed the monogrammed napkins. He pocketed a few—there was no one else around—and stashed a few more in his chinos. He would need them for base, where they never had paper or anything useful to wipe with. And his parents, for whatever reason, had refused to buy him things that the army was supposed to provide him—except sun lotion.

Back at the table, his mother was still yapping about Muslims and pigs, how their diets were no different than "ours" were. The same, she said, was true of their culture. They valued their families and home-lives.

"Dad," Shaul said, when his mother finally stopped, "Did you fix up the shop for your studio?" His father would occasionally dabble in wood, carving up downed limbs of cedar. And his sculptures were beautiful—the two in their home—though Shaul hadn't seen any new ones. He kept them stowed away in his private workshop, which is where he spent all his free time.

"No. I still need the tracks. The lighting isn't right on the overhead."

"Can I see them tomorrow?"

"What?" asked his father.

"You know, the ones that you've been working on recently?"

"No."

"Why not?" Shaul asked, though he knew better than to ask.

"Because they're my private collection."

"I was just thinking—"

"No," snapped his mother. "That gallery's closed to the public."

His father snarled and banded his hair. He signaled the girl with water.

His father wore a ponytail at age fifty-six, which was weird, because it hadn't yet grayed. His beard had filled into an immaculate white, though the back of him looked a bit skunkish. Still, Shaul wondered how his father had ended up with his mother, whom, he thought, was less striking. It wasn't her age or her face or her weight, but the ugliness with which she would talk: the way she braced forward and spoke with her lips, like two sandbags laid out on a tank hull. His father said nothing. The man barely spoke, but something about that was more honest. In fact, Shaul didn't even look down on his father for having chosen not to fight in the army. It was his personal choice not to serve in the wars. He just didn't believe in the effort.

The waiter brought wine, the cheapest on the list, and worse than the gunk in the army. It wasn't even kosher. Shaul studied the label, which denoted Australia and depicted a small hopping rodent.

"So listen," said his mother, adjusting her dress, a sleeveless black number from Zara. She had actually purchased the dress with the mall-issued coupons the army had sent him for *Pesach*. "I'm going in a couple weeks to a human rights rally in Ramallah."

His father was sniffing the end of the cork and trying to interpret the label.

"And we need to bring people, you know, some more Jews. I couldn't get enough at the meeting. So I want you to tell some of those guys that you're with and ask if their parents would join us."

"What?" Shaul asked.

"You know, the guys that you're leading. I tried sending emails, but the internet's down. Those idiots haven't figured out our account yet."

"You want me to tell the men in my platoon?"

"Yeah, just have them tell their parents it's that Thursday at six. We'll meet at the Qalandia Checkpoint."

"You've got to be joking."

"No," said his father. "I don't see what the big deal is."

"I'm not gonna say that my mom's against war."

"They already know who she is, Shuli."

"I don't think so. I seriously hope not. Not everyone has a television."

"Well, listen, Lieutenant." His mother looked him down. "If you're not gonna tell them, fine. But I need to bring people—you and your dad. And I thought it'd be nice to get others. Okay?"

"Okay. If you want, I'll go with. But I'm not gonna talk to

my soldiers."

"I've already got one. He's a friend from your school. And we might get a couple of pilots."

"Pilots?" Shaul's father looked up from his blond glass of wine and the blonde mane of hair he watched through it.

"Uh-huh."

"They're arrogant fucks."

"What difference does it make? They're respected."

Shmuel snorted. Then he unclasped his bolo, the one tie he owned. "Why, cause they like to bomb kids?"

"Look, Shmuel, we have to have somebody there besides all the peace-loving hippies."

"I'm sure you have friends, Lan."

His mother sneered, and his father set his tie on the table.

The dinner was painful but mercifully quick. The waitstaff knew they were not tipping. Soon, the dessert was brought out—a gelatinous shape, much like they had in the army. Shaul poked with his fork on its glassy, green edge. Inside it: the seeds of a melon.

Later that night, back at their home, which was about fifteen kilometers west of Jerusalem, atop the Judaean Hills, on a kibbutz called Ma'ale HaHamisha, Shaul went to visit his father's workshop. It was in the base of a three-story, crumbling, stone blockhouse that was set back high along a ridge. Flanked by tall Atlas cedars and Calabrian pines, all steeped in the night's glowing mist, it overlooked the fields at the base of the kibbutz, where Arabs had attacked in the forties. Dozens had died defending this lookout, and his father had turned it into his rec room. Of course, the doors had been padlocked, the embrasures lined shut, and Shaul dodged mudslides to get there.

He went alone, gripping his M4, which he was supposed to carry at all times. Plus the gun came in handy for excursions like this—and who knew what lurked in the woods.

He slammed his gun against the door's chained lock and some plastic chipped off of his buttstock. A few glinting creatures—greater mouse-eared bats—came screeching up out of the crenels. Undaunted, he kicked the steel door a few times with his boot and rammed the rotting hinge till it gave.

Inside, the blockhouse was musty and dark, but a bluish light dotted a ladder in back. He felt along the walls and failed to find a switch. Then he remembered his barrel-fixed Maglite. And he didn't have a clip in, but he thought that was wise on the off chance his dad kept a woman.

Sweeping the interior, as if on a raid, he discovered that his light barely shone. But towards the back, through the haze, he could make out some tall wooden shelves. They smelled faintly of varnish, or turpentine, pot—whatever his father had been doing.

Feeling a light nick on his neck, Shaul pulled down a chain from the ceiling. The lights went on up, and what he then saw is something he'd always remember.

Shining all around him in brightly carved wood were tiny glazed statues of soldiers—like the kind for a chess set, perhaps a bit larger, standing on bases of plaster. There were hundreds of them, all carrying guns. A couple bore canteens or stretchers. And there were cases for chisels, rasps, gouges, and paint, and rows upon rows of small soldiers, all armed.

The hell? Shaul thought. The soldiers all appeared to be uniquely carved from some fine-grained wood, maybe linden, or pear. He picked up a figure, which was sticky and round. The man seemed to be carrying an Uzi, like in the Eighties.

Setting it back, he thought he saw writing beneath it. He flipped the man over, and sure enough, there it was in red-painted, bold stenciled letters: SHAUL.

The fuck? He picked up another and saw it said Shaul. All of them appeared to say Shaul. A few more were grouped in a fighting position, aligned behind a wood tank.

Then he noticed a chair, which held a newspaper stack. Beneath it, he thought he saw photos. Lifting the stack, he unearthed a stash of VHS tapes and Dutch porn mags. This didn't surprise him. Shaul knew his father well. He had chosen to cut off the internet. He had done this because he was addicted to porn, and his wife had threatened to leave him. But what was this shit that was lining the shelves? Shaul was surrounded by three walls of soldiers in arms. There were other signs of life: a framed Coltrane poster, a crossword or two. Then an army of miniature Shauls.

In a way, Shaul thought, these statues looked nice. He was also impressed by his father, though he didn't understand why he'd bother to come and spend all his time on these carvings. Maybe he was building a reenactment of sorts, but of what, or for whom, wasn't clear.

Of course, it might have been his father, a Dachau survivor who'd somehow emerged from a death march unscathed. Newly settled, he'd signed up to fight in the Harel Brigade and widowed his wife at Latrun. Shaul was actually named for the man, and a few pictures haunted the walls of their home.

A bit spooked, Shaul pulled the lights and tromped back out to the rain.

Dimly, he sized up the door he'd dislodged. He tried to hook it back in its frame. But the base was unset and still edging out. He'd have to come back and repair it.

He rose the next morning, waking at six. His father slept late on the Sabbath. Shaul retrieved a few tools from inside the workshop and soldered the bolts to the panel. Somehow it worked, and the door looked untouched. But he immediately thought he'd regret it. He wouldn't tell his father that he discovered his stash. The pornos, Shaul thought, were irrelevant. But he wouldn't tell his father about the soldiers he found. The two of them would never discuss it. There wasn't any point, and nothing to be said, now that the door was reattached to its hinges.

He didn't really think he would die tonight. There wasn't much chance of that. Nonetheless, as Shaul lay along his cot in the officers' quarters of the Rachel's Tomb Outpost in Bethlehem, unaccompanied by his four subordinates, he thought he should phone up his parents. He had nothing to tell them.

A burning cigarette in one hand, his polished rifle in the other, he dimly gazed up at the ceiling—what was technically a dome precariously set on four squinches. The dome itself was plaster-faced, sagging, and unlikely to survive a full war, though somehow it had managed to make it through two or three centuries.

This room, which comprised the ground floor of a two-story, limestone-brick, moss-smelling manor, had been seized, along with the Tomb's near surroundings, several years back in an effort to buttress the fort. Now it housed the officers' quarters. A few faded tiles bearing Ottoman inscriptions lined the stone arches above. He tried to read them, but the inscriptions were Turkish and filmed with a layer of dust. One, he'd been told, said, "The Eye of God is on those who fear Him," of which he had little doubt.

He fingered the bright phone and decided not to call. And maybe it was a bane. Besides, it was almost eight o'clock. The food was set out. It was time to get his men up for the family meal.

Every Friday night at Rachel's Tomb, they'd have a family meal. Actually it was just the men in his platoon. But to Shaul, it seemed like a family, because they all hated each other and looked forward to venting at dinner. His soldiers would pile around a brown folding table, whose cholent he could smell through the curtains that divided his quarters from the neighboring hall. And frankly it was beneath him to sit with his men. Sometimes their shoulders would touch him. But it was only once a week and important for his men to see that their leader was human.

Tonight at the dinner, they'd have to discuss what happened last week at the checkpoint. This was the time when his soldiers could talk face-to-face as comrades and soldiers. And yet the dinner always took on this peculiar formality. His soldiers would wear their berets. Those who had yarmulkes—mainly Sgt. Pinchas, and Uri, a marksman—would preside with their bogus authority. But Shaul was the leader, and the ceremonial mom, and the one who would spoon out the cholent. He'd field their complaints, and look them in the eyes, and they would know where their sustenance came from.

There were regulations in the army that required giving food. And six hours of sleep was now mandated. Of course, if there was ever another war, which he knew there'd be, the soldiers would be at his disposal. And Shaul was looking forward to the one that would come, since he was creating a personal army.

But there was still the whole problem of what he'd say to his folks, they who spent weekends at protests. His mother was a Marxist. Or something like that. She went to the rallies with "comrades." And what was a comrade? She didn't even fight. His father had seen his share of the battles. But the man wasn't in them. He'd served the rear line, fixing up treads on the tanks.

And it was different here anyways, here in this war. The enemy was not immediately obvious. They weren't even Arabs, from what Shaul had seen. They were something altogether unnatural. They came with glass bottles, pipe bombs, and smoke. They hurled cement blocks from the rooftops and graves. And he never saw faces—only their acts, as if they were circling around him in flashes, fleeting. And they weren't even human. Just faces of God, recurring spots of an Image. They came with their bricks, though, their fury and wrath, flitting around him in sandals.

According to the reports and the stares of his men, Shaul had fought off a terrorist. *Killed* him, apparently, from what the men said and what they had read in the papers. And when he came back to base, later that day, last weekend, on the eve of the Sabbath, his soldiers were staring with sharp, puzzled faces, identical to the one he had shot. They wanted to know how it felt to have ended a life, to have taken the soul of a person. And Shaul didn't tell them. He didn't even know. He wasn't even sure that he'd done it.

But he'd have to bring it up at the table tonight. In three hours, they were staging an ambush. It wasn't a real ambush. It was a routine patrol. And the chances of seeing combat were nil. They would hike through the fields and the tombs to the west and set up a watch till the morning. No one would come. The Arabs rarely did. Last week had been a freakish occurrence—assuming that they came, and that there were Arabs at his post, and that Shaul had fired his weapon.

According to the sheets and the evaluations he filled, his M4 had discharged seven rounds. One of them was lodged in some dead Arab flesh. The others were still unaccounted.

Loudly, a toilet bowl flushed, and Pinchas returned, wiping his hands on his pants. "Hey man, there's a helmet in the bathroom, and the net's all messed up."

"See if you can fix that."

"Okay."

Shaul hitched up his gun and parted the room's hanging curtains.

Outside, his platoon sergeant was checking the rounds of the men who'd transported their food, which had to be relayed on foot thrice-a-day from Company HQ, the neighboring base up the street. Four barrels were raised towards the tall cinder wall. A couple helmets glanced down at the cholent.

They were in the Control Room, the outpost's main hall, which doubled as their command hub and mess. It spanned a sloping passage between the matriarch's tomb and the Ottoman home where they slept. The hall featured a PlayStation, stacked radio equipment, and about a dozen carved statues of Christ. These were olivewood figures, which the soldiers had looted from a neighboring pilgrimage shop. What they were intended for, he didn't know. One of them guarded the meat.

"Dror," Shaul said, "Get the rest of the men. Tell them it's time for their food."

His platoon sergeant held his thumb in the breech of a gun while a soldier pulled back its charger. "You want Yossi to come?" his platoon sergeant asked, referring to their most problematic soldier. Then he told Ivan to cock it.

"Yeah, why not?" Shaul said. "He's on mission tonight. There's no reason he can't come to the table."

"But I think he's on the sick-list."

"I don't give a shit if he's bleeding." Shaul said this loudly so that the others, and Yossi downstairs in the basement, could hear. Lately they had thought he was being sympathetic to Yossi, which Shaul had a hard time denying. Yossi had summoned every possible excuse for avoiding his chores and the missions. And Shaul had not laid into his soldier quite yet, because Yossi was a friend of the Captain's. The two had grown up in Ashkelon together. The Captain was one of his neighbors. Plus, Yossi was black—an Ethiopian immigrant—and was supposed to be a "mark of diversity." He was somehow a model of how everyone served and everyone fought in the army. Which was bullshit, Shaul thought, but he didn't say a word, because the colonels had deemed that important.

And Yossi, for what it's worth, wasn't incompetent. In fact, he was a physical miracle. In training, he had set a new infantry record for running 2k with his gear. And while he did about a third of what Shaul said, he was probably the best shot in their unit. He was also a marksman, when he decided to shoot. Last Friday, he had frozen on duty. Since then, he'd stopped guarding, complained about chafing, or said he was "allergic to pollen."

"I think he's downstairs jerking off," added Ivan.

"Shut the fuck up," said the sergeant.

The rifle bolts clicked. Shaul returned to his bed. He tried to listen close through the flooring. He could hear his platoon sergeant clomp down with boots and flick on the lights to their bunk-room in the basement. A couple groans followed, a low, tonsilar noise. It was the same one Shaul had made as a private. He hated that sound when he heard it in soldiers. Sometimes he'd make it for Pinchas.

"Up. Ten minutes. All of you, out. I want you outside and shaved," said the platoon sergeant. "Where's Yossi?"

"He in the back," someone peeped.

"What the fuck is he doing?"

"He's crying."

"Why the fuck is he crying? You know what, I don't care. Tell him get dressed and to get all his shit here in order. Dinner's at twenty-hundred. I want everyone out and seated upstairs with berets. Get moving."

At 1959, the soldiers were seated, minus one spot on the benches.

"Where's Yossi?"

"I don't know," said Boaz, the Moroccan, grinning. Shaul

wasn't sure what would follow.

Then his platoon sergeant went crazy. Dror's lips jutted out and out sprang a full list of invectives. "If that little *kushi* is crying again, I'm gonna give him a new chamber to grease." Shaul usually listened with curiosity to these remarks; it was the one thing that sergeants could do right. But this time he didn't. Instead, he just stared at his platoon sergeant's cranial features. It was terrifying, in fact, how he looked glad when he was mad and pissed when he was actually pleased. It might have been the steroids. Shaul knew he liked to lift and had gone bald by the age of eleven.

His sergeant stood up, the way drill sergeants do, carefully and deliberately rising. The others arched back. Physically moved. Shaul had selected him personally.

And Dror's neck was massive. He was under six feet but had more hair on his arms than a wooly. He backed away from the table, carefully, slow, shuffling his heels to the basement. And Dror always shuffled. No one knew why. It was as if he were chained to the concrete. It was terrifying to watch, the way that he moved. Even Jesus looked on in pure horror.

The basement door slammed and Dror shuffled in, clopping his boots on the steps. "Up." What followed was an exchange that Shaul couldn't hear and for which he wasn't feeling ungrateful. He thought he heard crying, a few muffled sobs, a rifle butt slam on a kneecap or bed.

Thirty seconds later, his sergeant emerged from the dimly lit nook in the hall. He ascended the staircase, rifle in tow, and parked himself down at the table. "He'll be here in a second." Nobody moved. Behind them, the radio cheeped.

Then Yossi came out with his gun on his back, his shirt still untucked from his pants. His eyes were bright red and his head was hunched down. It looked as if he might have been sleeping.

Shaul didn't know if it was deliberate that Yossi was wearing his pants by his knees. But he walked with a strut and his beret tilted left, like some kind of American rapper.

What the fuck is he doing? the others must have thought. This would require a conference.

"Excuse me," Shaul said, as his sergeant stood up. Dror started smiling ecstatically.

Shaul figured this was probably his cue to save Yossi from the wrath that would invariably follow. What Sgt. Dror could do included a variety of things involving shit stains, a toothbrush, his pillow. And Yossi would be here for a month with that stunt, with the bulk of it spent in the kitchen. Of course, that would have been fine for Yossi himself, since he preferred it to going on missions.

"Dror," Shaul said, putting a hand on his back—a muscle that ripped like a talon. "Tell Yossi to come up and meet me in my room. I'll deal with this one personally."

Shaul passed through the hall, all eyes on his back, and parted his room's hanging curtains. He removed the guitar from the foot of his bed and heard his sergeant say, "Get the fuck in there."

"And tuck in your shirt," Sgt. Pinchas snapped. "Gun goes in front at all times. Fix it."

Normally, Shaul would have sent him to jail without even pausing his dinner. He'd be off of the base for disrespecting a commander. But with Yossi, it had to be different. If Yossi were gone, Shaul wouldn't make captain. They were doing evaluations next week. Plus, they didn't have enough men to stand guard on this base. About thirty out of fifty had dropped for non-combat. And that was about the expected attrition. But they had a couple more slots to be filled. They'd beefed up the posts since Liav had been hit, not that it would make any difference.

"Yossi, come in here." Shaul parted the drapes. His soldiers were eyeing the cholent.

Yossi loped in with his head facing down and his hands curled up in his pockets.

"What's wrong with you?"

"Lieutenant,"—Yossi was the only one who still called him "Lieutenant," which Shaul could not understand; he told all his soldiers—it was army procedure—to refer to him here by his first name—"I'm fine," Yossi said. "Just a little worn out."

"What's with the shit before dinner?"

Yossi was still staring down at his boots.

"Answer me, Yossi. I'm talking."

His soldier looked up with two glazed reddened eyes. "I don't know, Lieutenant. I was tired, and I can't—"

"You know what, I don't even care. Here, come have a seat on my bed."

Shaul sat down on top of his duffel and pulled out a smoke from his shirt. He balanced his gun across the base of his knees with the barrel end pointed at Yossi. "You smoke?"

"I don't, Lieutenant." Shaul knew that he didn't but decided he was still going to ask. Outside, his platoon sergeant was barking at Ivan for having missed his stubble.

"Yossi, I want you to have a puff on my smoke. And I don't really care if it hurts."

"I don't—"

"I don't care," Shaul said, extending the Camel. "Take it." Yossi put the cigarette inside of his mouth—the wrong way, and Shaul corrected him. Shaul knew it wouldn't light now, so he broke off the tip and brushed off the spit on his pants.

"Here," Shaul said, handing him the filter. "Let's see if you can do it the right way." He wondered if he should be making some noises in here or start cracking his belt like a whip. "Take a deep breath, and pull through the back."

Shaul snapped the lighter, igniting a flame, and Yossi sucked air to his chest. He let out a cough, as Shaul had predicted, then he dropped the lit smoke on his pants. Shaul picked it up, brushed off the tip, and nestled the thing in his gums. "Listen to me, Yossi, I'll be frank with you. I've always liked you as a person. I think you're a good guy, a little confused, but that always seems to happen to soldiers. And what happened last week, with Liav at the blocks, well, I'm not really sure what went on. But I'll tell you this now, if it's because of that night, then I don't want you to have to endure this. If you can't take the army, that's fine. You can leave. I'll tell them it's because of your allergies." Shaul said this softly, which is the way that he spoke and found to be the most effective in leading.

"And if that isn't good enough, we'll think something up. In fact, I could get you a medal. If you want, we can say that you were injured last week or somehow were scarred by the bottle. I don't know. But we'll think something up. And you can leave here tonight. But I'm not gonna have you dogging. It'd be no embarrassment for you to have left the line. And I understand it's hard, what happened. We'll talk about it later, after the meal." Shaul knew they wouldn't discuss it. "But listen to me, Yossi." He took a long drag and thought that it tasted like *kushi*. "I want you to give me an answer right now. You're either in or you're out of the unit. No more excuses or bullshit tonight. If you want to go home, I'll arrange it."

Yossi knew he was bluffing. Of course he said "in," which Shaul had entirely expected. Shaul took another puff on the crackling smoke and offered it back to his soldier. Yossi declined, pushing it away, and Shaul stuck it in the kid's throat.

Yossi began laughing, as Shaul had expected. Then Shaul slapped him hard on the face. The slap stung his hand. Yossi looked up, fully shaken.

"If you're in my unit, I expect you to be tough. And that

means you will listen to orders. No more fucking around. You wear your pants at your waist. Now get, and go eat your dinner."

Shaul stood up. Yossi did not. Shaul thought about offering him a hand. He didn't. He turned to walk out and heard Yossi rise; his gun barrel clanked on the bed. Shaul didn't look back, but he heard the kid crying, coughing a bit with his throat. So he slowly reached down to his pack on the floor and pulled out two monogrammed napkins—two bent ones. He turned to look back, and Yossi was standing, reeling with hands on his waist.

He spewed out some throw-up, a whitish-green phlegm, that splattered the floor and a helmet. It was Boaz's helmet, by Pinchas's bed, and Shaul tried hard not to laugh. He walked over to Yossi, put a hand on his back, and said "here," as he held up the net.

They sat at the table, Shaul and his men. Yossi was seated beside him. Shaul thought about putting his arm around him, but that would require more cleaning. Instead he just smiled at his dandy black trooper, who had a look of demonic possession.

As Sgt. Pinchas finished blessing the challah and wine, Yossi stared down at the table. His face didn't move, and he didn't look sad, but Shaul couldn't guess what he was thinking. In fact, he never really knew what any of them were thinking when Pinchas said prayers at the table. Most were non-observant. A few were part-Christian. One was a Bedouin Muslim.

Thus far no one had spoken at the table, besides Pinchas invoking his spirits. So Shaul thought he'd start with a simple little topic. "Has anybody here talked to Orly?" Orly was the personal counselor for the base, a kind of social worker trained by the army. She came down to Rachel's Tomb at least twice in each month, mainly to help the new immigrants.

"I did," said Boaz, the Moroccan, hoisting a palm. Boaz was not a new immigrant. "She's coming next week, and I said to stop by. She's gonna spin my grogger. For Purim."

Shaul didn't know whether Orly was attractive or simply the only unveiled woman they saw. But for weeks at a time, she was their conception of what the female body looked like. She had thick, meaty arms and cumbersome breasts, which nearly emerged from her field-blouse's slits. The soldiers all knew every shade of her bras and the general order in which she would wear them. They could also recite every line that she wrote, because the others would study her clipboard. And she wasn't quite flirting so much as provoking when she told them, "It seems kind of hard here."

"—Yes," Shaul replied, since he would request his own sessions, alone in his room behind curtains. He'd strum his guitar, sing a few songs, and tell her his woes as commander.

Of course, Orly was taken, which Shaul now knew and would never reveal to the others. She kept all their hopes up just by coming each month. The sight of her justified guarding. And the reason Shaul knew that his mistress was taken is that he'd followed her once in his Jeep. He found her at the bus station—six kilometers north, in Jerusalem, with hands on a woman. It was an abominable sight, which he couldn't take. Her larger friend had a shaved head and piercings. And it was surprising, Shaul thought, because Orly was cute. Not like the ones at the protests.

"Are you kidding?" said Ivan, their medic, addressing the table. "She's greasier than a *bourekas*."

"You're just jealous," said Boaz, clapping his hands. "As if your pencil dick could arouse her."

Beside them, Yossi kept eyeing his plate, which mirrored his black, pointy chin. And he wasn't going to eat, so Shaul took his hand and set it on down in the cabbage. Then Yossi threw it off. Shaul thought this was good. The others stopped talking and watched.

"The reason I ask about Orly," Shaul said, "is that not all of us seem to be eating."

"Eat," said Shibli, the Bedouin soldier, who pointed his fork tines at Yossi. Of course, Shibli ate nothing besides *Bamba* and smokes and the occasional packet of Ramen. But as Arabs well knew, and Shibli above all, food was about more than just eating. It was an insult not to eat this—these three trays of meat with cholent and chicken and red fish. The scrod was sautéed in a vat's worth of oil and sprinkled with cumin and parsley. "This good," Shibli said. "What wrong, you no like? In Africa, you no fishing?"

"Fuck you," Yossi said, or seemed to imply by snarling his lip at the Bedouin.

The others returned to the food on their plates. They knew better than to worry about Yossi. They knew he was an issue and the number one problem. In the basement, he slept in the corner.

His soldiers talked some more about nothing in particular while pausing to chew challah and fish. They discussed a new bombing in Tel Aviv that week, which had ripped through a Promenade nightclub. And they talked about films—about ones they hadn't seen, but which featured good tit-shots or cleavage, evidently.

They went on for ten minutes, yapping from plates. Shaul leaned back from the table. He figured it was time to deliver the night's sermon, which he indicated by raising his barrel. "So," Shaul said, "we should probably talk about what happened last week at the checkpoint."

A shattering silence fell over the room. Ivan was forking his cholent. He stopped.

Shaul wondered if it was too late to retract the remark. It hung through the air like a bottle. Nobody moved, and nobody blinked, except Yossi, who picked at his cabbage.

"Well, the good news," said Shaul, searching for words, "is that Liav is coming back from Hadassah." The soldiers had sent him a get-well card, but nobody spoke of him much. He'd had some nerve tissue damaged along the base of his arm, but nothing to keep him off-base. "We should probably discuss what prompted the ordeal. You know, that whole thing with the bottle?"

His soldiers looked up: barren faces from plates. He still wasn't sure if they'd heard him.

"That was fun," said Ivan, the medic, thankfully breaking this silence. "I think we should do it again soon."

Somebody laughed then immediately stopped.

"What the fuck did you say?" said his platoon sergeant.

"Nothing," said Ivan, pursing his lips.

Shaul felt relieved by what the guy said. At least, it had lightened the mood some.

"Do forty," snapped Dror.

Ivan got up without saying a word and dropped to the floor by the table. He brushed off some challah crumbs, rolled up his sleeves, and counted off pushups in Russian.

"Anyone else got a comment?" his platoon sergeant barked.

Eight light green berets peered down in dismay from the table. Ivan's elbows kept creaking, a rickety noise, as if his joints had grown rusty since training. It was ridiculous, really, to make him get down. No one had done pushups since Basic.

Shaul thought about telling Ivan to stand so they could continue discussing the shooting. But Dror was still attending to his man on the floor, and Shaul didn't want to upstage him.

After a couple more seconds of ear-jerking creeks, Shaul repeated the question. Then he studied his squad leader, Pinchas, at the end, who was grinning and rubbing his hands. "Well," Pinchas said, "I wasn't there at the time, but I think I understand what went on. You guys just got scared. That kind of shit happens, especially your first time seeing combat." As if Pinchas had seen anything more than a couple of shots, which he'd fired one time as a warning—at children.

Yossi looked up from the side of his plate, as if he alone gathered the question. *What do you want me to say?* he seemed to imply by tilting his head to the ceiling.

"Keep going," Dror squawked at his man on the floor. Ivan's breathing was growing audibly louder. "Do sixty."

The other men shrugged or stared at their plates, ignoring what Pinchas had said.

"I'm sorry that I brought the issue up," Shaul said, "but I think we need to discuss it this evening."

"I don't know," Boaz said, shaking his head, as if he were still gauging the question. "We missed it."

"What?" Shaul said.

"We didn't shoot when we should have. I don't know how else to explain it."

Shaul nodded. Beside him, Sgt. Dror lifted his boot and set it on the neck of his soldier. Ivan's jawbone collapsed, smacking the floor. "*Cyka,*" he mumbled in Russian.

"I think it's just a matter of doing what you're told," Dror said, eyeing his victim. "Listening to orders, obeying commands— it's really just a matter of discipline."

Of course, Dror had been there, near the back of the tomb, and he hadn't rushed to the fighting. And Shaul had long suspected that Dror was afraid, which is why he signed on as a sergeant. It was a peculiar thing about sergeants—the big ones with fur who liked to lead men in their training. When it came to the field, they were quiet as mice and as useless as most of these soldiers.

"Well," Shaul said, as Ivan stood up, twitching his jaw like a gerbil, "I don't know what to tell you. If it happens again, we might all end up getting killed here. Who knows?"

"No," Boaz said with a determinant look. "That's not gonna happen to Aleph. I talked to the Battalion Commander last weekend, and I told him we're ready to fight now."

Last Friday, the soldiers had had a conference on-base, at Company HQ, a couple hours after the shooting. Shaul had listened through the trailer's slat window as the soldiers stood round in the office. The Colonel asked them what had happened, why nobody had shot. A couple men spoke or gave reasons—lame ones. And the Colonel was nice. He sat there and smiled. Then he said they would have to do better.

Afterwards, Shaul sat down with the man, along with five other commanders and listened as the Colonel explained that if it happened again, their whole company would go back to training. If it weren't for one leader—he pointed towards Shaul—their draft group would revisit Basic. And Shaul just sat there, at peace with himself, listening to words from the finger. As far as he knew, he wasn't even blamed. For some reason, the sergeants were scolded. And others. Which Shaul couldn't figure. But what did he care? He was well on his way to promotion.

As Shaul spooned out the rest of the meat for his men, he remembered to save some for the others. There were six who were guarding, six more on patrol, and two washing plates up at Company HQ. He had Pinchas set out plates with meat for each man, which he set on the bench by the gun oil. Eight rifles were leaned against the side of this bench, the guns of the men at the table. And it was probable, Shaul thought, that if anyone tried to steal from these plates, their first shots would be heard here in Bethlehem.

Shortly after dinner, and having dispatched his troops to their chores, Shaul sought a bit of solitude. Since his quarters were thronged and it was dangerous to go outside, he wasn't left with a whole lot of options, though he did have one place in mind.

He headed down the hall to Her Crypt. This was an ancient stone cenotaph, about the size of a Jeep, covered with silk, and housed away inside a pillar-lined, partitioned chamber. In the four and a half months that he'd been stationed at this outpost, Shaul had never gone in. This time he faced it and steadily approached its bright lights. Fortunately, none of the Black Hats were present; the Sabbath kept them away.

Squinting, he passed between two carved limestone pillars, each fronted with a cistern and vaguely resembling a cock, and down to Her arched inner chamber, where a chandelier hung from a dome. Beneath it, Her Mound was shrouded in a heavy blue mantle of lustrous velvet, which was richly figured in gold. Some ancient monument, undoubtedly. He wondered if Christ lay beneath.

Finally alone, Shaul dug out his phone and a tiny, creased photo from his wallet. It was a passport photo his girlfriend had taken last year. And the sight of her seized him, as it always did. She wore a sharp, puzzling grin. In fact, she looked like the Arab he had murdered last week by the checkpoint outside of this tomb.

After scanning the hall for any listeners, Shaul dialed, but she wasn't there. And he knew she wouldn't bother to answer his call. The woman had left him in August.

Besides, what would he say? *Guess what I did with my weekend?*

He tried to recall the last time that they'd spoken, when they'd gone for a hike in the woods. It was in the Galilee Forest, about seven months back, and they'd stopped to rest at a cliff.

It was a high escarpment of mastics and oak jutting out from the

Naftali Ridge. She was sketching the water: a far, blinking stream that threaded the south Hula Valley. They were five hundred meters up, possibly more, and the sunlight was bright on his face.

"I don't want to see you."

"What?" Shaul said.

"I don't think I can do this any longer." In jeans and a scarf, she was sitting cross-legged on a rock-face beside him, a spiral notebook and pencil in hand. And she looked almost monkish, still facing the valley, her hair blown about by the wind.

"*Shu?*" he said, meaning "what?" in Arabic.

"Don't give me *shu*," she said, turning to face him. The mascara ran from her eyes. "You know what the problem is."

"No."

"Take a wild guess."

"My mother?" he asked her.

"Honestly, it isn't her."

The past weekend, Shaul's mother had decided to make brunch. She had wanted to spend time "as a family." So he thought he'd bring his girlfriend. His parents knew who she was—and that she was Palestinian. He'd told them the first night that they'd met. And his father was polite—surprisingly nice. But his mother just sat there and sulked. She forced out a smile, a couple of shrill laughs, and shoveled out platefuls of salmon.

"The problem," said his girlfriend, sniffling a bit, wiping her tears with her scarf, "is that I see you three days a month. Less. And I'm risking my life to be with you. You know that, and you don't even care."

"I do." He started towards her. She pushed him back.

"If you gave a shit, you would call me. Or come. Or try to understand how I feel."

"But I took you hiking."

"That's fucking great. Maybe we could stop and have kids."

She zipped her fleece and she rose. "I've got to go, Shaul. I'm done with this stage. I'm ready to move on, and you know that. It's ridiculous that I'm still waiting for you, as if I were a little girl. Hell, you know the whole reason I came to this country was to marry somebody else."

"So maybe you should have."

"Maybe you should leave."

"I'm guessing you want a ride back."

"No," she said, rising. "I'll take a bus. And for your sake, I hope it blows up."

Her parents were Palestinian, but she was born in New York, where her father had served as Deputy Ambassador to the UN. Two years ago, he'd been called back, and he brought his daughter with him, intending to marry her off. She hadn't objected, at least initially, since she was twenty-eight and unwed. That didn't strike Shaul as terribly old, but for Arabs, that was near-death.

The first time Shaul met her was at a human rights rally in the West Bank town of Ramallah. It was the one to which his mother had dragged him, fittingly enough, he supposed.

That evening at the rally, which was in Ramallah's main square, a congested roundabout known as the Manara, he had slouched against a guardrail and smoked a full pack while his mother carried placards and posters. And his father was shitfaced, high on his life, his woodcutting, weed, or the aura and chanting. That's when it started: a couple of shoves. A little Arab boy ran with his fists up. More pushing ensued. Some police in blue vests held back some rowdy *shabaab*. A few rocks were thrown. A window was cracked. Others were screaming, "Death to Sharon!" And his mother in the center did not want to move. She kept waving her signs with the Arabs. They hugged. Shaul ran over and grabbed his father, who was watching the billboards above them.

"Let's go."

"We can't," said his father. "Your mother's engaged in the movement."

People were running: all madness and mess. A siren squeaked out through traffic. That's when Shaul felt it: a sharp jolt in his gut. Someone had punched his stomach. Beside him, the little boy was bent forward, cupping his fist. Then he ran off, giddily laughing. Shaul was keeled over, gasping for breath. The urchin had actually hit him. Shaul's father started swearing, "Ilana, let's go," but she was lost in the surge of the mob.

Pretty soon the crowd parted, and Israelis marched out with the Arabs, who held them in tow as they summoned the cabs. Shaul peered out at the buildings: a baker, a barber, brass *sahlab* dispensers, a cracked Arab Bank ATM, and all kinds of shit that was lining the road, dead animals hanging with parsley and plastics. He had to get out. His stomach still hurt, and that little fucker had knocked all his wind out. He didn't tell his mother, though, embarrassed as he was—two years to the day he'd enlisted.

As he hopped in the cab, along the ash-covered seat, something caught his eye through the window. She was standing in profile about five meters down inside a narrow, arched bookstore. Her brown hair was curly and tied at the back, though a single golden strand loosely fell to her cheek. Wearing a charcoal-gray wraparound sweater, tight jeans, and sleek, leather boots, she was skimming a paperback, biting her lip, indifferent to the maelstrom outside. She didn't look local; her figure was trim, and the book, he saw faintly, was by Edward Said. Plus, a small leather backpack was hitched to her arm and affixed with a button stamped FREE PALESTINE.

She turned. Her brown eyes quickly met his, widening a bit as she blinked. Then she smiled timidly, set down her book, and glanced all about the store.

He didn't know why, but he tapped on the glass, a quick little nick on the window. She didn't approach him, but she studied his face. Between them: a bustle of motion, pull-carts, and a stream of wide figures with sacks on their heads, all bursting with chard and *mulukhiyah*. He rolled down the window. The thing wouldn't roll. He reached for the door's rotted handle. It wiggled. Then he looked to the front where the driver was seated, discussing the fare with his mother. "I don't know," she explained, "to the Jalazone Checkpoint. If it's closed, you can go through al-Bireh. Don't stop."

Shaul looked out at the day's fading light: the streaks of gold, crimson and violet. A moon. Beneath it, the most beautiful woman that he'd ever seen was watching him with a grin. He banged on the door, pounded its glass, flung back the lock and the lever. It opened. Then the vehicle sped with his legs still inside. "I'm Shaul," he said through the window.

They drove to the Jalazone Point, where he showed his ID to the soldiers. They asked him: "What the fuck are you doing here?"

"I don't know," Shaul said. "My mother, she told me to come."

A couple of weeks later, Shaul went along to a protest up north near Jenin. Quite risky. It was suicide really, a Jew in that place. His mother was hardened and ready. She brought no signs, no placards or songs, only him and his father.

The town was called Ya'bad, a steep mountain village of slagheaps, goats, and chalked olives. The wadi was polluted, and the villagers reeked almost as much as their creatures. But he had the vague sense that his beloved would be there, intent, as she was, on freeing Palestine.

She was standing at the gates when his family arrived—grinding up in his father's old Chevy. They were forty minutes late, because they'd had to change a flat, and his father's S-10 had kept stalling. Her hands were dug inside a brown bomber jacket, and she was facing a couple of pilots—in t-shirts. An ex-classmate of his, Moshe, who was sporting a *kafiyyeh*, had evidently decided to bring them along at the behest of Shaul's mother.

Shaul wasn't sure what to say to the woman, so he went up to Moshe and said, "Hey there," ignoring her. He said it in English. It seemed a safe bet. But his ex-classmate responded, "*Keef haalek?*"—How are you? Shaul knew a bit of Arabic, had learned some in school, but not quite enough to converse. "*Qwayyes*"—all's good. Then the pilots started speaking in Arabic, as well, and the woman walked off through the field.

For a couple of hours, Shaul sat down and smoked on a ledge while his parents made a fence with the others and swayed. One played an oud, others tambourines. They were belting out Seeger's "We Shall Not Be Moved." And no one seemed to know her, this young woman who had come. She also hung back without singing.

The group marched along past the fetid ravine and a house that had recently been demolished. In its place stood block heaps and Rebar coils that clawed through the earth with a vengeance. It was an overcast day with long leaden clouds and a cool wind nipping the mountain. He sat on a block by the edge of the road and waited as the others trooped past him. And he knew he wouldn't greet or talk to her. For years he had encountered women he'd liked and not had the courage to speak with. He didn't like flirting or shooting it up. He didn't even know how to do it.

As the protesters faded, timbrels and all, beyond the ploughed ruins of a tiered olive grove, Shaul looked down at the rocks on the ground. Then he looked up at his beloved. She sat on the rock right next to his own, what might have been the stump of a kitchen, like granite. "I don't even know why we bothered to come. It's not like these protests are working," he told her. Then he realized he'd said it in Hebrew. "Uh, is no good," he said in English. "To come to dis place, is no work well in helping di Arabs." And it was embarrassing, really. He spoke better than that. His own mother had raised him to speak it.

She watched him with a muted expression. She was wearing sunglasses—huge tortoiseshell frames, which mirrored what was left of the sun.

"You understand English?"

"Yes." Looking down, she brushed off the dust from her jeans and tall boots. "That was you," she continued, "last month in the cab?"

"Yeah."

She folded the scarf on her neck. "You know, you can't just come into Ramallah like that and stare at a girl from a taxi."

"I didn't—"

"You know what they'd do there, if anyone saw?"

"Yeah," Shaul said.

She looked up. "They'd kill you," she said. "And probably me."

Shaul looked on without speaking.

"My name's Lina," she explained. "And I'm not a Jew."

"I'm Shaul." He smiled. "And I know."

It took him a couple seconds for the name to digest.

"I'm sorry, you said it was Ilana?"

"Lina."

"Ilana," he said, "is the name of my mom."

"*Lina* means 'tender,' or 'devoted.' It's Arabic."

"I see. And what do you do here?"

"I teach," Lina said.

"At a high school?"

"No, at a college."

"Which one?"

"It's called the Bezalel Academy, on the edge of Mount Scopus."

"I know it," he said. "You're an artist?"

"I'm trying."

"And where do you come from?"

"What?" she replied.

"I mean, where did you grow up?"

"I was born in Brooklyn. But my parents came there from Ramallah."

"Ramallah?"

"Yeah. A Palestinian girl. So watch what you do with your hands." She removed her sunglasses and glanced at the sky, adjusting a band on her head, a green one.

"Is that for Hamas?"

"What?" Lina asked.

"The band on your head, it's bright green."

"It's Fendi."

"Fendi?" Shaul asked.

"That's the name of a brand."

"Well, I guess that that isn't Hamas, then."

She had sparkling lip-gloss, a striped, collared shirt, and darkly-lined, wide, copper eyes. She didn't talk much. She played with her hair. Then she told him she had to get going.

"Where to?"

"I don't know. We can't really talk. I don't want to be seen with a soldier."

"A soldier?"

"I assume you're a soldier."

"How did you know?"

"You were talking to them by the cars. Plus your haircut."

He always forgot that his head was shaved. For six years, it had grown to his shoulders.

"So are you a soldier?"

"Not really," he said.

"So what are you?"

"A junior lieutenant."

"What's that?"

"It's like a rank or two below captain."

"You fight in the army?"

"Not yet," he said. "I'm in training."

"In training?"

"I'm learning to be a commander."

"To go fight a war?"

"I guess," Shaul said. "Or get married."

She laughed. "How long have you done this?"

"Served?"

"No, flirted with girls who are Arab."

"Not long."

"So you go to these villages?"

"Not yet," he replied. "I'm still learning things in the desert."

"But you'll go to these places—Ramallah, Jenin?"

"I hope," Shaul said. "It looks great."

"And what will you do there?"

"I'll kill," he said, as he flicked away a gnat from his shirt. Then he realized that she wouldn't catch his sarcasm yet, and he wished that he hadn't said it. "I'm joking."

"It sounds like you're not."

"I am," he explained.

"So why did you come to this protest?"

"My mother."

"Your *mother* dragged you here?"

"I guess, I believe—"

"What, that you'd like to meet Arabs?"

"No, I mean, I'm not for the army. I serve in it, though. But I don't really support what it does."

"You don't?"

"No," Shaul said. "None of us do. Except for the crazy religious. In fact, there isn't a single Israeli I know who wants to spend time ruling Arabs. You know that?"

"Not really. I'm new to this place. And I thought that the Jews here were killers."

"Uh-huh."

"So what will you do?"

"What do you mean?"

"What will you do in the villages?"

"I don't know. I guess some arrests, raids and patrols. You know how it works. It's an army."

"I saw you come into Ramallah last night. Not you, but a whole bunch of soldiers. They ransacked a building and plundered some homes. They left with a couple of kids."

"I doubt it."

"What do you mean, you doubt it? I saw it myself."

"They don't arrest kids in the army."

"Who does it?"

"The *Shin Bet* might do it. But they're the police. The army still tries not to touch 'em."

"Why's that?"

"Cause they hate holding kids. They always throw stones, and somebody comes with a camera, and shoots it. So they try not to do it."

"I saw it myself."

"That was probably the police, not the army."

"The same thing."

"No, it's not. Do I look like a cop?" He still thought his head was unshaven. "I'm not the police. That isn't my job. I like to hang out on the weekend."

"Oh do you? And what do you do?"

"I party," he said.

"What kind of parties you go to? With Arabs?"

"I wish. They're better than the Jews'. The Jews, they just like to get wasted."

"Sounds fun."

"Sounds fun?" Shaul asked.

"You know, I'm not really an Arab."

"I guess not. You lived in the States."

She shrugged. "And how do *you* know English?"

"My mother," he sighed. "Like you, she was born in New York."

"I'm sorry."

"Me too," Shaul said. "Plus, it's your name. It sounds like my mom's. Maybe I'll just call you my woman."

"Your *woman*?"

"Is that okay? I don't have one yet. And I like you much more than Israelis."

"You know, you're pretty cocky."

"Not really." He smiled. "I've always had problems with women."

"I'll bet," Lina said, as she rose.

"Seriously, you have to get going?"

"I told you, I gotta get back. And I don't want to get caught in the rain."

"You have your own ride?"

"Not really," she said. "But I drive."

"How'll you get home?"

"I came with some friends."

"Who?"

"Just a couple of soldiers."

"Not Moshe?"

"Yes, Moshe," she said.

"He got to you first?"

"Yeah, see, I'm already conquered."

Moshe, Shaul knew, was openly gay. Somehow he served in Golani. He was a fairly nice guy, a bit annoying at times, and disturbingly close to Shaul's mother. "How do you know Moshe?"

"I've met him before. You're nosey," she said with a smile.

"Just asking."

"He comes to my school and helps make art. He's doing this thing with the students."

"I'll bet. So you live in Ramallah?"

"Yeah," Lina said.

"Can I call you?"

"I guess. You're a soldier...I mean, if you want to have dinner, don't bring your gun."

"Okay," Shaul said. "But I can't—"

"Just give me a call." She reached in her handbag and uncased a small fountain pen. "You can write on my hand."

"What?"

"I want you to give me your number."

"Okay." He took her hand, which was fragrant and soft, and studied the rubble beside them. Nobody saw them, at least that he knew. Beyond them the homes were all boarded or razed.

"Just write down your number."

"Okay," Shaul said. "If this hurts, you can tell me to stop."

He looked at her face, the thin arch of her brow, which seemed to be colored with pencil, but wasn't. He knew she was Arab by the shape of her eyes. They were almond-shaped, narrowed, and judging. They watched him.

"Why do you do this?"

"What?" Shaul asked.

"Why do you come to these protests?"

"I told you."

"Uh-huh. Is that supposed to be a three?"

"Yeah," Shaul said.

"Okay, you can stop, cause it hurts." She took out her phone and sent him a text. The message said: "I WILL CALL U."

Indeed, the very next night, she sent him a note: "I HOPE UR ENJOYING RAMALLAH."

They went out on dates for a few weeks. The first thing they saw was a concert. It was a "Concert for Peace," or so it had claimed, at Ramallah's main cultural center. It was in the Sakakini Center, a repurposed manor of Ottoman stone, and she said they should sit far apart. Most of the attendees were suited or bejeweled. A dozen heads watched her sit down.

Then a string quartet began of young Arabs and Jews, interrupted by clamoring cellphones. The listeners kept talking, yapping at phones. The Argentine presenter grew testy and shushed them. Soon there was booing, followed by glares. The music returned. It was Haydn's "The Bird," and played with all the grace of a grenade going off. But he remembered the silence that followed the first movement, when nobody else had been talking—they shut up. That's when he saw her turn in her chair: that same dangling strand of gold hair laced her cheek. She glanced at him quickly, tied up her bun, and immediately turned to face somebody else. He thought of walking over and kissing her there, but the Arabs would have them both shot.

Afterward, he followed her home, and she bade him adieu with a text.

On each of their dates, he would travel alone, passing through checkpoints and crossings. He would always have to hide his army ID and show his American passport. And the border guards knew his family. His mother came through all the time with her network of comrades. But they didn't say a word to the men on his base, and nobody knew but his parents.

On the third or fourth date, when they sat on Lina's couch, alone in her Ramallah apartment (a huge loft), Shaul leaned in and took her left hand and said that he wanted to kiss her. She laughed. An uncomfortable silence was followed by stares, along with occasional talking. They discussed her new paintings, a book that she'd read—a memoir by Edward Said, which was "great"— and the rain through the season, how it hadn't yet come but soon would put out the protests that flared. She said no one would bother to stand in the rain.

In April, the violence erupted. Palestine became heat. War had arrived.

Shaul leaned in and they kissed.

Spiraling mortars were flung, basements shot out, soldiers fought mobs in the streets. And little kids died, wholesale in rain. Shaul lived down in the desert. He trained for six months while commanding a platoon on the desiccated pan of the Negev. He learned to seize hilltops, spread wire and lay mines, to chart his own course with Polaris. But what they didn't teach Shaul—what they didn't even say—is that a war isn't fought in the army. It is fought in a bedroom, in the quiet of night, under sheets and heaped blankets, in darkness, in angst.

When Shaul left the army twice in each month, he'd lock up his gun at his parents' kibbutz. Then he'd head to Ramallah alone in a cab, crossing by checkpoints and soldiers. When he arrived at her building, he'd go through the back, in the alley, where no one would see him. And they could only whisper inside her apartment, since her parents lived directly beneath her. A couple of times, they even knocked on the door, and Shaul made straight for the shower.

With the shutters drawn tight, her hair in his hands, his beloved would teach him expressions. "One day in your hand, one day in your arse." It was a way of explaining the weather. *"Kulna fi hawa sawa"*—"We're all in this air," or "we're all in the same boat."

He didn't really know what these Arabic words meant, but he liked watching her mouth the phrases. More importantly, Shaul did not love *her* yet, more like her beauty and glamor. She was nine years older, and much more mature, and she loved that he served in the army, bizarrely.

They'd kiss until dawn. He'd stroke her curled hair. She'd call him a kike or *yahudi*. Her soldier.

"Yahudi, you want this with French fries or rice?" She'd cook him string beans in her broiler, and burn them.

"I'll take French fries," he whispered.

"Those things make you fat."

He had put on some weight during training, oddly. Everyone else had lost weight there, but Shaul had not. His mother's cooking was surprisingly healthy, by contrast.

"So what should I do? Eat rice with my beans?"

"What's wrong with rice?"

"You're an Arab."

She squinted. She'd pull back her eyes with the tips of her hands and pretend that she'd come from the desert. "Would you like to see the tent now or later?" she'd whisper.

Shaul was already naked. "My conquest."

He'd peel back her robe—like cotton or mink, something so soft he could sleep there—and kiss her. He'd kiss her white breasts.

They bloomed on her chest. Arabs, he thought, were not children. They had childrearing hips, and childrearing minds, and he knew that this couldn't last.

She'd hold him.

They talked about battles or bombs of the week. Shaul was still in the Negev in training.

"You don't understand," he said. "They have to send tanks in. Otherwise, what are they doing?"

"It's children."

"Yes, but it's a war being fought. You think they'll go in there with Humvees?"

"Why go?"

"I don't know. That's not the point. The point is they're there and they'll win it."

"Oh, will they?"

"Of course, they shoot children, and of course that is bad, but the point is they're there, so it happens."

"I don't know," she whispered, "I don't even know. I don't want you to go into those villages, like they do. You know what they do there. And you know what goes on. It doesn't matter who's at fault, or what started—"

"It does, though."

"So why would you go?"

"I have to," he said. "It's the reason I serve in the army."

"To kill them?"

"No. To defend us from bombs. To stop all the Arabs you're sending."

She wasn't quite smiling, and she wasn't quite sad. It was something in between, and much darker. It was as if she were mocking him under her breath as she slowly reached over and whispered, "Why go?"

"I don't know," Shaul said. He'd lie on her bed as she'd fluff out her soft cotton blanket. "I have to. And what do you know about fighting a war? *Nu*, you've chosen to come here."

"I had to," she said.

"What do you mean *you had to*?"

"It's my home and land."

"That's fine," Shaul said. "You can take it. We'll leave it. You can have the whole West Bank. Here, start with New York. Why not Detroit or New Zealand? How 'bout it?"

She started to smile, but it was still kind of weird, as if they'd tapped into something much deeper: his conquest.

They hadn't made love, though they'd kiss every time. She was a virgin and wouldn't. Or couldn't.

"So why not make love?" he asked her in June. The two of them rarely discussed it.

"I'm Arab."

"What does that mean?"

"You tell me."

"I don't know," Shaul said. "It's a challenge?"

He knew she wouldn't do it, and in a way, he was fine. He was happy with foreplay and cuddling. But he wanted to be in her, to own this whole girl, to deposit his seed in her body, and store it, and come home to it there, every other week, in the very same place where he'd been. He couldn't. And it could kill a young soldier to come twice a month and do what he did with this woman: to rub all her skin and the depths of her back while grazing her neck and her earlobe. And what could he tell her? *I have to move on. I need to find someone to fuck me. Try serving.* But he didn't want to say it, had no way to prove that his love for this woman was deeper. And dearer. He knew what he should tell her—the words he should say—and which every woman wanted to hear first. He couldn't. He couldn't lie to this woman, because he knew what love was. He would feel it each night in the desert.

It was a supernatural feeling. It came with the stars. It came all alone while guarding and staring at the mystical earth, the heaps in their place, the broken black sands of the desert, their blowing, and the camps with their tarps as they flapped through the night and he stood with the strap of his weapon and wondered: would this earth soon arrive and swallow him whole, collapse his whole spine to his body, and eat him? Would it be a crashing white mortar, a twist through the dark, a tank shell or round of a .50? Would he taste all the salt and the fury of death? Would he risk his own life for his soldiers? He doubted it. These were unanswerable questions, which no god could foretell, and that was the beauty of living and being: it was an unending darkness, a beauty through peace, like the eternal great wrath of dark waters. He waited. He stood in the desert, alone with his gun, and he imagined these things he would tell her.

When she finally said, "Just put it in me," he stared, and he said that he couldn't.

She dumped him the next day. On the cliff by the rocks. It wasn't because she was Arab. It might be. But it was something much deeper, a cause in itself, like a rift that had formed in his body, and hers, too. It came from not bleeding, not fighting in war, but knowing that someday it'd happen.

"Look, Shaul. I'm tired of wasting my time. I love you. I can't wait forever."

He knew this. And he didn't want to hurt or lie to this girl.

Instead, he just shot at her cousins.

That Friday evening, thirty clicks north of Bethlehem, in the West Bank town of Ramallah, in a newly-built, glass-plated, palm-tree-lined mall, the Plaza Supermarket was bustling, swarming with shoppers and carts. Billed as the first "American-style grocery" in

Palestine, the store featured high ceilings, bright, spacious shelves, fresh produce and baked goods and fish.

Yet one shopper paused before the Oriental Goods stand and adjusted the band on her head. Even stuffed grape leaves came in a can, Lina saw, and all the hummus was Israeli-made.

She didn't like this. Not in her place, in her home. Nevertheless, she kept shopping, if only because the air here was clean, the prices were set, and the mall had a place where she could park.

Presently, she was shopping for fish with her great-aunt. It was called the *Sultan Ibrahim*, a red mullet fish that was impossible to get during curfews. But the store had been opened, along with other shops, for six hours on permission from the army. It was a "humanitarian gesture," according to the papers. Lina wasn't feeling too grateful.

The market was stocked, which was hard to believe. They must have circumvented the closure. They were short on the dairy, fresh fruit and eggs, but the meat and the fish were abundant. Her great-aunt had already made haste for the fish shelf while Lina hung back with the cart.

Around her, shoppers were arguing, talking about the war. It was mostly just women and children. A couple young men pushed carts through the aisles while their wives lagged behind with their veils. And it seemed as if the men were more insistent on those whenever the army held curfew.

The veils they had on were black ones and long—unusual, she thought, for Ramallah. They looked like Iranians, or Bedouins, worse—characters from some kind of movie, like *Star Wars*. They wore burqas with slits and hemmed satin robes—beautiful, almost, and flowing. And she wondered what it would be like to wear those one day, and if Skandr, her fiancée, would make her. He was a Christian, but one never knew with the Arabs who were born in these parts.

"Lina," said her great-aunt, breathlessly returning, "I don't like the idea of a village wedding. Your father's right. A hotel would be a lot nicer."

Her great-aunt had been talking about this for eleven straight hours. It was all she would do during curfew. Occasionally she'd knit or brew her sage tea or complain about Lina's not eating.

"I respect you for wanting to do it in the village, but the Mövenpick is much better. Besides, if we have it in the village, we'll have three thousand guests, and how are we gonna feed—"

They heard a boom. It was outside the store. The shopping cart shook in her hands.

"Get down," someone shouted. The ceiling lights flashed, and white powder plumed from the rafters.

Her great-aunt was still standing, carefully inspecting a labeled green tin can of olives.

"Get down," someone yelled, and Lina grabbed her great-aunt from behind. She steadied her shoulder and lowered her down, helping her sit on the tiles.

"It's coming from the Manara," somebody screamed. It was a woman across the aisle with the burqa. "Get up, get up," she yelled at her kids, who were huddled on the floor by her husband.

Outside they heard motors. A rotor blade churned, followed by sirens and whirs. It must have been a rocket or some kind of bomb. The Jews were attacking Ramallah.

Her great-aunt seemed content in her place on the floor. She asked why the olives had so many ingredients. "What is acetic acid?" Others were running with baskets in hand or babies clutched to their chests.

Lina stood up, gripping a shelf. She propped her great-aunt up by the waist. The woman got up and fluffed out her *thobe*. She checked to see nobody saw it. And she had knocked down a box of "3-Minute Tabbouleh," which she tried to return to the shelves.

"Just leave it," Lina shouted.

But before she could move, her great-aunt grabbed the cart and retrieved her package of fish. "I want this."

"Stay away from the windows," a custodian yelled, lugging a bucket and squeegee. Battered boxes were strewn about the waste-laden floors, and children were running with parents. In the center of the aisle, beside the iced tea, a young girl stared at the ceiling.

Lina ran over while her great-aunt pulled the cart and made her way down to the exit. "Where is your mom?"

"I don't know," the girl said. She looked to be seven or eight.

Outside the sky roared. It shook the tall glass. The parking lot flashed through the windows. Then the ceiling lights fluttered, dimmed and went out. A pink glow came on and replaced them.

"Come," Lina said, and she grabbed the girl's hand, leading her down to the checkout.

Her great-aunt was already in line with the cart, waiting to pay at the counter. The cashier was scanning the package of fish, whispering, "Come on, *Ya Allah*."

"I think it was on sale," her great-aunt told the clerk. He was frizzy-haired, dark, maybe Gazan.

Behind them, a lone orange cart was charting its course down the third aisle to the chocolates. People around them were screaming and cursing. Her great-aunt reached into her bosom. She pulled out her wallet, a gray plastic sheaf that she kept in her dress for safekeeping.

"I don't think it works yet. The power's not on." The cashier was tapping the scanner.

The girl whose arm Lina had held darted away to the corner. She embraced a tall man at the front of the store. He was wheeling a bread-filled stroller.

"You see that?" said her great-aunt, and she pointed to the glass, beyond which some faint smoke was drifting. It was about a kilometer west, well past the lots. Probably from the President's Compound.

The cashier kept punching the keypad. Others were pushing behind them with baskets. Through the glass Lina heard a few vehicles screech, and headlights swerved by the curb. A car alarm echoed. Somebody honked. Others were shouting in German.

To the right of the checkout, the tall man led the girl out through the glass power-doors—now working. They were followed by a woman—the Burqa she'd seen—carrying a cone with red sprinkles.

"I think I have a coupon," her great-aunt told the clerk.

"It won't even call up your debit."

"Can I pay in cash?"

"Yeah," the boy sighed. "Is this all you want?"

"Wait," Lina said, and she reached for a couple of Snickers. "Throw these in." Then her phone started ringing. It was Shaul, she saw. They hadn't spoken in months.

"Is that Skandr?" asked her great-aunt. "He's probably worried sick about you."

Lina clicked OFF. "He'll be fine."

"You know, if you'd like," said her great-aunt, as Lina popped the trunk of her Jetta, "we could have the *zaffa* in the village, still do the routine, and book the Mövenpick for that night."

"Okay." Lina looked out at the lights overhead, the glittering spheres of Balu'a. The streets were alive with sirens and horns and vehicles thrumming their engines. Her great-aunt would stay in Lina's apartment. Tomorrow they'd go to the village. But Lina had to get back and clean up her place. Skandr's family was coming on Monday. Plus, she had lessons to prepare, arrangements to make. She hadn't even purchased a dress. She figured she could always borrow her older sister's, but that was in storage in Queens.

Fretting, Lina drove back through the long, winding dark, avoiding the congestion downtown. She skirted the hills of Ramallah's west end, circling the banks of the wadi. She wound along a road that smelled like manure—the slaughterhouse site for a village—and past the water treatment and processing plant, the stables and pens of al-Bireh. She turned on the filter inside of the vents while her great-aunt stared out through the window, not talking. They had been here before—at least twice this month—and she never really seemed to mind.

Her great-aunt had been born before the Revolt, before the expulsion and *Naqba*, the *Naqse*, and before the Intifadas and protests that flared, when people still lived in the village in mud huts. And now she had a cellphone, a satellite dish, and a screenname which Lina had given her. Her screen name was Warrior0135, for the month and the year she was born. And it was amazing, Lina thought, that she wasn't even scared as the two drove up to her building. They parked on the street and hauled up the bags, pausing for breath on the staircase.

"You know," said her great-aunt, gripping the handrail, "whatever you decide, I'm sure it'll work out fine. All of this fuss about where people marry, who they invite, it's dumb. The important thing is that you've found somebody. You don't want to be alone, dear, like me."

Sometimes Lina thought about telling her great-aunt that for six months she had dated a Jew here. But it was doubtful that her great-aunt would even believe her—that, or she'd have her committed. At the same time, Lina thought that she might understand; her husband had died in the eighties. And Lina's mother always joked that they would set her aunt up with a vendor or priest from their village. Her great-aunt lived alone—all her children were gone, and she spent half her week stuffing peppers.

Inside, they drank tea. Lina's mother came and went. They didn't even hear the invasion outside. Finally, her great-aunt asked her how she felt about marrying.

"What's not to like? He's my cousin."

"Well, you've already made him wait a couple years."

"I have my reasons," said Lina.

The truth was that Lina had only met the man twice. They had gotten engaged last month. He wasn't bad-looking. Perhaps a bit simple, and perhaps a bit beneath her at that. But it was important for her father, since Skandr's father was a high-ranking government minister. And she didn't mind not knowing her future husband, since her former relations, which were much more involved, hadn't exactly worked out. Plus, this was still mysterious—even if it was arranged, or at the very least planned long ago.

Later that night, preparing for bed, her great-aunt asked to borrow a toothbrush, a spare. Lina had one in the shelf by her sink. It was a clear, plastic brush with a צ. The stenciled letter, Lina knew, meant Army in Hebrew, and Shaul had left it behind. But her great-aunt didn't mind, and didn't seem to notice, as she hefted the thing to her gums.

She let out a spit. Then she gargled and washed as Lina returned with some linen. "You know," her great-aunt told her, "men come and they go. And in the end, all you're left with is hygiene."

"I know."

Shortly after midnight that Friday, outside the Rachel's Tomb compound, a voice was heard screaming in the Bethlehem hills and the scrublands of northern Beit Jala. A hot wind beat down—the first since last June, though calmer than the winds of October. In a couple more weeks, the *khamsin* would blow and siphon the dew from the desert. It would pound all the rooftops and cobbled tin huts, rinse off the drainpipes and heaters, and carry. But this wind was calmer, like an augural breeze that swarmed through the graves and Aleppos.

Shaul felt it. He felt all the sweat and the grit on his skin and the stares of the soldiers behind him, who ran. He pictured his father at home in his workshop, sawing off legs for a soldier. His mother was probably awake now, as well, waiting to take testimony from him.

His patrol team, for their part, had just opened fire at a terrorist approaching their base. Or something. It was difficult to see—the air a wet haze—as they scrambled through the graves and down towards the unlighted street.

Shaul ran quickly, trailed by Ivan, then the other four, swerving like jackals. He turned to look back as they dashed through the rows and down to a wrought iron fence. There, they scaled a small wall, which Ivan fell from, and he told them to crouch by a dumpster. "Ivan, come with me. Boaz, you too. The rest of you stay by this wall and give watch." Shaul didn't know why he was whispering to them. The Arabs all knew they were here.

His men were kneeling on the curb of al-Aida Street, which sloped downhill from their base past some shuttered brick homes, a Che-stenciled wall, and a derelict mud field with olives and rocks. Towards the base of the hill, the paved road branched off into the sewage-lined maze of the al-Aida Refugee Camp.

"Vasily," Shaul whispered, addressing his light machine gunner, "cover those homes. If anyone comes out, you tell me. No shooting." Then Shaul sprang forward with Ivan beside him and the PRC squawking on Boaz. He fingered his trigger and steered the two left. He told them to fasten their safeties. As he emerged beyond the dumpster, he saw what they'd done. A small, ruptured body lay steaming in glass. The figure was youngish. A child's perhaps. And obviously not one with a gun, as they'd thought.

Shaul turned to look back at his soldiers again, and he heard a shrill cry from the buildings below. Dogs started yowling. The whole camp was up, about to descend on the victim.

"Boaz," Shaul thundered. "Call Company HQ. Tell them to set up a line this second. Get an ambulance out, and send the response team. I don't want them to wait for the Captain. And tell Sergeant Dror to send Uri out here. We need another marksman for cover." Shaul wasn't sure which man had opened fire first, but if he had to guess, he'd have said Yossi. And it was probably his fault for having scolded the fucker, much less encouraged his antics.

Grinning, Shaul fought back his tonsils, a lump in his throat. Then he turned to look down at the body. He didn't really doubt that his parents were awake. The only question was what were they doing.

In fact, about fifteen kilometers northwest of Bethlehem, at Kibbutz Ma'ale HaHamisha, Shaul's father was awake, having finished his carvings and stepped out for a spliff and a walk. He had wandered towards the lobby of the kibbutz's hotel and drifted inside its new spa. This was a towering structure of marble and glass that overlooked the Judean Hills. In fact, from its northernmost reaches, one could almost descry Bethlehem's shimmering lights.

Of course, Shmuel Braverman took in little of the perspective that night as he lay on his back in the sauna. The spa was intended for the hotel's paying guests, but he figured he was entitled. After all, he'd worked for thirty-one years in the orchards, not at a desk.

He hadn't even taken a vacation in months, which was more than he could say for his wife.

Wiping his face, Shmuel studied the boards in the ceiling. Probably European alder. Finnish, old-growth, and treated with wax or paraffin. He should have volunteered to build this damn place. He couldn't even guess what it had cost.

Earlier tonight, when he'd entered the spa, Shmuel had asked for a towel. The receptionist had snickered, "Vy bother?" Kristin was in her forties, a German to boot, with long, flaxen hair and toned arms. And her husband—a nice man, a man whom Shmuel liked—was no longer the farmer she'd married. Now he'd grown fat. He was triple Shmuel's size, having passed off his work to *Thailandim.*

And the least Shmuel could do was give Kristin a hand, so he helped her mop floors by the steam room. He was wearing his Speedo, a shiny black suit, though Kristin didn't seem to have noticed. He arched out his back as he bent to the floor, picking up spare cups of water. And she must have been impressed by the girth of his arms. He'd spent the last month hauling grapefruits. Then he thought about putting a hand on her back as she squeezed out the mop in the bucket. Instead he just watched those shins and firm thighs and the sumptuous line of her gym-shorts. She didn't look up or even say thanks. But she must have known he was watching. And she looked incredible for someone that age. She also taught step and Pilates.

"Zanks for your help. But zat's fine, Shmuel. Ah'll take it from here."

Then he moved to the sauna and sprawled on the bench, covering his gut with a towel. He thought about inviting her in for a drink or a Popsicle freeze from the cooler. He'd tell her: *Let's have a drink, just you and me. We've both scrubbed the floor, now each other.*

At that point he slept for what must have been an hour and awoke to gaze up at the ceiling. His back was steamed up, his face a pink peach, all wilted and puffy and burning. She must have let him sleep here, alone, undisturbed. Or maybe she was waiting to join him? Fantastisch. He seized the door and pressed on its pane. Then a blast of cool air hit his face.

Outside, the poolroom was silent and dark, and his eyes took some time to adjust. Between columns, the far orange lights of Kiryat Ye'arim zigzagged the pool at odd angles. Then he thought he saw movement. Sure enough, towards the lobby, an armed guard was peering in through a glass-paneled door.

"Shmuel, I thought you were here," the guard announced, entering. "Your wife needs to see you this second."

"What?"

"I don't know," he stammered. "She said it's your son. Something's gone on in the army."

"Of course."

Shmuel studied the guard, his thin, Russian face. He'd recently finished the army. Then Shmuel wondered if Kristin would have him each night. He wouldn't put it past an Israeli.

In darkness, Shmuel lumbered home past the banquet hall, sheds, the loud, smoking pipes of the laundry, the kennel, past the senior care building, where his mother still wheezed—she was probably up watching *Seinfeld*—past the hedges of myrtle and primrose and pine, the lawn-stage where he'd been Bar Mitzvahed and married, God help him, past the soldiers' apartments, where Shaul sometimes moped, the flagstone path edged with lupins and firs, past the library building, where his wife claimed to "work," and finally to the clearing with condos. The Bravermans' was last: a lemon-colored duplex of stucco and vines. A few grafted olive trees peppered the lawn, along with Ilana's herb garden.

She was standing in their doorway, hands on her hips,

glaring through the gnat-covered screen. And she didn't say a word; she just stood there and stared, silhouetted pinkly in her terrycloth robe.

And maybe they'd shot him. Shaul was gone. Tragic, Shmuel thought, but expected and wished for. Or maybe he had gone and eloped with that girl and gotten himself hung in Ramallah.

"I hope I didn't interrupt your swimming," she snarled, yanking the door, tilting one of her many chins to her shoulder.

"What happened?"

"My friend Moshe called. He said there was a shooting near Rachel's Tomb. No troops were injured, but I've been calling Shaul's phone, and of course he still refuses to answer."

Shmuel passed her. "Did he say what exactly—"

She shut the door. "All I know is there's one Arab wounded." Then she spun around. "Shmuel, are you high? Your face is all red."

"I've been steaming."

Snatching mint from her garden, Ilana made tea. She kept calling Shaul's fucking phone. At one point he picked up, but then all she heard was faint static.

Meanwhile, her husband was snoring on their crumb-littered couch, naked save his socks and his Speedo.

Ilana turned on the television—cranked to full blast. The cable was out. The dotted screen hissed. "Shmuel, put on the news now."

He fell off the couch. "There isn't any news until six," he groaned, rising.

Twenty minutes later, she brewed him a pot. Shmuel was asleep once again. "Our son still won't answer."

"I'm sure he's fine."

"Do you think we should go down to Rachel's Tomb and see him?"

"How would we go? My truck's in the shop."

"We could go on the bus."

"It's Sabbath. Besides, the checkpoint's closed. They won't let us through. And what would we say, that we're worried?"

"Yes. Is there some reason I can't be his mother?"

"He's fine."

"You know, I should just call up his Town Major now and tell him I'm rescinding permission." Because Shaul was their only child, his serving in combat required their consent. Of course, Ilana had been playing that trump for years—mainly, to get Shaul's help doing dishes.

Her husband got up and slowly approached her, placing a paw on her wrist. He smelled like chlorine, wood shavings, sweat, and that hooker who worked at the spa.

"Get off me."

"You know that he would never forgive you for that. And neither would I," he said, leaving.

"Whatever." Ilana sunk to the couch, put her head in her hands, and stared at this wreck of a marriage, and a carving of a sparrow, which Shmuel kept on the shelf beside a framed portrait of his father. "Why don't you go there? Would you do something useful? Instead of smoking dope in your workshop—"

"Oh, stop."

"Listen, Shmuel, I'm trying to be your wife, and to communicate with you. But you won't even hear what I'm saying."

"Which is what?"

"That I don't want to lose my son to this bullshit. You know how it is, with your fath—" Then she thought to add: "And at least that was for a defensible cause. This is just politics. It's childish, stupid. I mean, what the fuck is he doing in the Territories? Lining the pockets of Elbit and Boeing?"

"Look, hon, I know it's foolish. The whole conflict is. But he's an adult now, and he has to make his own choices."

"Make choices? He isn't even guarding the real Rachel's Tomb. Did you know that she's buried in Ramah? Go check the Bible."

"Whatever," Shmuel grumbled.

"Don't give me whatever. He's my fucking son. And the only one you'd allow me to have."

"You know as well as I do that that was your choice."

"Well, if I'd married a man who had money—"

"Shut up."

"Look, all I'm saying is that he should be in college, not a damn war."

"And I should be the head of Tnuva."

She dialed Shaul's phone, which didn't even ring. She left another message, half-frantic and screaming. Her husband returned to his place on the couch. Ilana stormed into the bedroom. She dug through a binder of bills and receipts and came up with the Town Major's number. She knew very well that neither man would forgive her. She dialed. Then she hung up the phone.

In the kitchen, she popped a few Xanax, dumped out her tea, and snatched down a bottle of Dom Pérignon. She had been saving it for her book's paperback release, but it was pretty clear that wouldn't happen.

Reeling, she stumbled to the sofa. She plopped herself down. The cushion was wet from Shmuel's Speedo. He was wide awake now. "What do you think?" she asked him.

"It's your fault he's dating an Arab."

She uncorked the bottle. "I think they broke up."

"Well, if that ain't a reason to toast."

In his dreams, he was floating along a dark desert path, when he came upon a woman clad in a flowing gown.

"Who are you?" she asked.

"I am Lt. Shaul Braverman."

"What do you seek?"

"I wish to know my own fate."

She had a dark, ghoulish face, and she was clutching a wineskin, or some kind of talisman. "Only a fool seeks to know."

He fell on his knees to beseech her, and he sniffed her warm crotch, which was scented with Arab perfume.

"Pleasure me, child. Then we shall speak of your fate."

As he leaned forward, she held up her arms, and he saw a ghost rising out of the sands. "This is your future," she said. Beside them, a hooded figure was walking with a cane. Clad in torn robes, his narrow face lined, his knuckles white as bone, he was picking his way across the dark dunes, blown here and there by the wind.

"Where am I now?"

"A Palestinian village."

"Which one?" Shaul asked her.

"Indur." Then she clutched his head and tore it off his chest. As she did so, he woke to his screams.

Early that Sunday, inside the Rachel's Tomb compound, Shaul awoke from troubling dreams to find himself transformed into a soldier. He was lying on his back with a greenish, Lycra-lined plate on his chest, and when he lifted his head, he could see that its Velcro tabs were sticking up, like mini-legs. He reached down to fasten them.

On his head he wore a helmet—a thick, hulking measure

in which it was not impossible to sleep, just undesirable, since rotating was a problem, and your neck normally cramped. His didn't, however. For a pillow, he slept on a worn vestpack, replete with eight clips, two grenades, an empty bottle of gin, a coat, several maps, and two water bottles. He also had a radio, which occasionally clicked, and some sun lotion he'd never used.

Why Shaul had not worn his boots while he'd slept would remain a point of some contention. But when he heard the explosion, which is what he'd just done, he grabbed them and knotted them up. It was a tricky maneuver, because he was running down the hall with his gun slinking down to his ankles. And he had heard the shot himself—he knew it was a gun—though the radio that was barking was unclear: something about signals, not getting their commands, Ivan was demanding a cigarette.

His emergency response team was scrambling for vests, piling into the halls of the Control Room. He told them to raise the barrels of their guns and cock back the rounds in their chambers. Then they ran through the halls, Shaul in the lead; Boaz was racing behind him. His radio kept blaring that a soldier was down on the northwestern end of the roof.

The weird thing about the army, Shaul began to think as he ran down the hall with his vest, the rifle stock clapping the side of his waist, his helmet jouncing up on his head, is that everyone was accountable to some other person. Everyone was constantly watched. People thought in war you were alone, by yourself, or left to your own personal devices. But there was no privacy in battle, and no solace to be found. Others were running behind him. And surely Rachel was weeping behind her silk mantle as he barreled down the hall past Her Crypt.

Outside, the streetlamps vapored the checkpoint and soldiers were kneeling on pavement, pointing strangely lit barrels, like luminant swords. Their faces looked drawn and misshapen. "Get down," someone shouted to the men at his side. Pinchas was crouched at a railing. Shaul kept running up the stairs to the roof and wondered why Pinchas wasn't captain.

And Pinchas was now watching him, and all of his men, as Shaul climbed up the brick-lined steps. He could feel his squad leader's eyes cutting behind him as he yelped his commands to the soldiers: "Night-vision on. Sets down."

In the reviews, they would ask what considerations had come to bear—what thoughts had now passed through his mind: whether he had stayed low beneath the bags on the roof, or shot out some gas to the street, or thrown up a flare to illuminate the graves, or called for emergency backup. Of course, Shaul was the main backup, the head of the response. The Captain would be joining him shortly. As would the ambulance, choppers and cars, whatever had prompted this shooting.

As Shaul rounded the steps and his boots clanked down— someone had laid down some metal sheets—he didn't feel scared or even confused, just agitated that he was constantly monitored; he would have to make decisions—here, all the time—with the knowledge he was going to be evaluated. The Captain would be here shortly, take testimony from Pinchas and the rest of his subordinate commanders. Shaul's boots let out a walloping creak; Ivan had laid down the tin sheets. He did this so the soldiers could sleep while on guard and not be surprised by commanders.

Shaul wondered if he'd have to report to the Captain that Ivan had laid down the metal. Shaul could say he'd done it to alert them to terrorists in case any tried to sneak on the roof, which was part true. And he didn't really want to get Ivan in trouble. Ivan, for all his shit, was his favorite. Besides, he didn't like having to report on his men; evaluations, he thought, were impersonal.

As Shaul reached the top step and quickly hunched down, crawling on his arms towards the kneeling group ahead, he knew he'd be demoted, or at least reassigned and transferred far away from this company. And that was fine to him then as he wriggled forward, approaching a handful of men crouched in blood. He'd miss all his soldiers, including the one who was wounded—and from the looks of it, dying. But that was just another part of the service.

Maybe he'd get an assignment at the Galilee Division, commanding the men who fixed tanks. Their job was to stare at the grass and the sun and await the next onslaught from Lebanon. And if there were ever another war, which he knew there'd be, he'd be relegated to the rear line. They wouldn't let him command in combat again. Not after this. Which was fine, because he wasn't cut out for it.

There were two kinds of men in war, Shaul thought: those who could lead others blindly; and those who could crawl on their knees above a roof and mourn for the death of a comrade. Shaul was neither. Maybe something in between. But at bottom, he was an ordinary person: not terribly compassionate, nor steadfast in fighting. He wondered if he should phone up the Captain.

It wasn't his fault that his soldier was sniped; he was surprised that it hadn't happened earlier. But they would blame him for not lining the roof with enough sandbags or stringing enough net from the tarps. Or maybe they'd blame him for sending this one up, since this kid was not equipped to be a soldier. Who knew what he was doing with that phone in his hand? It looked like he was sending a message.

The only problem, Shaul thought, is what he'd say to his folks, how he'd look them in the eyes and explain this. Not a day had gone by when he didn't remember them saying how pointless it was to be serving. And maybe they were right. Maybe he was wasting his time. And maybe he had caused the death of a soldier. Or maybe he was heroic for having led this fell charge, this occupation of the bereaved and the sullen.

He wouldn't tell his parents, nor Lina, by God, that he was going to be relieved of his command. What good would that do? What point would it serve? They would only have been happy to hear that. And he had nothing to tell them, no way of explaining the reason that he "fell" in the army. It wasn't because of cowardice, and it wasn't because of war, and it wasn't because he was an incompetent officer. And he wasn't above keeping his men up at night. He just knew that it wouldn't make a difference. There was no choosing in battle, no choice to be had. Bullets just exploded like sunlight. And if you had the unfortunate fate of getting hit by a shot, well, fuck it, you were better off dying.

He crawled on his knees. He felt the cold ground. He leaned on his waist by the dying. He felt his own gun and the sling on his neck and the weight of the pack on his stomach. And then Shaul had that strangest of feelings: the sensation that he was being watched. Not by a person or a commander below or any sort of god up above him. But something was transmitting: a synaptic pulse, like a beat that shot through his heart. As if his body was being charged with someone else's commands and of which he couldn't be certain. Others were leading him, pulling him around, extending his hand to this person, letting him feel this warming gray flesh, which was tinged with the ashes of cigarettes. His soldier was not smoking. That was from Ivan. Ivan was standing beside them. Ivan was staring at the night sky above, as if he was wondering what planet he'd come from.

2 SHAUL

1st Lt Shaul Braverman
2nd Pl, "Aleph" Co
_th Btn, _ Inf Brig

20 MARCH __

Dear Mr. and Mrs. Hadana,

I wish to express to you my condolences on the loss of your son. It was a pleasure to have served with him, and he upheld this country's most honorable values. He was a true exemplar of dignity, honesty, integrity, and faith, and it is with the utmost sincerity that I write to you as his commander.

From his early days in training, Yossi was a devoted soldier, one whom the others looked up to, and a shining example ~~of what an immigrant soldier can contribute in this country.~~ He was remarkably adept with weapons, as well as at running, and I attribute that to his ~~richly imbued gene pool~~ strong sense of character. He was a model soldier in many regards, not least of which were his compassion for his fellow soldiers and the exemplary behavior he displayed on our base. While he was perhaps less enthusiastic about the regular slew of chores, as most soldiers are, he chose to partake in them with the utmost conviction. He was also a leader among his peers and a striking display of how good conduct, combined with a firm sense of virtue, ~~can go far in this army.~~

Nevertheless, it is with a tremendous amount of sadness ~~and angst and depression~~ that I, that I longed for his death, actually. And it came as something of a shock, yes. But that's generally how combat seems to work in the army. They say good soldiers are the ones who go first, but your son was a regular fuck-up and belies the whole notion. In fact, most of the men on our base are relieved it wasn't them, but at the same time a tad bit disappointed that the number-one target, albeit black-skinned, and therefore difficult to see at night, was picked off so early. I do wish he had learned the fundamentals of hygiene, though he's not alone in that regard, and I can't help but wondering if that didn't contributed to his demise. He was a fine boy, however, in the sense that all of them are fine boys: too stupid to question this and therefore deserving. On the other hand, he might have been aware of what was coming, as a fair number of them are, in which case it's unremarkable suicide. Nevertheless, I write to you in pain, but not over the loss of a soldier. Something has overtaken me, something quite deep and to which I feel I am not emotionally privy. You see, I don't actually mourn for your son any more than the Arabs, or anyone else who's been shot with my weapon (they tell me). And while I didn't kill him, I spoke to him the night before last and asked him if he wanted to stay. Granted his choices were somewhat limited at that point—divided between jail-time and service—and admittedly it was probably an economic decision that prompted him to stay, as most really are, or maybe he just needed some counseling. Who the hell knows now? I don't really care. You should know this, though, Mr. and Mrs. Hadana: I loved your son Yossi in an odd sort of way. Not because he was an exemplary soldier or in any way possessing of virtue. But he was tragic in a way, as all soldiers are. Perhaps people, I guess. Now I'm laughing. Anyways, it will be a pleasure to meet you today at the graves. I'll tell your son "hi" when I see him (quite soon now).

Best regards,
Shaul
p.s. what could I do? It's not like I gave him his weapon (I did though)

The Family Braverman—as indicated by a small, engraved plaque on the door's beveled jamb, unadorned by any bell or mezuzah— wasn't one to air its grievances in public, notwithstanding a few bouts in a restaurant and the occasional Saturday morning brunch. That said, when Lt. Shaul Braverman—or simply "The Lieutenant," as Ilana liked to call him—returned home to his kibbutz that Sunday evening after the funeral, it wasn't to grieve with his parents. Indeed, his whereabouts were unknown to them at present, though Ilana could speculate a bit. Now she stood beside the forest on a trim gravel path, staring up at his most recent work.

What a bitch this is gonna be to put out. That's pretty much all she could say. She watched as the flames danced high off the roof, leaping up spectral and violet. A couple firehoses kept trying to beat back the flames, but the torrent didn't make any difference.

It was a three-story lookout, but the flames could be seen about as far west as Ein Kerem, she figured. Above, the tall funnel of smoke wound its way through the pines, trailed by crackling embers.

A light rain had come out and just passed overhead, which had helped to contain the damage. Still, the whole blockhouse was blazing—one ponderous mess—as Ilana looked on from the clearing below. And it was amazing, she thought, that for sixty some years, no Arabs had managed to do this.

Her neighbors beside her kept flinging their hands or shielding their faces and coughing. Hundreds had gathered: Arabs and Jews, volunteers, hotel guests and workers. They stood in their bathrobes, pajamas and shorts, all strobed by the flickering lights. And in the plains down below, along the Abu Ghosh roofs, thousands looked on from their decks.

It was an impressive display. She'd give Shaul that. He must have used gas, or explosives. A tanker kept dousing the structure with foam, but it didn't seem to make any difference. The rooftop kept belching out blankets of smoke as the sirens peeled up from Route One.

Around her, the night air felt sticky and ripe, and she regretted having come here in sandals. She hitched up her nightie, buttoned her flannel, and tried to kick the dust from her toes. It scared her, in a way, that her own flesh and blood could ignite the whole sky right before her. And she thought she'd be mad, but she wasn't just yet. At the very least, he had conviction.

Of course, her husband wasn't in there, as sad as that was, and neither was his friend from the spa. Shmuel had gone back to sleep when he'd heard, and her son had since fled with his duffel.

Ilana figured it was probably her job as a mother to inform Shaul he had a few problems. He was a threat to his family, his soldiers, himself. But she didn't have the courage to tell him. She studied her phone. Why would she bother to call him? She knew what he'd say. *I'm not coming home.* That's what he'd told her this evening.

She remembered the scene from earlier today, when she

was kneeling in her kitchen, searching for a plunger or lye. On the radio, Joni Mitchell was crooning, and the two-dozen shrimp shells, which she'd grudgingly purchased and then assiduously peeled for her ungrateful wretch of a son, were naturally clogging her drain. That's when she saw him padding up the drive. Shaul stopped and looked back through the tattered screen door. And she remembered his face, those caved, glowing eyes, like two gems brightly set in a skull.

Then the wooden door creaked, and the ghost-figure entered, clutching his duffel and gun. He was wearing wrinkled *Alephs,* his hands inked with soot, and a cigarette burned on his chapped lower lip. "Mom, I'm not staying. I've got to catch a cab. I just came to drop off my rifle and change."

"Where are you—"

Then he was gone. The wooden door slapped. He had locked up his gun to their bedframe and left.

"But I made you shrimp—"

He didn't even hear as he bounded down the path to Route 425.

She had thought about chasing him, but what would that do? He was just like his father, but worse. And she didn't even know what she was supposed to have said. What do you say in that context? *I'm sorry?* She knew about the man who'd been killed on their base, and the child they had shot before that.

Shmuel didn't. She hadn't told him. He probably knew, but she wasn't going to be the one to inform him. And when they heard about the funeral—things get around, especially on a kibbutz in the Center—she'd told Shmuel, "He'll want us to be there."

"But what would we say?"

"I don't know. Maybe *I love you?*"

And now he was gone. A flash in the night. He was probably off to Ramallah. She didn't even know what he'd been up to that evening, though she harbored a couple suspicions.

Then Etti, beside her, a witch with white hair, asked how this fire could have started.

"Who knows?"

"I heard arson," she said. "Something like that. And what did you say he had in there, your husband?"

Above them, the fireworks whistled and popped, like some errant street fair on Purim. "His carvings."

"Well, at least there weren't any people inside."

"Not that I know of," said Ilana.

It was a long walk back along the forested path as Ilana returned to their condo. She didn't even turn to look back at that wreck; she could smell it in the air like a furnace: Shmuel's carvings, his seven years' work, his pot and his porn, whatever he did in that fortress.

As she approached her front door, the neighbors upstairs—a young British pair who had recently started a family—emerged along the staircase, baby in tow, glancing down in alarm.

"It's one hell of a mess, just like I said."

The Rosenbaums looked at her, startled.

Inside her home, Shmuel was sprawled on the couch, scratching his balls, in a t-shirt.

"Well, they managed to stop it."

"That's nice," said her husband, unfolding *Maariv*. Then he turned to look up at the ceiling. A slow fan blade revolved in languorous swirls.

Ilana inspected her sink drain. "Why would he do this?" she asked, knowing full well that it was Shaul's mindless way of revolting. His "outlet."

"Who knows?" Shmuel said. Outside, they heard fire trucks wailing. "By the way, is the workshop all gone?"

"There's still a bit left."

"Well, I guess the place had it coming." He flipped to the sports page and said Milan lost.

"That's nice, dear. You know I'm a little bit worried about what's happened to Shaul."

"Is he coming back soon from...wherever?"

"I doubt it."

"You know, I made him some dinner. If you're hungry, there's shrimp on the table."

"No, thanks."

"Well, the police will be here soon. They know that's your spot, and they'll probably want to ask you what happened."

"I'll tell 'em."

"And what about Shaul?"

"He isn't here."

"And when he gets back?"

"He'll be leaving," Shmuel said.

"I don't think he belongs in a jail quite yet."

"Not for his work in the army?"

"I'm serious."

"So what should I tell them?"

"I don't know, a few lies. They wouldn't be your first this weekend."

When the policemen arrived later that night, along with the patrols and their neighbors, Ilana told them what had happened: just before dusk, she was tending the weeds in her garden and saw them—a handful of Arabs, migrants it seemed. Pickers who came from Qatana. They were wearing white headscarves and looked kind of mad. She thought that it might have been something. She watched as they hurried with shovels and picks down through the fence to their village. A young policewoman jotted down notes in her book as Ilana gave lucid descriptions.

And the Arabs had motive. They had done this before. Last year, they had burnt down a greenhouse. Of course, the neighbors all knew this: Etti and Dan, even Judy upstairs with her gremlin.

"It must have been the Arabs. I don't see why not. They have every good reason to do it. They should have. We gave them thirty-one to the dollar this year and docked a few more for the closures."

The Lieutenant Commander glared at Ilana. He was wearing a small, knitted *kippah*. Beside him, the woman—a Yemenite twig with those annoying red wire-frame glasses—just smirked. All the others were smoking. Most appeared bored. Shmuel sat up on the sofa. He was munching on shrimp, devouring legs. He'd offered them some before starting.

Later, Shmuel told them, "I don't know what I lost or how much is gone, but I think we should size up the damage."

"Really," Ilana added. "There were thousands' worth in there. All his work and his sculptures, not to mention that T.V., the new one we bought. We just got it set up for cable."

A couple men coughed or let out a sigh when Ilana claimed twelve thousand shekels. And no one thought much when they asked about her son and when he'd come back from the army. "Yeah, he was home here already, sometime around nine. He dropped off his stuff and left."

"Where did he go?"

"Don't know," Ilana said. "Probably out with his friends in the city."

"All the respect," a young trooper said, "for what the guy's been through this weekend."

She nodded.

As the troopers walked out, along with Etti and Dan—who

humbly washed plates in the kitchen—Ilana turned around to find Shmuel on the couch, asleep with his cheek on the armrest.

She slowly bent down to his garlic-smelling beard and planted a smooch on his skin. He grumbled. Then he pulled her beside him on top of the couch and said, "You know, I haven't cheated."

"I know."

"And I never would cheat you."

"I know that," she said. And for some reason, she still believed it. She kicked a few plates off the side of the couch and buried herself in his shoulder.

That evening, on his way to Ramallah, where he was planning to make amends with his ex-girlfriend, Shaul decided to make a quick detour—a pilgrimage of sorts—to the heavenly abode of Mount Zion. He stood at the Wall for several minutes and found he had nothing to say. He took out a pen and wrote a quick note, scribbling plainly in Hebrew: "Dear Lord, please grant me the girl. Is there anything else on this earth?"

He stuck it in the blocks, headed to the tunnel, and wandered down al-Wad HaGai.

Thirty minutes later, he was standing in the rain, in the pit of the souk, in the heart of the Muslim Quarter. The Old City was flooding, and it smelled of old stone and raw trash-heaps and incense and nutmeg and cats.

Hooded monks marched ahead through the smoky black gates, swinging brass chains with lit censers. And there were Arabs all around him, pushing their wares: sodden mint leaves, hibiscus, red cabbage, and lungs. They teetered through the plaza and under its gates, beneath the slabbed stones of the ramparts, above. Shaul looked up: that black, winter night. The sky overhead was now purple and clearing. The clouds went their ways and Shaul went his as he passed through the Gates of the Column.

It was *Bab-al-Amud*, as the cab driver had said when he dropped Shaul off along Yaffo. Now he mounted the steps—huge dolomite blocks—hugging his bag to his shoulder. And his sneakers were drenched. He should have worn his boots, but he didn't want the Arabs to see them. Stopping, he knelt by a handrail and lit a smoke with the Bic he'd just used to commit arson, and laughed.

Shaul kept walking, duffel in hand, past the lit stalls and their venders, their za'atar, boxed laundry detergents, stale coffee and beans, broomsticks and cumin, ripe jujubes, canes, and all these weird people—the Arabs, the Jews, the homeless, the hags, the untoothed and blue-freckled—with their stubbled chins, scarves, their cheap cigarettes, their fried chicken, phone shops, arcade games, their musk, and this whole sordid place, like the wreck of the earth. The most holy place on the planet, this city. Shaul didn't feel it. At the same time, he did. The ramparts were glowing above him in rainlight. And he knew God was watching, poking himself, laughing out loud on His cushion.

Shaul had only been to the Old City twice. He thought he should start making visits. He liked the dark churches, the brocaded stoles, the dusty prayer mats arrayed behind columns and doors, the smoking brass lanterns, gold Bibles and spears, the scents of burnt camphor and resins and clove. This place was quite holy, *because* they believed. People had chosen to make this. He knew there was life inside of these stones, as ancient and precious as he was, undying. Of course, he would die, and this place would melt as soon as they blew up the Temple. But they would rebuild it: the walls and the mosques, the Dome of the Rock at al-Aqsa, the churches.

Four-forty B.C. That's when they said Solomon had erected this fortress. Or ordered it made by the hands of his slaves. It was good to be king here and Jewish.

He took out his phone. The glass was webbed. It barely showed numbers or signal. But his mother had called, the army, his men, the Jerusalem Police, and his father. Not Lina. He scrolled through the names and found hers and called, and he said he would come to Ramallah. And it was weird hearing his ex-girlfriend's voice, like some spirit conjured up in a dream.

He sloshed towards the cabstand across Nablus Square, where Arabs were huddled by taxis. They waited with children, with bags and wet *thobes*, with smeared newspapers draping their foreheads, smoking. Or they stood behind columns, that black-checkered sky which passed through the night and the valley, above this. That sky would cross borders, the rift and divide, Nablus, Jenin, Tulkarem, the Green Line. The sky knew no limits. But these people did. One of them scratched at his tonsils and spat.

"Ramallah?" Shaul asked him.

His chin gave a tsk. Then a woman said it moved to the corner. She was a shiny-cheeked Asian in a sweatshirt and coat. Cambodian, maybe. A worker.

Shaul waded to the corner, where other men stood huddled inside of a market. It was a bakery shop, which also sold goods and those little egg pizzas they ordered. He got one. Then he waited for a van and watched it unload—Filipinos, reporters, and Arabs, all soaking. A young woman in dreadlocks and parti-colored braids passed him and spoke in her cellphone: "I cannot believe they has kill right then. They has kill in the street. This iz children, iz awful." Scandinavian, maybe. Shaul watched her go by with a backpack and thermos of water. Then she turned into a hostel on Salah-ah-Din and waved to some lecherous merchants.

Shaul sat down inside of the van. He wondered what she had been saying—if she had been talking about his patrol team earlier, the child they had shot at al-Aida. Then he asked a couple Arabs who sat at his side, stinking and wet with their perfumes, "Ramallah?"

"Ramallah," they answered.

"*Shukran*," Shaul said. Praised be to God and the Prophet.

More entered. When the shuttle filled up, the driver took off, passing the gates of the city and troopers and the blue blinking lights and the sirens and mess. Shaul gave his change to the driver.

At the front of the shuttle—a twelve-person van with carpeted seats like recliners and flowers and silver discs hanging from the driver's rear-view stenciled with prints of His Sayings—the driver was asking who had a pass, if everyone came with permission. Shaul thought about announcing that he'd let them cross, but then they would stop and beat him.

The ride was all silence. They passed through the hills, the settlements north of the city, a roadblock. They stopped at a junction, were greeted with lights and Border Police in a *Sufa*. The guards held their guns and their lights in the van, shining their beams in his face. He showed them his pass, as others had done. A guard answered back in bad English, "How are you?"

"I'm great," Shaul said.

"*Amerikai?*"

"Yes."

"Why you is go to Ramallah?"

"Vacation."

"You know zat is closed now."

"Okay," Shaul said. "I thought I'd just visit the checkpoint."

They let him. They took out some Arabs—some children in front and a woman who came without papers. She said something about kidneys, a transplant device, pleading outside with the soldiers. They hit her. And he watched from the window as the door was slammed shut and the vehicle sped off beside her. The others had papers, permission to go. Collaborators probably. Or dealers.

They drove on.

When they got to the checkpoint, the line was backed up about a kilometer south of the crossing. The rain had since stopped, and the place looked like hell. Garbage was hissing in dumpsters. Children were running, working the lines, selling their pretzels and coffee. There were tourists stranded, television trucks, a herd of soaked sheep, and a stalled APC. He thought he heard rumbling beyond the west hills—possibly tanks, or more thunder.

At the side of the road, he set down his bag and combed through his moldy belongings. Then he checked the south tower, a beige metal post, where soldiers were sleeping or farting. He pulled out a gas can and some spent HE shells, which he'd stolen from a Jeep back at HQ, and tossed them. Then he cut to the right of the long Arab line, passing by people with smallpox or plague, and down through the turnstile, flashing his pass, setting his bag on the scanner. He nodded to the guards, who called out his name while he smoked and sat down on the benches. Then he passed through the maze—the iron, grated lot, like a cattle-herding pen or a ghetto—and went on.

He thought he heard hisses, a few awkward bleeps, but those were directed to Arabs beside him. A few jackets pushed through with their VIP cards. Lawmen or friends of their leader. They shuffled along with their skins and fur hides. A black Audi waited to greet them.

An unusual number of Jeeps passed him by as he waited around for a van. There weren't any cabs with the curfew in force. He thought about hitching with soldiers. He couldn't. And there were all sorts of troopers and trucks rolling in: armored Humvees, Safaris, D9's, a *Bardehlas*. He watched the troops enter, shielding his face with the side of his hand to avoid them. He thought that this must be routine for this place. Lina was something to live here.

He found a lone cab, which had crept behind blocks. The

driver was fourteen or younger. Shaul asked him in Arabic: "You going to Ramallah?"

"A-Ram," he said.

"I'll give you forty to go to the fountain."

It was a yellow Mercedes without any plates, and the back cushion smelled like a urinal. As they drove through Kafr 'Aqb, more Jeeps rumbled by. The cabbie hung left through a village. He said it was illegal to drive here right now; they both could be killed for just standing.

"Okay. Try to avoid them."

"I will." The kid sighed. "Nice night to come to Ramallah."

The cab dropped him off about a kilometer south of the square by Lina's apartment. Then Shaul gave him a tip of twenty-one sheks for risking his life for a patron, a fair price.

Then he headed east with his duffel and coat, skulking through darkness and buildings. He saw the flitting shadows of people in alleys, children with rocks in dark corners. They were ducking behind dumpsters, bumpers and pipes, awaiting the convoy of soldiers. Shaul heard the Jeeps coming—their churn through the night—as they rumbled up Main and al-Nahda. And it was even louder, he thought, outside of those Jeeps than it was in his own in Beit Jala.

Kids waited. They crept with their rocks and their bricks and their slings, like David edging up to Goliath, or heathens, and they skipped between buildings, dashed down the streets, joining their friends in dark spaces. What the children didn't know—or didn't seem to care—is that it wasn't that hard for the soldiers in *Sufim* to hit them. When the men didn't shoot them, this was a choice. It was like hitting plaques in the desert. You did it. And you listened for the ting, like a tiny little chime, and the plunk of some weight on the gravel. And the kids here were stupid. The ones by his base had accidentally stumbled upon him. But the ones in Ramallah, they wanted to die. They wanted to face down the troopers, like chicken. And did they think they were playing with green plastic toys, or the rides that they saw at a circus? Shaul heard the Jeeps whirring, their slow-rising drone, wheezing and clacking and stalling, then grinding. They were a couple blocks south, just past the bank, rounding the strip of Qaddura.

A gunshot rang out like a thwack on a can, clunking off a steel shutter.

He was kneeling on the curb of Mughtarebeen Square, which divided five streets with a fountain. There were Arabs all around him—dozens by cars—swarming in packs through the alleys and racing. One of them picked up a brick with his hands, slammed it on the ground, and took pieces. Another one crouched in the wet alley light, holding his forehead and singing. They were men of every age, fashion and weight, bearing armbands, *kafiyyehs*, and crosses. They zipped between buildings, puddles, and lamps. An ambulance idled beside them, in darkness.

Shaul bolted towards an alley and squatted by cars. Across from him, a young man was peeing. The man looked him down. Through the streets, they heard armored trucks revving their engines. These were impossibly loud—even louder than before, as if they wanted to punish the children, and him. Then headlights swung out along al-Nuzha Street, as bright as Ezekiel's vision.

Shaul picked up a rock and threw it towards the Jeeps. Then he ducked behind a raised shutter. He did this to show them—the packs at his side—that he wasn't a Jew in Ramallah. Then he sprinted towards a building north of the square. The corner door opened. He went in and squatted. A masked man was kneeling. This man had a gun. On second thought, a Nesher Malt bottle. And it was stoppered with a rag. He reached in his coat. He pulled out a yellow Bic lighter, and lit it. But he didn't light the rag. He felt through his shirt. Then his eyes came to rest upon Shaul.

"How are you?" Shaul asked.

The militant leaned with his back to a wall. A staircase rose through the darkness above him. The front wall had block windows, a ledge with some stains—coffee grounds, maybe, or syrup. A pencil. The light through this window shone gauzy and pink from the streetlights outside in the square. And the door was ajar. The man held it back. The Jeeps' drone was getting closer and louder. It shook them. Beside Shaul, this soldier—in knit-rib balaclava, checkered red shirt, and tan cargos—was waiting. His eyes glistened whitely, beneath their two slits. He whispered to Shaul to be quiet. "*Uskuut.*"

Then the vehicles came and rounded the square, illuminating the blocks of the window. Still squatting, Shaul balanced himself on the wet cement floor. An apple core shone on the staircase above him. Soon the room became quiet and musty and dark, and the militant stared with a grimace. "*Amreekee?*" he asked.

Shaul nodded and grinned.

"Why you here?"

"For a visit."

"*Ya Allah.* You see what they do here?"

"Yes," Shaul said.

"Why the Jews come to Ramallah?"

"Your guess."

Before Shaul could move or even sit up, the militant rose with the bottle. He dashed past the staircase and out through the door and down to the light of the circle and stopped, where he was contoured brightly beneath the pink glare, about five meters down from the fountain. Leaning, he seized the bottle and gathered the wick and ignited the rag in his jacket. And he looked like a sculpture, or some ancient frieze of a hurler bent down with a disc. The bottle sailed forward, silent in the light, and broke on the Jeep's coming hood. The flames sparked up and quickly steamed out as a gun barrel rose through the rear hatch.

"Get down," Shaul shouted. The man didn't move. *Fuck.* Without even thinking, still holding his bag, Shaul sprang out and tackled the man by the waist. They both fell, and a gunshot clanked off the door. Shaul rolled sideways, having broken his fall with his bag.

He didn't even turn to look back at the man then. He sprinted away from the square. As he did, another shot boomed through the night.

Gasping, he ran past the buildings, away from the light, down the dark stretch of an alley and west. Then he heard a loud wailing, an ambulance blare, and the sound bombs that cracked at the Manara. Dozens ran past him with bricks and lead pipes, like some medieval mob on a rampage. Then he turned at the corner, stopped and looked back. An ambulance pulled to the fountain. A couple medics hopped out with their bright orange vests, shouting in Greek or Italian.

Shaul set down his duffel and rubbed at his eyes, removing the sweat and the gravel. Then he jogged past a streetlight hanging from a line. A yellow light signaled for caution.

He wasn't even sure if that Arab was dead now. If he wasn't, he'd surely be soon.

Shaul wiped off his face. His elbow was scraped. He picked up his duffel and ran. He could feel himself sweating and heaving for breath, mildly glad he was alive.

Around him, the city looked strangely quiet as he ran, much calmer than when he'd come for the protests or Lina. And all the places he'd gone to—Ruqab's for shakes, the Checkers for burgers and donuts, and Palsoft—were boarded and shuttered or stripped of their wares, all since the uprising started. The whole town looked deserted, minus the fog and steam sifting up through the grates. Plus engines: he saw the Jeeps blinking far to the north, down al-Radio Street, past its tower. And there were helicopters gliding, skidding with blades, circling north of al-Bireh.

Exhaling, he turned and looked out from a precipice road, a sheer cliff overlooking the wadi. He could see western Tel Aviv, its pale, leaping lights, like a spectrum of dots on the shore, and the slopes of al-Tireh, south, his kibbutz, his parents at home in their bedroom, the workshop, or that funnel of flames as it danced through the night and commingled with smoke from Ramallah, above him. Up through those buildings, those tall angled lights, Lina's apartment was waiting. There were two-dozen buildings of approximate height, but only one had been built with a penthouse.

He climbed through the city, past the stables and park, a small wading pool used during summers—now vacant—a Romanesque manor, walled orchards with fruit, ripe kumquats and loquats and daisies, McDonald's, and up the stone steps that led to her street, through the wrought iron gates of her building.

Inside her courtyard, he crouched by the gates and searched for the keys in his duffel and found them. Then he took out his thermos and wrested the lid and doused off his head with the water and drank. And he thought about calling her, buzzing her name, but the power was off in her building. So he entered her hall—twin doors on each side, each of them bolted in silence.

Behind him, the light through the transom fell hazy and gold, and it smelled of wet Pine-Sol and diesel. He shut the door and mounted the steps, climbing five flights with his duffel. There were families with children inside of these rooms, though all he could hear was his steps.

At the uppermost landing, he stopped by her door and stared at the light—an amethyst sky lit the window behind him. Ramallah was burning, his family in flames, Jerusalem blew through the distance with choppers. And amidst all this silence, this madness and mess, Lina was taking a shower. He heard her.

Forty minutes prior, just as she'd stepped in her shower, her cellphone rang on her shelf. The tune was Bach's "Fugue in D-Minor," a ring she'd assigned to her ex. She let it go a little bit, then reached past her towels, her Chanel No. 5, and a couple back issues of *Vogue*. Finally, she resolved that she couldn't put him off. Not that she had much to tell him. "*Shu?*" ("What?")

"Lina, are you home?"

She cradled the phone. "Why?"

"I'm gonna stop by for a visit."

"What?" She groped about for the handle. The hot water stung her, burning her back. She almost dropped the phone in the water. "When?"

"Right now," Shaul explained.

"But you can't," she said. "I'm...not ready."

"Don't care."

"You're crazy," she said, louder than she'd have liked. "The checkpoint is closed."

"I'll make my way through."

"*Yanee*, there's tanks in the city. I hear them."

He hung up the phone. She checked her watch. The shampoo was burning her eyes. She was supposed to meet Skandr's family tonight, but the army had shut the streets down. And she didn't even know what she was supposed to tell Shaul. *I'm sorry, dear, I got engaged?* He'd had his chance. He'd balked at her gestures. And she'd risked her own life for that fuck—not to mention the career and reputation of her father, who'd just been appointed Ambassador.

She dried herself off with a towel and shaved. She plucked between her brows with tweezers, and rinsed off. She threw on her best jeans—the oldest; they fit—and searched behind the stove for the bourbon. She didn't even know why she was doing this now. She was supposed to get married in June.

When she answered her door, at a quarter to one, Shaul was standing in jeans and a t-shirt. He was holding a duffel, an enormous black bag, and his cropped hair was gleaming with water. His elbow was bleeding, his jeans caked with soot. "*Salaam*," he whispered.

"Shut up and get in."

She shut the door. He studied her place. His eyes shone bright in their sockets. She lit a couple candles, which she kept on the stove, and turned to appraise her ex-boyfriend.

"What's in the bag?"

"My socks and my shirts."

"Why did you come here?"

"I had to."

"For laundry? Did anyone see you?"

"I don't think so," he said.

"If anyone did, we're both dead."

He sat on the couch. He studied her floor. She offered him tea and a biscuit. He took it.

"What can I get you?"

"I don't know," Shaul said. "How about a kiss?"

"I'm a virgin."

"I know."

She sat on his lap, upon his oily blue jeans. He brushed back the hair from her shoulder, and kissed her. She tasted his tonsils. He tasted like smoke, and the grime in his nails, and the army.

"Why did you come here?"

"I had to," he said. "There's something I wanted to tell you."

104

"Okay."

He stared at the floor. He pulled out his pack. He took out a joint and he lit it. Then they stared at the evening outside through the blinds, the shooting that flashed off the buildings.

They kissed on the floor. They almost made love, madly rubbing and naked and silent and wet. And he kissed her lips and her hands and her thighs, and for a second, she felt herself quiver.

Then they moved to the bedroom. They swam through the sheets. As he kissed her and held her, he said it.

She blinked.

"Lina, you need to know this. There's something I want to tell you."

She was looking at him deeply. Clearly, she knew this was coming.

"I love you."

"Shaul, you're a kid."

"No, I'm not."

"You are. You don't know even what love is yet."

He had nothing to say. He had nothing to say to this woman. He had spoken his heart. And she believed what he said; that's why she'd chosen to say this.

"I don't love you," she told him.

"Not at all?"

"No."

"Then why did you say that in August?"

"I don't know."

They slept for three hours. She slept. He thought about his parents, the Arab he had shot, and why he no longer loved his girlfriend. Needed her, however, if only to complete this whole process of self-destruction.

"Lina, I want to have sex." It was 4:55 in the morning. In an hour, he would leave for the checkpoint. "Lina, wake up. I want to have sex."

"You really are a little kid, Shaul."

"Am I? Why?"

She turned her head over to sleep again. He stood up on the bed and started to dance, a dance he had learned in the army. It was called the "Shakshuka." It involved shaking his arms a lot and swinging around like a madman. He pounded his fists, shook his whole head, kicked out his left leg and right. She didn't look up. She pretended to sleep. At that point he reached down and kissed her. He pulled off his boxers, put his dick in her face. She threw him off the bed, and he fell.

He stood. "My name is Shaul S. Braverman, and I am a lieutenant in the Israeli Defense Forces Army. I am here to arrest you for terror. You can leave this house unharmed. If you do not, I will be forced to take action, and I will secure my own entry."

She did not respond.

"I repeat, if you do not get up, I will be forced to take action. Please think about your life and your family."

She looked up. "Shaul, get the hell out. And take your bag. I don't want that shit in my apartment. Your ganja."

"Lina, I'm horny."

"Just get the fuck out. I want you to leave. And I don't want to see you here again. Go."

He put on his jeans, his belt and white shirt. He considered making tea at her counter. He studied her kitchen, the room where they'd slept, the spot where they'd kissed on the carpet, her sketches. One was a view from the Naftali Ridge, angrily daubed in black.

As he started towards the front door, Lina came out. She was wearing her white cotton bathrobe and slippers. And she was holding a toothbrush, the one that he'd left, eyeing him redly and crying. "Please take this."

"I thought you might want it."

"You can keep it," she said. Then she turned and stamped down to the stove. She rinsed off a glass and clicked on the flame. Then she swung around to face him. "Look Shaul, I'm sorry. I didn't really want you to go. I'm just mad that you came here and did that, and I—"

"Did you mean what you said?"

"What?"

"In the bedroom last night?"

"I don't know," Lina said. "I'm confused now. I'm sorry. Look, I don't want to hurt you, and I didn't mean to say—"

"It's fine. I'll get going."

"Wait, Shaul. Stop—"

Outside of Lina's building, the streets were all silent, minus the din of some construction workers distantly drilling. It was ten after five. The sun wasn't up, but the sky shone hellishly violet. A pink mist of haze weltered up from the east above a large billboard for yogurt. The Jeeps all appeared to have come and gone. He wished he had flagged down a ride.

Shaul turned to look up at her building again—the tall glassy complex with shutters. Her building had been completed in the early Nineties, back when the exiles came here. Now her parents resided on the third and fourth floors. He thought he should stop in for a visit. *Hey pops, I tried to fuck your daughter. It didn't work out. You wouldn't have a few sheks for a cab ride, would you?*

He stalked to the fountain and south up to Main. No sign of the shootings or clashes. In fact, about ten meters down from where he dove for that Arab, two elders were smoking a hookah. One of them watched as Shaul went by. "Peace be upon you," Shaul muttered. The other one sipped at a glass of mint tea while stacking a coal with his tongs.

Shaul turned to look back at the scene of the crime: the thick blocks of glass in the window. To the left lay a stall whose shutters had been raised. Inside was a cage full of hens.

There were holes in the walls of the Jerusalem Bank, where soldiers had shot at the riots and killed. Beyond them hung posters of martyrs who had died, most bearing human-sized rifles and grinning. One looked familiar, a face Shaul knew: the man he had shot outside Rachel's.

He looked for the face from the building last night, though all he had seen were the pupils and breath. Plus these were older, all faded and ripped, like headshots awaiting their filing. Another looked familiar. A girl that he knew. A martyr who had come from Daheisha, near Rachel's. She'd blown herself up just south of his base, outside a Jerusalem market. And she looked kind of sexy, with her eyelashes curled, a cream-colored veil and rouge lipstick. Like Lina. He thought he would date her. But now she was dead. Maybe she came with a sister. They all did.

Sometimes he wondered if Lina would do it: blow herself up at a market. She could have. She had the permission, the papers to cross. She'd probably wait for a discount or bargain. Or maybe she'd do it inside of the mall while fucking a clerk in the storeroom. Or soldier. Or one of those builders, those men who came by. "Cousins" she knew from her village.

He had forty minutes before his bus would depart, the one he would catch at the junction, and transfer. Then he'd stop off at his parents' kibbutz and pick up his gun for the army. Of course, he'd have to avoid being seen at his home—he figured he'd come from the forest. Then he'd catch a ride on the Jerusalem line or hitchhike with settlers to Kfar Etzion. He'd be back in time for the meeting at one. He was supposed to read maps with the Colonel and Captain. Or they would discuss, while Shaul would sit and ponder his fate with the others.

Of course, what he realized then as he stood by the bank, eyeing himself in a window, is not that he'd die—he wasn't that brave—but that he still hadn't gotten his hair cut. He couldn't talk to the Colonel or Captain like this, much less yell at his soldiers. And maybe that's why his own girlfriend rejected him. He didn't even look like a soldier.

He could always go back and get his head shaved at home, but the others might ask what had happened. And he could use his electric when he got back to base, but he always left clumps by his ears. He could go to a barber in Zion Square, but those would be closed or expensive. Or maybe he could find a place around here. There had to be one that was open. He had a few minutes— enough for a shave—and the Arabs were cheaper than nothing.

He walked past the market, the stalls and green sheets. A peddler was hawking some carrots. He had a glassy blue eye. The other didn't work. Probably a cousin of Lina's. He asked him, "*btraff ween enah baqdar...*" Shaul snipped with his hand, miming scissors. Then the vendor gave a look as if it were a briss Shaul sought.

"A haircut," Shaul told him in English.

He pointed.

It was weird, Shaul thought, or uncannily real, that nobody here seemed to notice or wonder that a war had been waged here late in the night with armored trucks, tear gas, and weapons. The only real signs of an invasion last night were the scuffmarks and rocks on the pavement.

Near the end of the souk, towards Qalandia Street, he came to a shop with a barber. A spiraling pole sat outside the windowed shop, which was sided with logs like a cabin. And there were children inside, about a dozen on a couch, watching a gameshow in Hebrew.

He entered. "*Salaam al-alaikum*," Shaul told them. The young teens looked up with their mustaches, tracksuits, and sweaters.

"*Alaikum wa-salaam*," a couple kids said. The older ones stared at the channel.

"*Msakkar?*" Shaul asked.

"We open," said a kid of indeterminate age. He might have been fourteen or forty.

"Can I get my hair cut?"

The urchin looked back. "Yes, you enter. I cut you."

"Okay." Shaul walked inside with his jeans, a white shirt, and a duffel that smelled like a body.

"You welcome," said the kid with that curved Arab smile and the waxy orange cheeks of a jackal. "You welcome."

"*Shukran ktiir.*"—"Thank you very much."

"What you want? You want shorter?"

"I guess."

"Where you from?"

"*Amreeka*," Shaul said.

"Oh, you like Michael Jordan?"

"I do."

"You know, he good nigger. Fly through the sky. We need this in Ramallah. You know that?"

"I do," Shaul said as he set down his bag and thought about asking the price first. Yet that would be rude. As Lina once said, you never talked price in Ramallah.

Shaul sat in the chair. He looked in the mirror. About six future martyrs were smiling behind him. Several sat on the couch. A few watched the set. One of them flipped through the channels.

Then a news show came on. It was satellite news: al-Jazeera, or some Arab station. It showed a dozen tanks heading in here last night and up to the home of their leader. There were pictures of his compound, several Arabs, dumb guests, helicopters pounding the rubble, explosions. But there wasn't any footage of the Jeeps at the fountain. All the cameras, he supposed, had been taken.

Then a couple kids asked if he had come here this morning.

"Yes," Shaul said. "It looks great."

"You see what happen outside the jail?" an older one asked from the sofa.

Shaul looked up.

"Two Jews they come here. They enter the town."

Shaul looked at the kid, then the channel. The news showed some pictures of soldiers who died. Two soldiers, it seemed, in Ramallah.

"What happened?"

"They bring Jeep here, enter this place. They try to make killing in secret."

The news showed some footage of mobs in a street. The masses were swinging a body.

"What is that?"

"It Jew," the kid said. "They come here with guns." The others looked up from the sofa, still smoking. "And they come in. But we get them first. We make fight at the jail."

"No kidding?"

Shaul listened closely and tried to make out what the veiled Arab woman was saying. Two soldiers had been stranded. They had driven here alone. The mob dragged them out by their feet. And they were held in a station by the Arab police, who tried to fend off the riots. Then they were pulled from their cell and thrown to the crowds. One man was torn into pieces and burnt. Another one escaped or tried to get out, but it wasn't really clear what had happened. He died.

"You like scissors?" asked the barber.

"Electric is fine."

"I do both."

"Just electric."

"Okay."

Shaul looked out at the cold, passing wind. The sun was now bleeding into the city. It lit up the buildings with wide, angled stripes and stopped at the nook of the market.

"So now they gone," another kid said, craning his neck on the couch. "The tanks came in already. They pick up dead and they leave. They come back. Soon they bomb whole entire town. You know this not make a difference. I know this. They kill us. We kill them. What difference it make?"

Shaul flinched.

"But you no worry. Good you here. You tell world what happen."

"Okay."

"You reporter?"

"Yes," Shaul said.

"You tell American people."

"Okay."

Shaul watched the young kids through the mirror on the wall. The barber was draping a smock. He was twisting the cords behind Shaul's neck, preparing the noose for the hanging.

"You no worry. America fine. We only have problem with *Israeleen*."

Shaul looked back at the kids on the couch, all puffing away, like tiny, dark, lair-nesting dragons.

"Reporter good. Come to this place, tell of the suffering people. We suffer. They make trouble, many die. You know what happen at Manara?"

"What happen?"

"Many killed there. I see many die. You know, I see man, he look like you, last night. And they make picture, reporters who come. They tell world what happen."

"Okay."

"Why we fighting? Why we want kill? You know we want peace with *Israeleen*. We all want. But they come, and they take ourz land, and they try to kill Arabic leader."

The Arab looked up with soft, angelic eyes, like a cherub, or Arab, or Lina. They all were. Tiny green serpents with teeth and wet fangs and that gelled hair that spiked from their foreheads. They asked him: "How short you want?"

"Number two," Shaul replied.

"Like a soldier?" They laughed.

"Make it longer."

"No problem."

A couple kids smoked and watched him obliquely, tipping their ash in a palm. "No good," someone said, "what they do to these men. No good to do, even soldiers." Another one tsked and studied his cigarette, snapping the wheel of his lighter. Two more were seated in chairs by the back, flipping through pages of hot rods and singers.

The children looked twelve, but the one with the smock who ran his wet hands through Shaul's hairline looked twenty. His chin bore a line of tiny black fur, like Lucifer's almost, but thinner.

"Is anyone else here?"

"What?" asked the kid.

"Who is the barber on duty?"

"I." Then he kicked down the pump and elevated Shaul, tightly gripping his shoulders.

One kid got up and walked to the chair. "You want Fanta?" he asked with a bottle.

"No, *shukran*." Shaul looked up at the set overhead, which showed an Arab inside of a building. He had blood-covered hands, all shiny and red, and he was waving to a mob from a window. It must have occurred here sometime before dark. That explained all the tanks at the crossing.

"You no worry. I cut good." He was licking his lip in the corners.

"Just do what you can," Shaul replied. "I have to get going, so quickly—"

"Okay. No problem. You our guest. You welcome in Ramallah."

The barber reached down, plugged in the cord, and held up the vibrating razor. He smelled like cologne, talcum and sweat, and the Arab he'd grabbed at the fountain.

A couple minutes later, when they'd shaved his whole head and successfully lopped off his sideburns, Shaul told them, "Thank you. That's fine. *Shukran, ktiir.* But I really think I should get going."

The barber looked up with a barbarous face, his meaty thumb pinching the razor. "No go."

"I think I should go."

The barber looked back through the mirror. "I shave you." Then he promptly bent down to a shelf at his side and pulled out a strop and a razor—a straight one. He looked in the mirror. Shaul looked back. "It no trouble. You guest here." He smiled.

On the couch along the wall, six children leaned forward. One of them slurped on a Fanta.

"No problem." Then the barber unlatched the long blade with his hands, turning the tang on the pivot. "I careful." The smooth blade was glinting, reflecting the light of his hands and his teeth and the window.

"No, thank you."

"Yes, no problem." The Arab reached down and squeezed

out a fistful of lather.

"I quickly."

There on the table, the straight razor sat, gleaming with light on a towel. It had a cherrywood handle, a rounded French point, and a shank that said MADE IN RAMALLAH.

"I careful."

He laved Shaul's cheek with a dollop of foam and pressed it around with his fingers.

"I have to go now."

"No, stay," the man said. The children behind him were smiling and smoking. Others had joined them, piling on the floor. A couple more peered through the windows.

"No problem," one said. "You our guest. No worry. You welcome."

Shaul wasn't sure if he should be scared or appear to be honestly grateful. He didn't feel scared. He could take this one out. The others would give him some trouble. And he should have brought his gun. He had left it at home, because he didn't think he'd get through the crossing. He would, though. He could have said where he was going, and what he now did, and why he had come to Ramallah: a woman. They'd understand that. All soldiers would. Every man had his conviction and cause. But what would that get him? And where would he go? The two soldiers had come here with weapons and died. He could always use his hands and fight his way out. He suspected he'd get to the square.

There were about a dozen inside, ten more on the street, and hoards between here and the market. He could run to Shufa'at Camp, Qalandia, south, but he wouldn't make it out to the checkpoint. He could hold up a cab by using one of their shears, or the bright thing that passed for a razor. But the Arabs had guns here. All Arabs did. They kept them at home with their women and children. And even children had guns here, and pitchforks and swords, flaming bottles, and pipes, and scythe fingers. They had bashed the men's heads in using fists and bare hands. If the tanks hadn't come, they would have eaten them.

Shaul looked at the ceiling. His head tilted back. He thought about Lina, her answer, his lover. He knew that she loved him. He knew that she'd lied. And that's what you get for an Arab. And she knew he would come here. She saw this whole thing. She had probably planned the invasion and lynching. And she was watching him now from her room up above, probably instructing the barber. She was the lieutenant, the one man-in-charge—and here he was dying a martyr. Like Samson. And all these horrid creatures, like Lina's own clan, bracing to razor his neck.

He rose. He had lather on his face. He wiped the gook off. Then he said to the barber, "I'm going."

"Why you go soon? I no finish shave."

"I have to," Shaul said. "An appointment."

"A what?"

"I've got to fuck a woman."

A couple kids laughed.

"Laugh all you want. It's your cousin," he mumbled. "How much for the shave?"

"For you, zat free."

"Why?" Shaul said.

"You guest here, *ajnabi*."

Shaul reached in his pants. He took out his cash, set a few bills on the table, and left.

"*Salamtak*," they shouted.

"And peace unto you." He ran through the streets of the city. He carried his coat and duffel in hand, and he thought about going to see her.

As he fled past the buildings and bullet-pocked walls, he noticed that no Arabs had emerged. Strangely, the streets were all silent. *Were the troops coming back?* Then he glanced inside a coffeehouse window. A couple of Arabs were perched by a screen.

In fact, a few more did the same thing next door. He couldn't quite tell what their televisions showed, but he could swear it was a wet, naked girl. *The fuck?*

Shaul kept running down Qalandia Street. Soon the clouds opened up, and it rained.

As Shaul reached the south station, he walked by a Jeep. He recognized the flags of his Battalion. His soldiers? They were carrying guns inside of their truck. It was Ivan and Boaz—no sergeants, bizarrely. They slowed at the checkpoint and waved to the guards. As Shaul saw them, he heard Ivan whisper, "*Blyad.*"

"Why are you here now?"

"A mission," Ivan said.

"What kind of mission?"

"An errand."

"Okay." Shaul rounded the back, and he climbed in the cab, and he said they should head to Route One. And he couldn't even guess what they were doing out here, though it looked like they'd stormed the Sahara. The rear fender was missing. The windshield was cracked. And the grenade case he'd raided for charges was open. "It smells like a bong here."

"Wouldn't know about that." In the driver's seat, Boaz was smiling.

"What was this, a joyride?"

"I guess," Ivan said. "And where were you?"

"Making an arrest."

Shaul directed them west to his parents' kibbutz, where he had to run in for his rifle. When he got to his home, he found his mother and father asleep on the floor by the sofa. He didn't wake them up. He gently stepped through the house. Then he saw that his parents

117

were naked. With socks on. The sight was disgusting. It shivered his neck. He picked up his gun and left.

Outside, the Jeep waited with his soldiers inside. He told them to scoot, he would drive it.

They drove through the forest towards Bethlehem, south, and out along 60 to Rachel's. And when they pulled through the gates of Company HQ, Shaul told them: "I don't know what happened. I don't know what you did when you were off base, and you didn't see me this morning."

They nodded.

They gave the Captain the keys to his truck. They didn't give papers or answers. They stood there. Shaul then explained that they'd had a tough day. The roads had been closed. There were lynchings.

When his troops were dismissed, Capt. Avi faced Shaul. "You look like you've been through a war."

Shaul sighed.

"I don't know what that shit was with the soldiers this morning. We'll deal with it after the raid. You're leading a *Bardehlas*. Go get eight men. I suggest you choose soldiers you trust."

Shaul did as instructed, perusing his ranks. It didn't take him long to decide.

Later that night, as Shaul sat on his bed, poring over their plans for invasion, he glumly looked down at the day's latest news, which the Colonel had delivered from Battalion HQ. There wasn't much news that captured his glance. The army was besieging the Nativity Church. And two soldiers had been killed by a rampaging mob, not far from where he'd been in Ramallah. But what caught his attention as he flipped to the back was a dispatch from some foreign press. He couldn't quite believe what was written in print, though he didn't really doubt it had happened.

Palestinians Complain Israelis Broadcasting Porn from Captured TV Stations

Agence France Presse

RAMALLAH, West Bank. Porn movies and programs in Hebrew are being broadcast by Israeli troops who have taken over three Palestinian television stations of Ramallah, irate residents of the besieged West Bank town told AFP Monday.

The offices of three local television and radio stations were occupied by soldiers, a few hours after tanks and hundreds of troops stormed the town in Israel's biggest offensive in years against the Palestinian Authority.

The soldiers started broadcasting the porn clips—considered extremely offensive by most Muslims—intermittently this morning from the al-Watan, Ammwaj, and al-Sharaq channels, the residents said. [...] Israeli foreign ministry spokesman Emmanuel Nachshon said any such broadcasting was "shameful," but said he was not aware of the Israeli army's involvement.

"I cannot believe that Israeli soldiers would engage in such despicable behaviour," he said.

Semites had no half-tones in their register of vision. They were a people of primary colors, or rather of black and white, who saw the world always in contour...This people was black and white not only in vision, but by inmost furnishing: black and white not merely in clarity, but in apposition. Their thoughts were at ease only in extremes. They inhabited superlatives by choice.

—T. E. Lawrence, *The Seven Pillars of Wisdom*

This made sense to Shaul. He had been engaged in a war now for several decades of his life—he was approaching twenty-two—and the battle zone that was Rachel's Tomb was only the most recent and distressing one. Frankly, the war with Lina, as well as the one fought at home with his parents, were given over to weird bouts of passion. There was no predictability in the matter, nor logic to govern it. It made thorough and complete sense to him that his father would try and mold him into the shape of a soldier. It was also frankly relieving to him to realize that his mother possessed the same indomitable spirit that he did, as well as the woman he had dated. Of course, women were another matter and governed by their own, separate discourse. That wasn't one he'd care to analyze yet, seeing as how he didn't feel he had the proper tools at his disposal.

Nevertheless, when he arrived back at Rachel's Tomb that Monday, preparing for the incursion on Tuesday, and equally dreading it—if not the incursion itself, then the altercations which would ensue when he returned to his quarters and set about informing his mother what had happened in the battle; for she would wish to know what had happened, and she would telephone him regularly, and if not him, then his Captain, and his Adjutant, and possibly his own men, assuming she hadn't yet obtained all their numbers from the District Authority, of whom she was said to have reputable contacts—it was fairly clear to Shaul that Lina's

Arab nature could be investigated further, if not fully delineated.

The contents of Shaul's duffel bag featured a diverse array of items, including his glass pipe, tracer rounds, two and a half liters of aged British gin—purchased at discount in Bethlehem—a soldering gun, Frisbee, magnetic tape, pliers, a rotting army tooth brush from Lina's, a few condoms he had yet to employ, and a Hebrew-Arabic dictionary that he'd regularly peruse in his free time, which wasn't much these days. He also had a copy of a book he'd purchased at the Jerusalem Central Bus Station. Most of the works there were the sort commonly cleared from American Jews' shelves: Leon Uris, James Michener, something by Abba Eban. But what Shaul stumbled upon in this second-hand shop is a work that he held in almost singular esteem and considered to be a modern-day classic. It was called *The Arab Mind*, by one Raphael Patai, and it featured multiple chapters on women. One of them was entitled, "Extremes and Emotions, Fantasy and Reality." This was a veritable treasure-trove.

Patai opens the chapter with the above-cited quotation from Lawrence. He then talks at length about the Arab's rather "polarized" worldview:

> *If I were inclined to seek a correlation between the Arab temperament and the natural phenomena found in the environment, I would refer to the wadis, those rocky, narrow ravines in the desert which for most of the year are dry and dead, and then, on a few occasions when rain falls, possibly miles away, are suddenly transformed into tearing, raging torrents, rolling down big rocks and destroying everything that happens to lie in their way, only to subside again a few hours later as quickly as they rose.*

In some ways, Lina's premeditated response was governed by

weather. Whether or not she chose to say she loved him ultimately hinged on questions of mood-swing, and these, in turn, were governed by strange flights from reason—predictable, perhaps, on a climatological scale but wholly unknown to him at present. Naturally, all women were governed by the moon, much like the tides it created. Their bodies seemed to operate in conjunction with gravity, and it was said of the females who served in the army that entire regiments of them would menstruate in sync, assuming they had lived together long enough. There was no predicting the fatal mood swings of Artemis, her wild cries at midnight, but the Arab himself could be gleaned insofar as he perceived the world in terms of opposites. According to the Arab disposition, a man was either enemy or kin. And Shaul appreciated that distinction. Serving in an army long enough would give you that perspective, and he started to suspect that the Arabs' proclivity for extremes had less to do with any innate disposition than the mere warlike conditions in which they'd subsisted. This, as it were, might owe itself to centuries of imperialism and the fact that they had been dominated for several ages.

Of course, it was older than empires; the Bible itself contained evidence of such outbursts—David, Saul, Job—and he had no doubt that a Jew like himself, or at least one who had been living here long enough, would start to entertain such fantasies. Patai writes:

> *What the Arab mind does is to elect purposely to give greater weight in thought and speech to wishes rather than reality, to what it would like things to be rather than to what they objectively are.*

This, Shaul knew, was the predicament. No honest admission of their feelings was possible. To the extent he loved Lina, he could barely even say it, and she, for that matter, was dishonest. The truth of the matter was that she loved him, and he was in love with the idea of loving her. This bothered him extensively.

More pertinent, perhaps, to the invasion this week and the lynching that had occurred in the Manara was a passage on the Arab predilection for violence. Patai cites Wilfred Cantwell Smith, the noted Orientalist, who sought to explain the "Arab proclivity for mob action" in terms of "a number of psychological factors." According to Patai, "What emerges...is the picture of a human type which readily and frequently throws off the restraint of discipline and, especially in mass situations, is likely to go on a rampage."

Shaul was not convinced that the Arabs, including Lina, had ever possessed such a concept of discipline. Certainly Boaz didn't, unless he were succored into having it—hence, basic training. Nevertheless, Patai analyzes the difference between the Occidental and Oriental worldviews, and he sums up what he perceives to be the great mystery of that divide:

Why one group is characterized by such oscillation between the extremes of self-control and uncontrolled outbursts of emotion, while the life of another runs its even course, is one of those tantalizing questions to which no satisfactory answer has yet been found.

Tantalizing, indeed. Across from his cot, and down the hall through the curtains, a half-dozen soldiers were greasing up the bolts on the Negevs. These were long, metal guns with cylindrical barrels—they actually looked like penises, with their compressed buttstocks and retractable wings, all of which were bunched neatly behind them—lined in a row. The actions and assemblies were disassembled, resting on a bed of flannelette in front of each weapon. Boaz was licking his lip.

"According to both Freudian theory and experimental psychologists, there is a definite linkage between aggression and sexuality." Patai goes on to explore, in fairly convincing fashion, "the sexual repression-frustration-aggression syndrome of the Arab personality." Patai's book was written in '73, several months before the October War—Patai was Israeli—and Shaul had to wonder what sort of advances had been made since then in unveiling the Arab persona. In particular, he would have liked to offer a couple emendations on women, as the chapters seemed preoccupied with males and pent-up sexual frustration. As relevant as that was, it didn't go very far in explaining Lina's reaction.

"Shaul," Boaz asked from outside of his room, "do you want us to take down the mortars?"

"Not necessary."

Across from him, Sgt. Pinchas had set about reading his scriptures. He seemed to have returned to the Bible this week, rather than his regular run of *Harry Potter*. Perhaps he was moved by the war.

"Pinchas," Shaul yelled to his squad leader, "get the rest of the men up, and tell them to get down here. I want to have a quick meeting."

When the rest of Shaul's soldiers were gathered and spread out before him in the Control Room, slumping on the benches and looking somewhat bleary-eyed, if not exhausted and in tatters, he told them, "All right, you guys know what's going on tomorrow night. We've already discussed this. I hope you had a good leave. I don't think the invasion will take too long. We're not expecting too much resistance. Special Forces already did a mop-up. We're doing the shit-end, house-to-house, clearance. That sort of stuff. We're going to have to enter some buildings. You already know about all that. You discussed it with the Captain. However, at this point, I feel privileged to tell you, as some of you already know—I'm sure all of you know by now—that at one point in my life I was romantically involved with an Arab girl. Still am, in any case, though that hasn't seemed to pan out yet."

A couple guys laughed, thankfully.

"And as you may or may not know, after that screening last night, and the unfortunate events which preceded it, I don't think the Arabs are going to be thinking too highly of the Jews here. Needless to say, when we go into the homes tomorrow, you should be on your bestest behavior."

A couple more laughed, and Shaul did, as well. They had that look of estranged sadness in their eyes, all of them, the kind that is vented not in fury, nor emotion, but merely by killing. And he had no doubt that they would do that tomorrow evening.

"However," Shaul told them, "when we go in there tomorrow, this isn't a blood hunt. We're not out to hurt anybody. I know you guys are probably thinking about what's happened. God knows that I am. But that isn't a reason for fighting. And it has nothing to do with our job in the army. You hear me? Boaz? Ivan? Uri? You listening?"

That night, the soldiers concluded with the preparations for battle, including the oiling of the weapons, taping, the occasional prayer-hymn, and a sermon, which Shaul delivered privately, to himself, in the confines of his bed. He wrote in his diary:

Behold the Arab mind. Behold how it works. I take comfort in it, really, knowing that the world in which we live really isn't that complicated. Despite what everyone makes of this conflict, the ruminations and sermons, the speeches delivered, all on the subject and the specimen of Arab, these are all bogus and superfluous, jaded. Truthfully, I believe, and I know this in my heart, that the Arabs are no different than we are. It is just a part of the mode of becoming.

Nevertheless, my heart agitates me. I feel myself unduly attracted to the woman, torn by her, swept up in all-consuming passion of the sort poets often write about, artists often paint, but which few have ever fully experienced. For I have seen these things. I have seen the way the world works. And it has left me in some comical daze, some passion from which I feel I can never fully be rescued. I understand the appeal of the religious tracts. I understand the pull to Jehovah. I could never become a part of that, mainly because I was brought up with a skepticism towards doctrine, but I realize now, after all my days of warring, that all thinking is fruitless, and the only certainties we have are those which we live by.

He continued his writing in earnest. He did not heed the call from the Captain, who instructed them to sleep well tonight, for tomorrow they'd be fighting past midnight. He gripped his phone tightly on the side of his bed, between his soiled sheets and his pillow. And he thought about calling her, dialing her name on the cracked, oily pad of his phone. He couldn't.

Patai writes: "It is safe to conclude that in comparison with the West, the realm of sex constitutes more of a problem for Arabs and hence elicits more concern and more preoccupation."

Grinning, he decided not to call.

The morning before the invasion, up at Company HQ, while his soldiers were eating their breakfast—a delectable assortment of fried eggs, gruel, and reconstituted guava juice—and others shuffled through the doors of the double-wide trailer that comprised their company mess, Shaul sat in back of the steel, crusted kitchen, which spanned an adjoining hatch. He didn't care to eat with his soldiers this morning, not even in this facility, and he preferred the company of the cooks in the back, who were less obtrusive when it came to dining officers. In fact, Shaul needed a bit of privacy, as he'd set about writing in his journal extensively since last night. He detailed his encounters with Lina, and he felt somewhat bad about writing these things down, because he knew that anyone on his base could gain access to these journals, provided he was willing to sneak into his bedroom and sift through his duffel bag—as soldiers were prone to do, evidently. Nevertheless, Shaul described to the fullest extent possible everything that had happened with Lina. He also described his experiences with his parents, his mother, the incident in the workshop, and everything else he had endured while serving in the army. He was up till early dawn. Moreover, Shaul found something strangely therapeutic in writing about his experiences, as if he'd obtained a certain measure of peace just by divulging his thoughts. And while he worried that others might obtain them, he had no doubt that in some other setting, somewhere perhaps far from this warzone, someone else would probably be having a similar set of experiences, elsewhere, but they would no doubt be the same. And that was the beauty of the matter, as well as its strangeness.

He picked at his eggs and looked up at the Captain, who was instructing his subjects through the windowsill. Shaul watched him as he stood by their tables, holding a cup of yogurt in one hand, his rifle in the other. The Captain was talking to them. They were nodding their heads in approval. Shaul did not know what the Captain was speaking about, because frankly, he wasn't listening. He was thinking of Lina; he was thinking of the times they had spent together—how they hadn't been happy times, exactly. In retrospect, they were bitter ones, and most of their time was spent arguing. But maybe that was the conundrum: that time could never be enjoyed as you experienced it. Joy always seemed to work in retrospect—even if you were acutely aware you'd enjoy it. And he had been at certain points. Especially while he was fucking her. Or trying to, in any case. He also remembered taking a bath with her, holding her skin tightly, pressing her, kissing her long back, watching the curve in her butt cheeks, her upper hips, looking at the way she could stand up and dry off, and knowing very well, as he sat beneath moonlight, in the thin, misted clouds of her mirrored sink, that he loved her. That he had to have loved. Even if it were sexual. Even if it were purely passionate in character. Even if there were no logic or explanation to govern it. And even if it was base love. In fact, even it was based on some conquest, a routine submission, he knew that he loved her, and that should have counted.

At that point she'd dry off. She would look at him softly. She'd turn her whole head, her wide hair, her flapping mane, and she would be staring down starkly, watching him with flustered eyes, like she wanted to make love to him, like she wanted to be his conquest, to be owned, that he should possess her, but she couldn't yet, because then it would be over, and everything after that would be rudiments, peaceful.

He didn't even want that. He didn't know what peace was. And she didn't either. Peace was the consolation of the defeated, the wastrels. This world was energized. It was meant to be conquered. It was meant to be had. He knew that he would go back and talk to her soon, and if not her, then another million Linas. For even if she spoke to him once, and even if she said that, her words would mean nothing, for he didn't hear them. He didn't have to.

"Shaul," said the Captain, walking into the kitchen, dumping his plate in the metal sink, "come to my office at noon.

We have to have a talk about the weekend."

"Okay."

YOSSI

To stave off attack, the soldiers exited the Rachel's Tomb Outpost by one of two routes. The first was through the main corridor, past the matriarch's tomb and front gates. The second, by way of the basement, led through a heavily reinforced door, past a small gravel yard, and down to the hill's terraced graves. Neither route was preferable to them, and they did their best to vary it up.

Friday night's was through the basement. Six men departed, hastily breaching the cold. Their breaths hovered whitely as they bounded through the graves in the dark, crouching and pointing, feeling their way through the crumbling rows of chipped tombs. Most were hewn limestone, about elbow-height, and fringed with a layer of moss. Towards the base of the hill, the stone labyrinth seemingly continued in a sprawling array of flat roofs, scintillant cables, and pencil pines cloaked by the haze.

Stumbling northwestward, the men's tag-and-dash movement ground to a halt when Shaul held up a fist. Then he summoned Yossi, who, panting, knelt at his side.

"Can you see the road down below?" the Lieutenant softly whispered.

Yossi peered out through the tombs. The row's walls faded inward and stopped at a fence about twenty meters down, past a prickly pear hedge. Beyond, a couple cars shone out along al-Aida Street, which sloped downhill from the gates of their base. "Yeah."

"I'll be around the corner with the others. If anyone goes there, you signal." Then the Lieutenant ran off through a cloud of white dust, which powdered Yossi's Aquila.

Yossi wasn't feeling scared now as much as relieved to finally be out on patrol. He'd done this route a few times already, though not since the attack of last week.

He laid himself out on the cold, ashen floor. Pine needles stuck to his elbow. Sweating, he kicked out his bipod, planted its legs, and cushioned the stock on his shoulder.

On his left was a small, narrow slot in the tomb. It was roughly the width of a body. A few more lined the walled tombs up ahead, though most had been filled in with mortar. This wasn't. This one was open, and it smelled of wet rot. The inside was caved like an igloo. And dark. He could make out the remnants of leaves on the ground, and a lumpy, blue packet of *Choco*. The Arabs were said to store bombs in these graves, though this one looked otherwise vacant. A bit curious, he extended his hand towards the cave's open floor. The black earth was soft on his fingers. He wondered what it would be like to be buried in this place, if someone would seal it behind him.

Around him, the team was fanning out in an L-shaped formation overlooking the road to the camp. It was where the attackers had come from last Friday, or so Shaul had said in his briefing. Yossi hadn't paid much attention to the speech, because he never really found that it mattered. It was just he and a team of five other guys. If any Arabs came through, they would shoot them.

He lowered his cheek to the comb of the stock and fingered the guard on his barrel. Then he nestled forward, edging his cheek to the suction-cupped lid of the eyepiece. He pressed his eye forward to the quiet inside, and a universe opened before him. It didn't seem real: just flittering dots, bright jade-colored grains and their patterns, colliding. Then he toggled the view and focused it softly, revealing the streak of the road.

Through the slot on his left, he could hear the faint click of the PRC radio receiver. Boaz was switching the manpack to squelch, and others were taking positions. They would be here for hours—days, it seemed—through the pitch black and dawn of the morning.

Yossi remembered the sound of the explosion last week. At the time, he had been manning the roof's north post. The attacker had run beyond his own field of view, but Yossi knew he could have run to the ramparts and fired. He hadn't moved. He'd just sat there and stared—at what, though, he couldn't imagine.

He wasn't even sure what he'd been thinking about then. It was probably his girlfriend, Keren. He had just sent her a text-message saying he wanted to see her again. Or maybe it was the backgammon game on his phone. He was about to win ten in a row.

And she wasn't even his girlfriend, really. The two hadn't spoken in ages. She had left for America, gone with her aunt. She wouldn't come back to this country.

That's why, he knew, he had refused to take orders or go on these stupid patrols. He thought that he should have explained himself better, earlier, when the Lieutenant had grilled him. He could have said what had happened: that his girlfriend had left. But the Lieutenant would not understand.

And he couldn't believe that his Lieutenant had slapped him. At dinner, Yossi thought he might shoot him. But as he held the gun tight now and pressed to his cheek, he also felt surprisingly grateful. For what, he didn't know, but he thought the slap was good. In a way, he didn't mind the Lieutenant. The rest of the soldiers all hated him and wouldn't even bother to see him. But the Lieutenant wasn't racist. He hated them all. And that's why he had bothered to slap him. Or maybe he was just being considerate then, reminding his man of his duties.

Yossi checked in the scope and watched the bright lights, the flooding of night on the pavement. And the way the dots moved, so steady and sharp, it reminded him a bit of his girlfriend. She wasn't real; she was more like a dot. She just flitted and darted through blackness.

He wondered what he'd say if she ever called, how he'd explain what had happened. He knew he wouldn't tell her that he'd frozen that day. Maybe that his rifle had jammed. Or maybe that the Arab was already dead and he didn't want to risk his own men. Either way, she'd be impressed that an enemy died, that his unit had seen real action.

He kept picturing that guardbox, that booth where he'd sat, the old Coke bottles gleaming with urine. He wondered if he should have been standing at that point, and whether it would have made any difference.

Then he remembered what he'd been thinking about: it was the time she came over for dinner. It was a Passover Seder, about two years ago now, back at his parents' apartment.

He remembered that night because they brought home a goat-head. His father said he wanted to bless it. He said it was part of a ritual slaughter his family used to do in their village. In Africa, his father said, his uncle would cut it before the first night of the Seder.

They had all sorts of weird traditions over there which Yossi thought, or had hoped, they'd abandoned. And he'd never seen a goat like the one that they brought, because his parents were trying to adjust: to be more Israeli, and less Ethiopian, though for some reason they insisted on doing it.

So his father set the goat in the sink for the meat, and Yossi's girlfriend looked on in stark horror. She liked it, she said. It was good that they did this. Yossi tried to take her out of the kitchen.

"No," Keren said. "I think it's really nice. My parents don't even celebrate *Pesach*." Why she had come, he still didn't know. She had asked what he was doing on break. And he couldn't say no, though he found it kind of weird that she wanted to visit his parents. After all, they hadn't even gone out together, though they'd once shared a Sprite on a bus.

Her own parents, she'd said, had just gotten divorced. She lived with her mother in Ashkelon. Her father lived north near the Haifa Port and managed a biotech startup.

She had come to Yossi's school at the start of that year, and she took all the photos for yearbook. She had met his mother once at the shop in the mall, where his mother worked developing photos. After that, Keren sat beside him in English each day, and usually, he'd copy her tests.

Still, he wondered why she wanted to visit his parents. Maybe she thought they were funny. He was always embarrassed about the way his father looked. He still had the cane and the *kuta*. At least his mother had abandoned her sash, but she had the tattoo on her neck. When she began working at the mall, her boss said it was fine as long as she learned to speak Hebrew.

Their apartment was small. He was sorry for that. It was a kitchen, two beds, and a sofa. He slept on the sofa. He was rarely alone. But his brothers were down at his uncle's. And when he came back from playing football that night, he found Keren with his mother in the kitchen. They were talking and chopping up parsley and meat. His mother said they had met at the mall again. She said she had recognized Keren by her dreadlocks and braids— she was white, but she "looked like a *kushit*."

They seemed to get along well. Plus, Keren was wearing her bracelets. They were large silver clasps on the base of each wrist, which his grandmother brought from their village.

He was embarrassed about the room and the shelf by his couch, where they kept a toy doll of a soldier. At least they had the computer, which the rabbis had brought last year, when they came for a visit.

The rabbis had come to talk with his father. They had wanted to make him more religious. And his father hadn't been very religious before, but soon, he started living the Bible. He said that it would help with his job on the bus—no one would scream at a *kippah*. Plus they got money and food from the store and all sorts of gifts from the service.

As they stood in the kitchen, his father read prayers. He barely even knew how to read. Beside him, Yossi's mother kept patting a pot, as if it were a familiar ritual.

What he couldn't understand was his mother saying prayers. Sometimes she visited the Wall with her friends, but she never said prayers at the table.

And he didn't understand why they were saying these things, much less why Keren was nodding. They chanted, "And there shall be an offering of goat for your sin."

"I thought that we stopped this a couple thousand years back, you know, when they took down the Temple," said Yossi.

"We did," said his father. "In exile, at least." He held up the goat's dripping head. His thumb was pressing back the bloodstained ear. Then he brushed the brown fur with his finger. "Can you smell this? The offering's fresh. It's an atonement for all of your sins."

He couldn't be serious. And worse yet, Keren was listening. They hadn't even been alone on a date yet, much less committed a sin.

"Here," said his father, "you need to bless it. You give it a kiss on the ear." He turned the head in the sink. Then, with a gold-handled knife, the one for the bread, he cut a small slit in the tonsils. A pink lump protruded, gleaming with puss. His father leaned down to smell it. Beside him, Keren was pinching her nose, and his mother was humming the blessing.

"The son will go first," his father announced. He pointed the bread-knife at Yossi.

Then his mother reached down for a small silver cup, which she set on the tray with the matzah.

If there is one angel or voice among the thousands that can vouch for the goodness of man, then God shall be gracious and say unto them: "spare his own life from the pit. For I have found a ransom." His flesh is as tender as that of the child, and the goodness of man is restored.

"Yossi, bend down and kiss it," said his father.

Yossi was mortified. He couldn't even move. The worst part was Keren was watching. She liked it. She stared at the creature, its ruffled, brown hair and the glassy black eye, like a puppy's. She looked up at Yossi, her narrow brow raised, as if to say, why are you waiting?

The goat-head smelled awful, like vinegar, death. Plus, his mother had sprinkled on cumin. Water beads clung to its gummy, black lips. Yossi leaned forward to kiss it. His own eyes were closed. The animal's weren't. He thought it would turn up and bite him.

"Here," said his father. Yossi opened his eyes. Two fingers were parting the incision, which leaked. "Kiss it right here, right next to my thumb."

Yossi edged forward, pursing his lips. They no longer felt

like a part of him. And the stench was even greater as he drew himself in. Behind him, he heard a loud gasp.

He turned around, and his mother was laughing hysterically.

What the hell? Yossi thought.

His father sighed.

Keren came over and hugged him.

"What the hell are you doing?"

"Yossi, please don't get mad. We just wanted to see if you'd do it." Keren smiled. She was holding his hand. It felt kind of nice. At the same time, he wanted to slap her.

"What hell are you—"

"When I met your mom earlier outside the *shuq*, she said someone gave her this goat-head for free. And we were thinking, what could we do with this? She didn't have a pot..." Beside her, his mother was bawling.

"Are you kidding?" Yossi wiped off his mouth. *What kind of mother would do this?* He imagined what the flesh would have done to his lips. "I almost kissed the dead face of a goat. Now tell me what the fuck you were saying."

"Yossi, watch your mouth," his mother replied. She was rinsing her hands in the sink.

"Watch my mouth? How can I? I almost got it poisoned with goat blood."

"We weren't gonna let you kiss it," said his mother.

Then his father looked up, gave a slight sigh, and threw the goat's head in the wastebin.

That was the weirdest: his father had been in on it. A man who actually believed in the Bible. He wasn't too religious, at least not at heart, but it wasn't like him to go mocking their customs.

After that, they ate dinner, and Yossi ate well. His appetite wasn't diminished. They had chicken and fish, which was spicy and skinned, and he picked at the bones on his plate. His mother still laughed. His father said little, except to ask Keren some questions.

"No," she replied. "We don't do any of this stuff, except for that thing with the goathead... Actually, no, I didn't even have a Bat Mitzvah. My parents never went to a synagogue."

"And so now you live north?"

"Yeah, not far from the beach, about twenty minutes south of the mall."

"You like it up there?"

"I do, quite a bit."

Yossi thought about eating the goat head.

After dinner they made love. Actually they didn't. He just escorted her down to her car. Her parents were rich. She had a Volvo Sedan, though she said it belonged to the start-up. It had shiny, black windows and chrome, fitted caps and a moonroof that gleamed like a saucer. As she paused to get in, she stopped and looked back, as if he were supposed to come to her.

They had only known each other for a couple of months, and they never really talked after classes. Sometimes she'd stop as they passed in the halls and tell him, "Yo Homie," in English.

"Do you want to go to our formal?"

"What?" Yossi said. She had asked him the question in English.

"You heard me. I think they're having it sometime next month, after our graduation ceremony. I don't know, maybe, it's stupid."

He hadn't even thought about bringing a date, except maybe Sara, his cousin.

"Um, yea, I guess. I don't see why not." He could feel all the fish in his stomach.

"Good," Keren said, and she looked at him strangely. He could tell that she wanted to kiss him.

He thought he should go over and reach for her hand, but he didn't even know how to do it. She stood there. She waited some more, then she got in her car and drove down the road without headlights.

The formal was ceremonial and too dark to see. Everybody in the room was on chemicals. Yossi sat next to Keren. They talked a little bit. After that, she went home with some friends of hers.

The next day she called. She said she'd had a good time. She was wondering if he wanted to have ice cream. "Uh, I don't know," he told her. "I'm not into that. It kinda hurts my head when I eat it." She laughed on the other end. She must have thought it was a joke. It wasn't, but he was glad that he said it.

For the next couple months, they went out on dates, but he never found the courage to kiss her. Sometimes, on his parents' computer, they'd watch his old films, including one with a hero named Braveheart. She fell asleep on the couch, but Yossi did not. He was stunned by the sight of this warrior. He thought that someday—in about seven months—he would fight in a war just like this one. And maybe he'd return home to find this young girl and save her from some evil conqueror. Like Alex—the man who she saw on and off, a Russian whom she claimed was a "friend" of hers. He was into hard drugs and D.J.'d at clubs, including the Dolphinarium.

But as she lay on his chest with her head near his lips, he could smell the warm scent of her dreadlocks. There was dandruff there too, and some sort of braid. She was as lovely as the Princess of Scotland. Lovelier even, and more real to him then. Though she wore too much gloss on her lips. She looked like a slut. He liked that as well. He laid her head down on the pillow.

"You can sleep here," he whispered in her ear, which had all sorts of metal and piercings.

Her eyes opened up, and she gave a pained look. "I have

to go, Yossi. But thank you. You're sweet. Maybe I'll see you this weekend."

She picked up her bracelets, which she'd set on the couch and his mother had apparently given her. She made her way down to the door and looked back. Yossi was still on the sofa.

"Are you going to come say goodbye?"

He didn't know what to do. If he went there, he might have to kiss her. But he couldn't stay here—that would be rude. So he got up and went to the kitchen. He picked up the knife on the tray for the bread, and then he slowly walked over. He held the blade up to the side of her waist.

"What are you doing?" she asked, backing away.

"I want you to have this."

"What?"

"It's a gift," he explained, "from my family."

"I can't accept this."

"Why not?"

"Cause it's yours."

"Well, I'm giving it to you as a present."

"What for?"

"I don't know," he said. "I thought that maybe you'd want it. In case you have bread with your family."

"But it's your parents'—"

"No, it's not. It was a gift from some men."

"Uh, okay," she said. "You don't have to do this. But that's really nice of you, I guess."

He thought that it might have been a stupid thing to do, but then she reached over and kissed him. Her lips felt warm, and he imagined the goat head. She tasted like smoke and the gloss on her lips and that mint gum she chewed before English.

They stumbled towards the kitchen, against the hard sink. He wondered if his parents would wake up. And she didn't seem to care as they embraced in a lock. He imagined that his mother was watching.

It went on for ten minutes while wearing their clothes. They touched every part of their bodies. When they were done with their touching, she pulled herself back and gave him a kiss on the forehead.

He reached for her again. She said she should go. She turned to walk out of the kitchen. And Yossi felt weird—weirder than before, and even weirder than he'd felt at the formal. This had been his first kiss, except for that time when Sara had sucked on his neck once in grade school.

Keren opened the door, smiled a goodbye, and started down the hall with her gift. And she almost scraped the knife against the balcony rail. Near the end, he saw someone was watching. It was Avi, his neighbor, an Ethiopian soldier, who was six years older than him. Avi was already a captain in the army. They used to play football together. He didn't say a word as Keren walked by, bearing a small weapon in-hand. Avi just stood there sorting his mail, wearing fatigues and a t-shirt. And his t-shirt had a picture of an alligator on it—the symbol of Avi's battalion. He looked up at Yossi, gave him a nod. Yossi smiled and closed the door to his apartment.

Yossi felt awesome, though equally confused. And he wasn't really sure what to do next. And he wasn't even sure which he appreciated more: the kiss or the nod from the Captain.

He looked at his apartment, its white-painted walls, the bookshelves and fruit on the table. He was proud of himself, and his country and land, and he knew he was ready to fight now.

She dumped him the next day. At least, she never called him back. A couple times they met at the movies. She came with that guy who had a tattoo of a bull and probably evaded his service.

Yossi did not. He enlisted in the army, and he requested Avi's battalion. In training he thought about writing Keren a letter, and he did once or twice without sending it.

Keren, I'm sorry that things didn't work out. I hope that you're happy with Alex. Maybe when I'm done with the army next week, we could go out and get some more ice cream.

No. That sounded corny.

We could go watch a movie—which she would have slept through. *Or swimming*—but he didn't know how.

Definitely nothing which raised the possibility of a kiss, since it couldn't match the one that they'd had.

He wanted to fuck her. That was for sure. But kissing seemed like an impurity.

So I was thinking that maybe I won't see you again. You know I might die in the army.

Who was he fooling?

Well, maybe I'll come at the end of next month, if you're not too busy with—

Enough of this crap. Yossi stood by his cot. He was in training down south in the Negev. It was Saturday morning, their one time for rest, and he was sitting in his tent with his squad. He threw down his notebook, reached for his rifle, and went out to piss at the trailers.

A couple minutes later, when he returned to his tent, he saw that his notebook was missing. It was a small, spiral sheaf, not very light, but it must have blown off of his duffel. Around him, the others were sprawled on their cots, sleeping with arms over their eyes.

Towards the end of the row, Ivan was reading, and Boaz was sewing a button. Yossi asked them if they'd seen it.

"*Blyad,*" Ivan said. "What, do I look like your mother?"

Boaz didn't bother to look up from his cot. Beside him, though, Uri was praying. His phylacteries were on, those black leather straps, but he got down on his knees to start searching.

They searched out the back, around the gravel and posts, beside the cigarette butts and the Coke cans. No sign of the notebook or even his pen. Somebody obviously took it.

Fuck 'em, Yossi figured. They were always playing jokes. Someone would eventually return it.

Nobody did. But he was glad it was gone. Later he heard that she left. She had gone to Los Angeles, where she was going to make films and live with her aunt in "The Valley."

He thought that someday she'd make a movie about him and everything he'd seen in the army. He had seen quite a bit, though no real war—that is, until the shooting last week. And he wasn't even sure if that shooting was real, though he could still hear the clanking bottle.

Forty minutes later, Yossi awoke on his gun. He heard a rustling noise in the cactus. It was twenty meters up, flapping and wet: a wheatear, or maybe a bunting. It clawed at the buds of a prickly pear pad, then it scrambled up the ledge of the wall.

Yossi slid back the cloth on the face of his watch and pressed down the button for glow. It was a little past twelve. Soon they would go. The Arabs were not coming through here.

He rubbed his watch, a Tough Solar G-Shock, which Uri had lent him last fall. Yossi liked how it looked, how it felt on his wrist. Like a deep-sea diver's or sailor's. A commando's. It even had a clock that he'd set for L.A. on the off-chance that Keren would call.

He closed his left eye and entered the scope. Nothing had changed in the darkness. Just the streak of a road—black, steady, and lit—and the insects that zapped through his filter.

Yossi centered the hairs on the cactus below. The wheatear was flapping its wings. It was bathing itself in a drain along the wall. He thought about blowing it open.

And he still had to pee. He crossed his legs, and he knew that he shouldn't have had *Choco*. He had wolfed down a couple of packets before leaving, since he hadn't touched a thing at dinner.

He picked up his M4 and slowly crawled backwards, scraping his elbows and kneepads.

"Yossi, the hell are you doing?" the Lieutenant harshly whispered.

"I gotta take a leak."

"Do it against the wall. And stay down."

Yossi crawled forward with his barrel on his wrist, then turned to face the mossed tombs. As he hefted his pack up and unhooked his belt, the Lieutenant whispered, "Be quiet." A couple men shifted in the rows to his left. They were probably trying to sleep.

As he sprung himself out, all clouded with dust, the gravel bits piercing his elbow, he clenched his insides, but he knew he couldn't go. His weight was all pressed on his stomach. He could hear the Lieutenant, or someone beside him, whispering "*shokist*," or fuck-up.

As he eyed the low, hollow slot in the tomb, he tried not to think about Keren. Then it came out with a sparkling hiss. Piss trickled down to his ankle. Fuck. He'd managed to piss himself. He knew this would happen. There was always some shit on a mission.

He leaned to the side and let it run down: a bright orange puddle of gravel, steaming. He could make out some ants as they ran for their lives, and the headstones above him were glinting.

Most of the slabs bore long Arab names, like Abu someone or another. And the years of their dates—1040, 1212—were hard to make out with their symbols. He wondered which people were buried here—and if they would mind getting watered.

He shook out his boot, kicking up dust. He could hear the Lieutenant beside him, crawling. Yossi dug through his pockets for a tissue or two but only found a vomit-stained napkin. As he bent down to wipe off his ankle, he heard a soft noise down below, like chirping. But it wasn't a bird or a radio signal. It was footsteps below on the street.

"Shit," Yossi said, as he flung himself down. A small figure emerged on the street down below. The graves became silent—utterly still—as soldiers peered out from their rifles.

"Yossi, you see that?"

"What?" Yossi said, fumbling for the sling on his barrel. His bipod was open. The legs were unset. The reticle's view was upended. He thought he saw something—what looked like a bird. A small, greenish infrared person. The person was passing behind the parked cars. He was carrying a sack, or a bucket.

"What is that?" the Lieutenant whispered from the row to his left.

Yossi could barely make out the translucent shape. It kept fading in and out of focus. "Don't know. Might be a terrorist."

Below, the man stopped and glanced all around, as if he had heard them talking.

"Is he carrying something?"

"I think," Yossi whispered. His voice echoed strangely through his ocular rings.

"All right, I'll go check it out. Vasily, give cover. And Yossi, you keep him in range. Everyone quiet. I'm moving down. Don't move unless I give orders."

The footsteps continued below through the tombs, like some kind of clap through a tunnel. Yossi looked to the left, where the Lieutenant had run. A dust cloud had settled behind him. He was racing through tombs. Chasing, he stopped. He knelt and peered out through his ACOG device.

Yossi's throat tightened. His trigger-guard shook. He could feel a pulse in his chest. The terrorist, he figured, was thirty meters down and moving left through his Mil-dots. The rise, he knew, would be positive two, possibly less at this pressure. He didn't even know what he was supposed to do. *What if the man had a gun?*

Below him, the Lieutenant yelled "*Waqf*" in Arabic.

The terrorist started to run.

"Stop," the Lieutenant shouted in English. "Don't move."

Just as he said, the graveyard flashed with a boom. Gunshots followed like bangs on a drum, and the night opened up all around them.

Slicing rounds pounded the street down below, clanking off metal and pavement. Blue lights skipped up and streaked through the dark, whining through air with a fury. And there were tracer shots soaring like hot, coral darts, whirring through air in slow motion.

Yossi looked in his scope. He wasn't even sure if he'd shot. He hadn't. His port cover lid was up. The cartridge was locked. He could still hear the banging inside him. He looked up. Others were shooting, a deafening noise. It came from the rows all around him. The tombs were black, brightened, whitened with smoke. The fields were alive with their shaking and flashing. And it came from behind him, through branches of trees, where Uri was perched in the balcony nest; his barrel kept belching out thin orange flames and sucking them back with a sputter. Below him, the Negev kept whipping its chain, thrashing its belt on the gravel. Its tracers kept zipping and zapping with light, keening through air with a whistle.

"What the fuck's going on?" someone was shouting.

Near the grave border, beside the stone wall, the Lieutenant was yelling, "Get down. Get down. Get the fuck down. Everyone, hands off your weapons. Cease firing."

The chain barrels rattled. The firing stopped. Gun barrels ticked all around. Yossi looked out at the tombs and black night and the plumes of gray smoke as they parted.

He checked in his eyepiece. Too bright to see. To his left, he could hear someone running. He focused. He could make out a small yellow curve on the street, what might have been the neck of a person.

The Lieutenant was yelling, "Get the fuck down. Everyone, hands off your weapons."

Gun barrels clanked and fell to the floor. Shell casings rattled on concrete.

He didn't even know what was happening, though others were re-fastening clips.

The Lieutenant kept yelling, "Everyone down. Take your hands off of your weapons. I'm coming."

Yossi leaned forward and wiped off the soot from his lens. The handguard was greasy and cool to his touch, and the air smelled like rotten eggs.

He crouched on one knee and checked in his scope, trying to see what had happened. He could feel the warm air and the hot yellow sky as it fizzled and spun in his view.

Then he saw movement on the street down below: a glint of skin in the mist. The light sparkled brightly inside of his scope. He turned the knob for the focus. The fence was still grating and whining below. Beyond it, a small arm was bending.

Then the Lieutenant called out, far from the road, "Ivan, get down here this second."

The medic ran down, fast through the graves, clutching his rifle and kit. He was bumping and weaving, threading through dirt, as other men rose up beside him.

From a cellphone recovered on the roof of the Rachel's Tomb Outpost:

Outbox (27)
1 Message(s) Marked for Deletion

Keren, I know we haven't talked. Just wanted you to know, before I enlist, that I do this for you.
(Draft Saved)

Keren, I'm going in now. Wanted you to know I lov
(Draft Saved)

Keren, why am I doing this?
(Draft Saved)

Keren, I'm enlisting now. I miss you.
(Message Sent)

Wazzup baby, you no good? Why you no write me dis lettah? Sweet thang. Youz trippin me sugah?
(Message Sent)

Keren, girl, damn, youz playin me, fool. Whazzup wid dat? Why you no write me girl? Me love you long time. Sucky sucky
(Draft Saved)

Keren, I need to talk to you. The army here sucks.
(Draft Saved)

Keren, things are good here. They're making me a marksman. Said I would have to do a lot of fighting, you know. I'm up for it.

What's up with you?
(Message Sent)

You're still not writing me. That's cool. I guess you got things to do in L.A.
(Draft Saved)

You got a man there or something? Who you playin me with hizzo?
(Draft Saved)

Please write me, Keren.
(Draft Saved)

Keren, something bad today. Guys in my unit. One of them injured. Firebomb. Maybe you saw it on the news. I looked for myself on the television. Didn't see it. Maybe you could record it, if you see me.
(Draft Saved)

This is your number, right Keren?
(Message Sent)

It's good to hear from you. But I don't understand what you meant by that. We're not dating or anything. Why can't I write you?
(Draft Saved)

Keren, something happened. Need to talk.
(Message Sent)

Keren. It's bad.
(Draft Saved)

Keren, um, I killed a man.
(Draft Saved)

Keren, I shot a girl today. She looked a bit like you. Maybe a bit darker. She was ugly.
(Draft Saved)

Keren, I'm sorry. I'm sorry you're not here now. I love you.
(Draft Saved)

Keren, I did something terrible. Help me.
(Draft Saved)

Keren, that was fun. The army's really good now.
(Draft Saved)

Fuck you Keren. And fuck all your boyfriends
(Draft Saved)

And fuck your mom too, that white whore
(Draft Saved)

I'm sorry Keren. I have nothing to say to you. I just want you to know that I lov
(Draft Saved)

Keren. Please write me. I miss you.
(Message Sent)

Keren, I'm coming soon. I don't know when or how, but I'm coming.
(Draft Saved)

Keren, I'll find you.
(Message Sent)

Keren. I miss you. I know you think I'm weird, or not right for you. And maybe that's right now. I don't know. I don't even know what to do here, or what I've done. But I miss you. I know that.
(Message Sent)
(Message Returned. Error 147: Number Disconnected)

This guard duty sucks. I need to go now.
(Draft Saved)

00000000000000011
(Message in Progress)

BOAZ

The last thing that Boaz Abutbul would recall about stepping on the boy's ear and grinding it into the pavement is that it was a particularly solid feeling—within himself, as if he had conquered something, stepped on someone, and it wasn't just an externalized object; it was a part of himself now, an obstacle he had defeated.

Previously, he had been horrified by violence, or at the very least aghast by its presence in his life. When he was home from the army last month at his girlfriend's apartment, they were eating olives together and she cut her thumb on the can. Her hand had started bleeding, and Ruti didn't say anything. She just wiped it. But Boaz was horrified. He clutched her in his arms, held her, unsure, at first, what to do. He looked for some gauze in her bathroom, and when he didn't find any, he returned with a handful of tampons—the ones that she kept beneath the sink. He pulled out the white cotton. Then he bit off some dental floss, which he also brought with, and tied it around her thumb. He wasn't sure what to do with the tampon's white string, so he tied that as well, and all the cotton bloomed red, like a rosebud. But it didn't stop her from bleeding, so he tied it a bit tighter, and then he realized that he'd tied it too tightly. Ruti said that it hurt. And she was also laughing. Boaz wasn't sure why she was laughing, but he realized she was laughing at him. "What's wrong?" she asked. "You've never seen a little blood before, soldier?"

And the truth was he hadn't, with a few small exceptions, until now, late Friday, out here on this road, where the dead body lay curled on its side, clinging to the strap of a gym bag. He kicked the boy's wrist with the tip of his boot. The tiny hand didn't release it.

"Here," Boaz said, and he spat on the child.

Then Ivan began pulling his vestpack. "What the fuck are you doing? Get off her. *Chto za huy...Chyort voz'mi.*" Ivan was swearing in Russian.

Behind him, Shaul kept watching the field, a rocky olive grove rimming the north. A line of white oaks still clove to the west, lighted by an aubergine sky.

Ivan looked down at the flesh on the ground, crinkling his brow in discomfort.

"What are we gonna do?" Boaz asked. The body they had shot was a child's. And it might have been a girl, as Ivan implied. The brown hair was cut short in a bowl. Bright pieces of flesh trailed off from her side, glistening clumps by her forearm. Boaz thought about going over to kick her some more, but Ivan was holding his vestpack.

"Get away from her," said Shaul, turning to face them. "Ivan, there's nothing you can do for her now. Go get the others, and tell them to cover that field." Ivan ran off, rifle stock bouncing, his face curled up in dismay.

Boaz stepped back from the body on the ground. He loosened the sling on his rifle.

"I don't want you to see her," Shaul said softly. "I don't want you to see what we've done."

We, Boaz thought. He hadn't even shot. But he was hoping he could still take the credit.

Her face was looking out in Shaul's direction. Boaz went over to see it. But before he could get there, Shaul reached down and picked up the strap of her gym bag. He held up the strap. It was shaking in his hand. He set it on top of her face.

"Get back," Shaul said. "I don't want you guys to see what we've done."

It wasn't even clear whom he was talking to. Only Boaz was standing beside him.

Boaz backed up and leaned on a car, one of several that was shattered nearby. The front seat was smoking. The hood said UN, and pieces of skin flecked the door.

Shaul still stood with his gun in one arm. He was looking straight down at the body. "Why did we do this?"

"What?" Boaz asked.

Shaul looked up with an electrified, ringing expression. His blue eyes were watered, blinking and large. He looked straight across and he muttered, "Why?"

"What?"

"Why did we come here...to do this?"

"What?"

"Shoot her?" Shaul said. "Don't you see what you've done? Don't you see that you're holding a weapon?"

Boaz didn't know what his commander was saying. Everyone around him had fired. And he hadn't even shot, because his rifle had jammed. He had forgotten to clean it this morning. By the time he unloaded and relocked the clip, Shaul had told them to cease—which, Boaz thought, he would eternally regret. He considered firing rounds in her body.

Shaul started brushing some spears of dried grass, a patch of barren brome edging the road. "I don't even know what I'm doing," he murmured. "Or why we would bother to come..."

Boaz stood up and adjusted the straps of his radio. It kept pinching his shoulders—this wide, angled box. It was worse than on hikes during training.

Shaul kept brushing the grass with his hand, shutting his eyes, lightly shaking.

Boaz walked over and faced Shaul then, not sure what to make of his commander. Behind him he could see their patrol team dashing and crouching down next to the field.

Shaul looked down at the child on the ground. Tiny flies picked at her hair. And she was wearing white Reeboks, like the kind for a boy, except they were small and stained red. Boaz studied them. He wondered what this girl had been doing out here, fifty meters down from their base. The curfew was gone, but the rules were in place, and this was a restricted area. A green line.

"Help me with the body."

"What?" Boaz said.

"You heard me. Lift up from the ankles. We're moving her."

"Where?"

"I don't know," Shaul said. "Further up towards the base."

"Why?"

"So your fucking friends don't get charged with murder. Unless you want to pretend she was armed."

Then they heard the roar of Jeeps starting up, far past the base, on Hevron. He could see their faint headlights—their liquescent glare—as they swerved past the gates of the Tomb.

He moved her. He wasn't sure if he'd do it, but he reached for the body, and the body felt remarkably lifeless. Like lifting a dead sheep, which he'd done one time while driving down south to Eilat. And the soles were soaked wet with what might have been urine. Glass pieces clung to her forehead. But he didn't see her forehead. The gym bag still covered it. Gooey blood dripped from her ankle. He threw her.

Then Shaul got mad. He said some foul things. He picked up the girl from her shoulders. And he pulled her by a dress strap, which ripped in his hand. Then her head smacked the ground, and he swore.

Boaz waited and watched, and he waited some more, and he wondered what Shaul was thinking. He turned to face Shaul. Shaul looked down. Shaul was watching the body.

Then Shaul got up. He told Boaz, "Come." Boaz followed along with the radio. The two scampered out there, alone towards the field, leaving the road and the body.

"We'll set up a watch from the north," Shaul said, addressing his five crouching men. None of them paid much attention to him. They were fixed on the ambulance's lights. Beside it, two Red Crescent medics were scooping the body, their reflective gear glinting with stripes. Downhill, huge crowds had gathered along al-Aida Street, howling and flailing their chests. Shaul instructed his men not to shoot them. "No more excitement tonight."

Guns shouldered, they crossed through the fields, past the crackling stems of barbed goatgrass and sage and pale flax. They tramped down a mudpath and up through a shelf of gnarled olive trees older than Jesus. Then they came to rise of chalked boulders and spurge. Shaul told the others to wait. He climbed up on boulders and above the high rocks and turned out to face Route 60.

Boaz knelt down and raised his Leaf sight, coughing and rubbing his eyes. Then he reached in his vest and dug out a tissue. His allergies constantly bothered him. And here in this field, with all its pollen and dust, the conditions around were like murder.

He crouched in position with an arm on one knee and took a quick sip from his jug. He screwed down the cap and Velcroed the pouch and wondered when they would be leaving. He was facing clear gravel, steep slopes of the road, the turnoff for Gush Etzion.

As the ambulance wailed its loud bleats heading off and more soldiers arrived from Battalion, their Jeeps screeching up with their dirt-rattled brakes, their vehicles slamming and steaming, Boaz looked up at his commander above him, Shaul up high on the planet: a tall, distant figure, alone on that perch, like some kind of chanter of weather.

Shaul's gun was slung down from the side of his waist and his helmet was facing Route 60. Bright lights shone out along the base of his stock—the approaching of *Sufim* and Humvees. And he was holding his phone out, studying its dial, as if he weren't sure how to use it. Suddenly, with a flick of his wrist, Shaul tossed his phone towards the bushes.

Boaz couldn't believe what he'd seen. He wondered if Shaul had lost it.

Then Boaz looked down at the soldiers around him. Vasily was twisting his eyepiece. Behind him, Yossi was dialing his phone, texting someone in secret. And behind them Uri was holding a prayerbook, the one that he used at dinner. But he wasn't saying prayers; he was flipping its sheets, stroking and thumbing the pages.

"What are you doing?" Boaz asked.

Uri looked up. "Nothing," he said. "I'm reading."

"Saying a prayer for the dead?"

"No," he replied. "I'm saying a prayer for the living."

URI

At 0600 on Monday, all of the non-guarding soldiers of 2nd Platoon were dispatched to Aleph HQ, the neighboring base, for an impromptu company briefing. Then, after thirty-seven minutes of standing in formation and listening to the Captain discuss emergency procedures, they retired to the mess hall, where they ate for twelve minutes, until the First Sergeant called out their full names.

"Uriel Friedman, you take the showers—and when you're done with that, come see me for more work."

Uri went to the supply shed and grabbed three full white bottles of cleaner, a bucket, some gloves, and a mop. He didn't understand how a man could have been killed on their base and they were expected to go on with their work. It was as if it didn't even happen. They didn't mention his name. They only talked about emergency procedure.

Remember to wear your boots when you sleep, and it isn't because of rules and regulations.

Behind the HQ barracks, in the trailer for showers, Uri scrubbed the floor with a mop. He peeled off a tissue, which stuck to the shelf, and beside it, the case for a razor. The case, he knew, was neither his nor Yossi's, but the thought of it clenched at his throat.

He thought of last Friday morning—the last time that they spoke—when they were standing here at the sinks. Uri was shaving. It was ten minutes before an inspection, and he had to hurry, because he hadn't yet polished his weapon. He was patting his lip, wiping a cut, when Yossi asked if he could borrow his razor.

"What?" Uri asked.

"The razor in your hand. I need to use it for just one minute."

"You need it right now?"

"Yeah," Yossi said. "It'll just take me a second."

"I don't know," Uri said, eyeing Yossi's face. "I don't think the Sergeant'll notice."

"He will. He's been on my case. And he gave Ivan a week for his stubble."

"Um, I don't know," Uri said. "You don't have anything at all? Can't you use Boaz's electric?"

"It's dead," Yossi said. "It needs to recharge. Here, just let me use it a second."

"I don't know," Uri said, biting his lip. "You know what... all right, go ahead and take it. And when you're done with it, keep the blade. I got a whole extra sleeve in my bag."

Uri did not. It was the last of his blades, and he couldn't afford to buy extras. He was saving this last one until he got paid—next month, or whenever that happened.

"No, thanks," Yossi said, fingering his chin. "You know what, I think I'm just gonna wing it."

"No, it's really no problem. Take the blade."

Yossi looked back through the mirror. "I don't want it," he said, and he turned to walk off, grabbing his rifle and kit. His towel was slung over the back of his shirt, and it was the last time the two of them talked.

What Uri now remembered was the smile Yossi gave, the way he exposed his teeth. His teeth shone white and bright against his lips, like most of the Ethiopians.

But Uri didn't feel that he was being racist with him then, which is how Yossi must have seen that incident. He just didn't want to exchange blood with anyone else, regardless of where they had come from. And he didn't see why he should have to live the rest of his life on an assumption that was patently false. He wasn't a racist. Others here were. And he had gone out of his way then to help him.

Aside from that blade, Uri gave him his watch after he got a new one in training. It was a Casio G-Shock, a really nice watch, though he doubted that Yossi had appreciated it. But watches were always a big deal in the army, since they were your only real item of personal wear, and they said what kind of soldier you were. If you had a Casio G-Shock, you were known to be serious, because the glass wouldn't break or get scratched. If you had a Timex or one of those generic brands, you didn't give a shit and only bought one for the clock. And if you didn't have a watch, which had been Yossi's plight, it meant you were poor here, or otherwise new to the concept of measured time.

Yossi, Uri knew, had come at age six, arriving on a plane with his family. And in training, Yossi could tell time with his hands by holding them up to the sun.

But Uri didn't regret having hesitated with the blade, and he didn't feel this was racist. He knew about the diseases that Africa had and everything that went on in that continent. Yossi himself was probably clean, but there wasn't any point in risking it. He knew in the army that presented a problem, since they were supposed to "shed blood for each other." But they'd only been on the line for five quick months, and he had yet to see blood from a soldier.

Of course, that would all change late Saturday night, when Yossi got shot on their base.

Uri didn't even get to see the body for himself, since at the time he had been out on patrol. All he had seen was the roof's damaged end: a chip in the thick wall of concrete. It was shaped like an axe, with no sign of the blood or the brains that were washed with the hoses. He had even gone to guard there a couple times since, which for some reason, he didn't find troubling. He just sat on the stool, playing games on his phone, and wondered if Yossi was watching.

Now he filled up a bucket with steaming white water and mixed in a bottle of cleaner. He splashed the cement floors and the pipes overhead, the mirrors, sinks, faucets, and ceiling. He wondered if the chemicals would burn through his soles as the water level rose to his boots. The drain, he could see, was clogged down below and he'd have to reach down and unstop it.

He untied his watch and slid it through his belt. Warm water seeped through his socks. He hated this job more than anything else, no matter how many times he had done it. He looked at the windows, where light filtered in, spraying white rays from the sandbags. He decided that he would rather go get shot on patrol, since it was better than lifting the drain cup.

He stuck his hand in the water, between his two boots, and located the mush-cluttered basket. He pulled it up by the rim, and there was avocado inside, some sort of fur. Water trickled down to his feet. As he returned the grate to its hole in the floor and wiped off his hands on his pants, he realized that his watch wasn't on him. He panicked for a second. Then he remembered it was tied to his belt.

Late Saturday night, which seemed half-a-year ago, he was patrolling the fields to the north. He was climbing over boulders and yellow thorn brush when he heard the report from the hills. It was just he, his squad leader, and five other men, and no one thought much at the time. Arab kids were often setting off firecrackers near the base, and they had gotten fairly used to explosions. It was late, though; it was almost three in the morning, and they thought it was an Arab car backfiring. They continued on their way through the dried-up ravine, while Uri walked point by the Sergeant. They checked in their scopes and night vision sets, surveying the grasses for movement, and kept moving north for ten minutes in silence with just the rustling sounds of their vests.

Then they heard static and shouting on the radio. A flare shot up in the sky. It blocked out the moon and lit up the fields. The trees around them looked purple: gentle silhouettes of brushes and pine, tinged dark red at the corners. Above all their helmets and up-tilted faces: a flaring pink sun in the sky, burning. It reflected off pupils, the barrels of guns. Nobody bothered to move then. It was as if they were frozen or stuck to the earth, enamored by what they had seen.

Then the radio said that a soldier was down at Carmel-One, Two-Aleph. That was the guardbox on top of their base, where Yossi had been on watch.

Yossi was dead before they got to the gates. That much they knew from the radio. They sprinted the whole way, a kilometer or more, and Uri tripped and fell flat on a rock face. He broke his fall with the base of his gun, and he wondered how he didn't manage to shoot himself. He struggled to stand, saw that he'd cut up his hand, and scrambled to catch up with his squad.

The watch, he now knew, was unscratched by the fall, but he still had the marks on his hands and face. And the whole thing seemed like a dream to him, much like the rest of the morning. He didn't remember the perimeter they set up or any feelings of fear that he'd had. All he could recall was the moment he fell and his legs had given out from under him: he was floating through air, above the white rocks, facing the mouth of the canyon.

Cleaner from the floor stung his right hand, eating its way through the scabbing. He knew he shouldn't have stuck his hand in that drain without having put on some gloves. He rinsed off his hand, and it stung him some more. His scab wounds looked fleshy and white.

These scars, it seemed, were the only living proof of what happened to Yossi this weekend. Of course, there were other little things, like his empty blue bunk or the unfilled slot for his helmet. He had also written his name on a bulletproof vest, which was stacked in a pile in the hall. No one had since bothered to use that vest, even though he had been wearing a different one. Maybe they thought that the ink would wear out if others continued to use it. But there were dozens of names on each of these vests, and most had since finished the army. There was a tradition here, though, that you never crossed out any names when you found them on an item of gear. This was why soldiers were always losing their shit—because nobody could ever identify anything. Gear was recycled and everything got shuffled, except for Yossi's green vest at the bottom.

But the Captain hadn't even spoken Yossi's name since they found him curled up on the roof. It was almost as if there was an unwritten rule that nobody talked of the deceased. It was weird how it worked here, these army superstitions—like not wishing anyone "good luck" before a mission. There was also a custom before each operation that you never took photos of soldiers. This, it turned out, was a pretty stupid thing, because they didn't have any pictures of Yossi. The only photo they could find to submit to the press featured his girlfriend hugging him at his formal. The girlfriend was smiling, clutching his neck, and Yossi looked as if he knew what was coming.

The water level rose again by his feet as he spilled out another foam bucket. The next drain, he could see, was clogged up as well. A tornado of hair swirled above it.

Fuck this, he figured and picked up his gloves, which he'd set on a hook by his rifle. He left the whole bathroom in a grand, flooded mess with his *kova* cap still on the sink ledge.

When he came back to get it, ten minutes later, the water was gone from the floor. He looked in the mirror and sized up his zits, the scratches that marked his forehead. And his hair was getting long. He'd have to buzz it again. Maybe in time for a picture.

Outside on the pavement, he set down his mop and knocked on the commander's trailer. "I'm done," he said. "And I'm tired of this shit. I'm ready to do a patrol." The First Sergeant smiled and patted his back. He said the Captain had sent him a message: "You're free to go home, to take an early leave. He wants you back by tomorrow."

Of course this would happen the one time in his service when he didn't actually feel like leaving. He wanted to stay and do some arrests, if only out of service to Yossi.

"Go home and get laid. And get some more sleep. You're gonna need it, starting this week." The First Sergeant explained that late Tuesday night, they were staging a raid on al-Aida. The camp's ground, he said, was contested turf, and they would undoubtedly see some action.

Uri knew that the leave would not be a gift and that he was about to endure some fighting. And if he were to survive what he saw, which he started to doubt, he was going to have to get rest first.

The First Sergeant told him to report back to base by tomorrow at ten in the morning. He said that he should also get his head shaved at home, or the Sergeant would do it himself.

Uri thought about calling up a couple old friends. He had gone to a religious academy. But the only thing they ever did was read Talmud or pray, neither of which seemed too appealing. He wondered if any of his friends from the army were getting a leave for the night. He telephoned Boaz, Ivan, and Shibli. None of them said they were going.

Uri hitched a ride in the back of a truck that was delivering food to the checkpoint. Then he flagged down a Jewish settlement bus, which brought him up north to Jerusalem. He caught another bus to the Tel Aviv station, where he bought a cold beer and a sandwich. He thought he should call up his mother at home and tell her he was coming to dinner.

Of course, his parents both knew what had happened this weekend. They had come to the funeral service. But he didn't really feel like dealing with them now, since to them, it was just a reminder. His mother once told him: "This is what you get. It was your choice to serve in the army." She was talking about the time when he fell in training and fractured a bone in his wrist. And when they talked Sunday morning after the attack, the only things they discussed were arrangements: how he'd get to the funeral; if he needed a ride; what his parents could do to "support" him. They hated that he served but acknowledged his choice—as long as he maintained the religion.

Instead of catching the bus up north to Haifa, which is where he lived, he went to the bank and deposited his check, which they had given him upon leaving the base. He knew that for Yossi he was obliged to spend it on something entirely personal. Razor blades didn't seem like the appropriate choice, and he wasn't about to purchase a Bible.

At a kiosk he bought a bottle of Jack, some chips, and a packet of Camels. Then he took a quick bus to the Tel Aviv beach and laid his head down on the sand.

When he woke up again, two hours later, the tide was up to his boots. The sun was low and flaring red. His rifle weighed down on his chest. He brushed himself off, gathered his bag, and threw out the liter of whiskey. He would have stayed on the beach for the night, but it was probably going to rain. He walked down Allenby and Ha Ya'arkon and found a neighboring hostel. He rented a room, which had flowered, blue sheets, and he sat down inside the running shower. He cried a little bit—for what, he didn't know. Then he dried himself off on the floor. He put on his jeans and his last clean white shirt and decided to go for a walk.

He thought he should get his head shaved first, but all of the barbers were closed. And the clubs were deserted, the bars emptied out, because of the bombings that month. It was a little past twelve and the streets were still wet, slicked with the glaze of gasoline.

He only knew of one place that would be open at this hour, though it wasn't exactly a bar. Boaz had once recommended it to him and said he was a regular customer. It was near the Old Central Station. The place was called "The Tropic." It was famous in the army for servicing soldiers and even offering them discounts.

When he arrived in the district, he noticed the bums, mostly camped out on the streets. African men were selling bracelets and gum. A few of them offered him Ecstasy. He could see the lights of The Tropic up ahead, but the place didn't seem that appealing. Maybe it was the thought of Boaz having sex, but he decided that he'd look for another. He roamed through the streets until he settled on a place that probably had a lot less traffic. It was in the back of an alley, alongside a wall, with a rusted green iron door. The sign overhead looked welcoming enough—it was a tiny, bright, pink neon heart.

When she heard the knock, she was making coffee at her dresser. She preferred instant, because it didn't stain her teeth the way filter did. And she had exceptionally good teeth, which she maintained with rigor, using peroxide strips, a pharmaceutical rinse, and dental floss made in America—she didn't trust anything made inside Israel. Back in Chisinau, her uncle had been a dentist, and he told her that teeth were the most important thing in a profession. That was back when she still talked to the man—his family had raised her since birth. Now they never talked, though she continued to send checks and said she was employed as a cleaner. Which wasn't, she figured, entirely untrue, given the state of her clients.

She left the electric pitcher to boil and gave a quick nod to the mirror. Behind it, Vladimir was sorting his mail. She could hear the rustling slips.

He was a good man, Vlad. She wished he made more, but his salary wasn't out of her pocket. He had also once broken a couple legs on her behalf, and for that she was eternally grateful. And the guy never asked for any favors in return. She suspected this was because he was gay. Sometimes, when her younger clients came in, she could hear a few jerks from his stool.

His one-way mirror looked out on the entire room: a windowless, pink-walled cell. The spot where he sat was connected to a hall that adjoined the neighboring dance club. The club was now closed, due to repairs or some sort of dispute with the owners. There were all sorts of people living upstairs—Filipino and Cambodian workers.

But when she heard the knock, Vlad's papers stopped flipping and she guessed he had moved to his chess games. Back in the Ukraine, he was a "Candidate Master," which was apparently a high designation. These days he'd play about four games at once, each on the screen of his laptop. And she knew he was smart, though he didn't say much. He also did her bills and accounting.

She set down her mug and powdered her chest. She put on her lipstick in patches. She stepped up on a box beside the green door. Through the peephole she could make out a yarmulke. *Great*, she thought, *another Black Hat*. The religious were shoddy with tips.

When she opened the door, she noticed his rifle, which was slung around his arm like a purse. "I'm sorry," she said. "You can't bring that in here." Vlad would never allow it.

The young soldier nodded and pirouetted back to the street.

Since the bombings had started, it had been a slow month. The Arabs stopped passing through checkpoints—and they tipped. The Jews themselves were scared to go out, and the tourists had been non-existent.

"You know what, it's okay," she called through the alley. He turned back around with his gun. She glanced at the mirror and heard no dissent. And her hair was looking blonder than usual. Just that morning, she had dyed it again, because that's what they all seemed to want. "You can come in," she continued. "Just to look around. And don't worry, you can take your gun with you." The boy looked cute. He had long, lanky arms, and he looked like he might be a virgin.

He grinned. "Um, I was just looking."

I'll bet, she thought. "Why don't you come and have a seat? I'll make coffee."

"I don't drink coffee."

"Well, maybe you can have something else then."

She held the door in, and he came.

"I'm Evelyn," she said, shaking his hand.

"My name's Boaz," he said, and she knew that it wasn't, since soldiers never used their real ones. His right hand felt warm and sticky to the touch. She wondered if he'd come from a bathroom.

"Nice to meet you, Boaz." She thought the name sounded vaguely familiar. "You can call me Eva, or just Eve, if you want. Here, come have a seat on the sofa."

She lifted up a newspaper, which some Arab had left. He had paid an extra hour just to sit there.

"I don't have a lot of money. And I don't mean to be rude, but I was wondering if we could talk about the price."

She sat down on the plush couch beside him. "It's okay," she said. "We can work around what you've got. But it's two hundred sheks for a suck and fuck."

"Any position?" he asked. So maybe he wasn't that new.

"Any position except anal."

"Um, well, maybe we could do just the intercourse part, since I don't have enough for a suck."

She thought she heard a soft laugh in the mirror, but the boy didn't seem to hear. "It's no problem," she said. "How much do you have?"

"I only have 120 shekels."

"I'm sorry. You're going to have to leave." She never went below 180—group standard.

"But wait," the kid said, "I've got a nice watch." The boy was still seated as she smiled and walked to the door. "It's a Casio G-Shock. You see, it glows when it turns to the side." He demonstrated for her, and at first, she thought he was kidding.

"That is a nice watch."

"Yes, isn't it?" he said. "They gave it to me as a present."

"Who did?"

"The army. That was back when I finished my training. They said I was the best in my draft."

"And that's why you're here now?"

"No," the kid said. "I'm out on the line. I finished my training in November."

She smiled. She liked his brown eyes. They were rounded from drink. And she liked his red bush of a haircut. His chapped lips were sagging, somber and low. He reminded her a bit of her father. He had once been a soldier in the Afghani War, judging by one of his pictures.

"So, I was thinking," he continued, "that you could take the watch along with the 120 shekels. And maybe that way you'd do a good thing for this country and help out a soldier in need."

"I think you should keep the watch for yourself. Just don't tell anyone what you paid."

He nodded.

She unbuttoned his jeans, which were tight at his knees and clung to the bones of his waist. She pulled up his t-shirt and noticed his chest, which was remarkably thin for a soldier. His ribs were exposed, his stomach flat, and his arms tanned red like a farmer's.

She smoothed out the sheet on the beige massage table. "Come here," she said as she patted it. She undid her robe, which was cotton and white, and rubbed some light oil on her breasts. The smell was vanilla, which she always liked best, because it drowned out the smell of the clients.

"Come here," she said again to the boy, who was appraising the couch for his gun. "You can leave it over there. It'll be fine."

He hopped up on the table beside her.

"You're pretty," he said, and he seemed to have meant it, judging by the part in his lips. His dick wasn't up, so she stroked it a bit. His shaven chin smelled like tobacco.

"You can touch me," she said, pulling his hand to her breast. It sat there like some kind of dead animal.

He let out a groan, an uncomfortable wheeze, as his balls clumped tight in her hand.

"It's okay," she said. "Have you done this before?"

"Not really," he said with a smile.

She did it often with virgins—at least three times this week—though none of them came wearing yarmulkes. One of them had been a worker—a Thai, evidently, though she barely understood what he said. Another one came with his father and brother, and all three of them finished in seconds. The third was a young Palestinian man who was planning to get married this week. He invited her to his wedding, and when she respectfully declined, he told her he'd bring her some cake. They all went inside her with the condoms she gave them, and she felt nothing except the sparkle of finance.

But with the Orthodox she always felt a warm sense of spite, and she enjoyed corrupting their youths. Their men always scowled as she passed on the street, as if they weren't regular clients.

She caressed the boy's hand and tickled his thigh. She buried her head in his stomach. His skin fluttered tight and bunched with each kiss along the red fur of his happy trail. His cock grew hard in the palm of her hand, and she climbed up on top of his legs.

"You want pink or dark blue?" she said with a smile, reaching inside of her robe.

"Um, I don't know," he said, cringing a bit, as if it dawned on him suddenly that others might have been here before him.

"You know," she said, "you have a very large dick," which

succeeded in putting him at ease. "Here," she said, and she gave him dark blue, even though the pink ones were thinner.

She held his hand. "Do you want a bit of help?" He was debating which side to roll down.

"Uh, yeah," he said.

She slid it on down. She could do it with only two fingers. "Do you want to be on top?"

"Uh, okay," he said, with that shrill, piping laugh that only the Orthodox gave.

Then she thought about Vladimir, that he must be online, because his mirror wasn't making its noises. "Are you ready?" she asked.

"You bet." He slid inside her with confidence. He went too far up—all of them did—and turned a bit to the side. *Slow down,* she wanted to say to him, but this she never said.

He breathed heavily at first and then not at all. His brown eyes were starting to water.

Sweating, he moved back and forth in flashing red thrusts, and she wondered what he was thinking. Probably of his mother—most of them did, at least the first time that they started. No, she thought, probably his father; this one was obviously beaten. She could see a few welts and scars on his brow, though those might have come from the army.

"What's that?" she said and pointed to his brow. He didn't look up from his fucking.

"I fell," he said as he wiped off his face. Then he cradled her back with his hands.

"Sorry," she said and touched his left cheek. His skullcap was dangling off him.

She felt like she wanted to kiss this young boy ever since he called her "pretty." She knew that she wasn't—not since the repairs—though something inside him had meant it.

Her face still showed signs of the beating she had suffered alone in this apartment in August. It was from the District Police, a "personal friend," who had come to collect on the payments. And it was partially her fault for not having insisted on obtaining a bodyguard like Vladimir sooner. But at the time she had worked for a small-time affair that was edging its way in the market. Of course, after the incident, the gang wars ensued. The men who now owned her were decent. They were a much better lot, with connections all around, and promised they'd see to her safety. And the cash wasn't bad—at least till last fall, when the clients stopped coming to visit. But her owners, she knew, would still put her up as a reminder of debts from the city.

And she no longer even hated all the sex that she had. Occasionally she found it pleasing. Of course, the heroin helped, but she didn't do much—just a couple quick dabs for the evening.

This soldier, however, kept pounding her insides, and she felt nothing but the churn in her stomach. She realized that she hadn't eaten since ten in the morning. After this, she would go make a salad.

His pelvis kept jabbing up and to the right. His cheek muscles clenched in his jaw. She could see that his eyes were trying hard not to focus and that this one would require some effort.

"Here," she said, "why don't we try from the back?" She knew that he wouldn't have asked. But all of the soldiers wanted it this way. It had something to do with the army, she figured.

They tried it for a bit. He reached around to her breasts and fingered the braid of her vulva. He wasn't too hard; she could feel him inside as she pressed herself on to his stomach.

She tossed her hair up and onto her back. The sight of it was usually enough for them.

A couple minutes later, she felt him pull out. He turned to look down at his watch.

"I gotta go," he said.

"Are you sure?" she asked. She wasn't sure why she had said this.

"No, it's not gonna happen."

"Why? What is it? Is there something wrong with the way that I look?"

"No," he said. "It's me. I'm sorry. I think you're one of the prettiest women I've seen."

It was strange, she thought. He seemed to have meant it. His dark eyes held her gaze. "So what is it?" she asked. "Is it the position we're in? Do you want me to try with my mouth?"

"Uh, I don't know."

"Let's try it," she said, as she reached for his waist and bent down.

The blueberry didn't mask the spermicidal taste, which was horrible, no matter how many times she had mouthed it.

A few minutes later, she could see it wouldn't work. His legs were still glued to the table.

"Here," she said, "let's try something else." She peeled off his condom and threw it.

"What are you doing?"

"I don't mind," she said. "Just try not to go on my face."

The boy didn't hesitate. None of them did. She only ever did this with virgins.

He laid his head back on the pillow and sighed—undoubtedly thinking of his father.

She throated him up and down with her chest, breathing in air with her nose. She knew that she was good—had been told so each day—and that not even a faggot could stand this.

"I can't," Uri said, ten minutes later, parting the hair on her face.

"What is it?" she asked, wiping her mouth. She seemed to be checking the mirror again.

"I don't know. It's something in my head. I don't think I'm going to finish."

"Do you want to talk?"

"Not really," he said. "I don't even know what to say."

He didn't know why this woman kept asking or what he was supposed to tell her. There was no cause he could give, no reason to explain. He didn't even know why he came here.

He examined her eyes, her immaculate teeth, that strange, calm draw of her breath. Her face was exotic, like it wasn't quite white, and it sent a shiver through the base of his spine. "I think I should go."

"No, stay," she said. "I won't charge you any more—as long as you wear that skullcap."

He wasn't quite sure what she meant by the remark as he pulled up his jeans and his shirt. "Here," he said. "You can take the watch. I'm gonna get a new one tomorrow."

"No," she said. "I don't want the fucking watch. Just take your stuff and get out."

"What about the money?"

"You can keep it," she said.

"Okay." Uri rose from the seat. He picked up his duffel, his gun and his clip. He tied a quick knot in each boot. Then he took out his wallet and counted his bills, setting them all on her sink. He left her two hundred. The watch was worth more. But this woman would not even take it.

He shut the door and walked through the alley. He sat on the edge of the street. He lowered his head into the skin of his hands, and he could feel the beat of his heart.

NAHLA

That Friday evening, beyond the west hill of the Rachel's Tomb Outpost, a small cemetery choked with Aleppos, and blue garbage bins stenciled UN, a sultry wind gathered and bounded off the laundry-draped homes, clacking tin, overhead water tanks, rattling the loosely-set panes. This was the Aida Refugee Camp. Population: 4,012.

Inside one of the warren's north buildings, a two-story, poured cement home, a young girl peered through the curtains of her room at the purpling wash of a sky. She had delicate features, and her downy cheeks glowed in the light. Outside, the muezzin's call echoed, though Leda didn't care to pray.

She rolled out the mat. Since the curfews had started, it wasn't easy, because she had to keep her head below the window. That's what her father had told her. And he had boarded it up once with a long sheet of wood, but then she had a hard time breathing. She had asthma. The yoga was good for her. That's what her mother had told her. And her mother knew well. She was a doctor. Or, at least she would give out the medicines. But everyone called her doctor. Her shop was downstairs. Sometimes she'd come up and join her. Right now she was across the hall arguing with her dad. They were talking about her uncle.

She could hear them yell as she spread out the mat, using her hands and her feet. And she didn't see the point of yelling all the time when people were standing right by you. But it's all they would do, yell at each other. Sometimes her mom would make pudding. Her dad would complain that the pudding wasn't sweet, and her mom said they were all getting fat.

Leda wasn't sure if she was fat or if she was one of the thin girls. She felt in between: round in some places and long and bony in others.

She stretched out her arms and lay along the mat. She could feel the cool sponge on her cheek. It felt crinkly and soft, kind of like her dad when his beard wasn't coated in pudding.

She kissed the mat, and she kissed herself—at least, she blew a kiss in the air. She grabbed it with her hand and put it back on her cheek. Then she breathed in some more air.

Lately she hated doing this stuff, but she felt like she still had to do it. They couldn't go outside or even walk around and her kneecaps were starting to tighten.

She wished she could jump up and cling to the walls, bounce from the floor to the ceiling. She would swing from the light-set and pounce at her desk, claw at her bed and the carpet. But this was much better. Better for the house. To her mom, that was really important. They had lots of guests—people who'd come and visit her family's apartment.

Most of these men were friends with her uncle, and her mom didn't like them at all. But her uncle's home was no longer around. At least, that's what her father had said.

She wondered if maybe she could go live in the sky, because there was plenty of room up there. Plenty of birds and pheasants and swans, and no Jews that she'd have to be scared of.

Sometimes the Jews would come from the graves and point with their guns at her window. And she wasn't really scared. The boys from her school would throw rocks in the graves, and they were the ones who were scared. They would hide behind tombstones, dash down the rows. A couple got hit with a bullet. One of them died. That's what she heard. Though she hadn't seen anyone since school closed.

She liked being home, drinking tea with her dad and doing yoga right here with her mom. But she wanted to go outside and take a break from this place and maybe get a bottle of Pepsi. Her mother wouldn't let her drink Pepsi at home, though sometimes her father would sneak it. He brought her a bottle early last week, and she was saving it under her mattress. She also enjoyed Coke, but she liked Pepsi more, because that was the one with Britney. She had seen the ads on the television set—back when they still had the antenna.

She remembered the night when they got rid of the antenna. Her father came home with a dish. He put it up outside of her room, and that's when her mom started crying.

This was over two years ago. This was when she was four. And it was weird, she thought, how she remembered these things, because she barely remembered her brother.

Her younger brother had been in the hospital then. He had some kind of problem with food. He stayed away for over one week, and then her mom said he was gone. And when her parents came home from the hospital that night, her dad brought the dish for the set. It had lots of cartoons, and some really good shows, but her mom said that they couldn't have sugar. Her father got mad, and he threw down the dish. Then her mom went to live with her aunt. She decided to come back early last year, and since then, they hadn't had sugar.

Sometimes her mom would make honey-syrup cakes or this pudding that tasted so weird. She used this gray bottle of liquidy stuff that took a long time to come out. And afterwards Leda had to go to the toilet, which she really didn't like to do. So she stopped eating sweets. And she didn't really mind. The only thing she missed was the Pepsi.

And Britney Spears, who wasn't even on. Now they only watched the news.

She took out the tape with the Asian music on it and set it down by the mat. Then she clicked on the lid of her new cassette deck, which her dad had brought from work. He had said she could keep it for as long as he was here, because the post office closed during curfew.

The music began playing soft and then loud. It sounded like blowing wind. Then water crashed down against some far rocks, and she could hear the tingle of stars.

She lit up a candle, which she kept by the chair. The candle smelled like banana. She liked banana; it wasn't too sweet. Not as sweet as the melon.

The air smelled nice. It was pleasant and warm. She no longer heard all the shouting. It might have been there, but she tried not to think as she breathed in and out of her lungs.

She sat along the mat with her legs spread apart and her toes curled up from her feet. She took a deep breath and she thought of the stars—the ones that she heard on the tape.

She could still hear the shouting outside from the hall. It kept interrupting her breathing. The men were still there. They were talking about war, or whatever it was they discussed.

The power flashed off in her room and the hall. The music and lights went off. The waves stopped crashing, and the candle flame flicked, hissing along the table.

This was not good. It happened last week. But at night, it always took longer. Then her father called out: "Leda, you okay? Stay where you are, sweet. I'm coming."

"I'm fine," Leda said as the flashlight approached, spotting the door, then her face.

"Is everything okay?"

"Yeah," Leda said. The flashlight was right in her eyes.

"I'm gonna run down and get gas for the stove."

"Can I come?"

"No, stay where you are. I want you to sit at the table."

The flashlight left, and so did her dad. Leda sat down at the desk. She drew on her hand with a rose-colored marker: two circles and then a diamond. She held up the face and talked to her hand. She asked herself how she was doing.

"Fine," she said. "It's warm in this place. I want to go out for a walk."

"You can't do that," her hand mumbled back. "You know there's still a curfew."

Well, fuck the curfew, she wanted to say, but her parents would never allow it.

"Fuck" is what the boys all said—the ones she used to chase. But they weren't interested in her. Not anymore. Maybe it was because of the cola. She needed the drink to give her some life. It made her whole head feel sparkly. She thought that the boys probably felt the same thing whenever they threw rocks at the Jeeps.

And they hadn't lately. Things here were calm, especially outside of her home. She didn't understand why she couldn't run out and get a quick drink from the store. Her cousin's shop was down on the corner. They also sold *Bissli* and nuts. Her mother had said she could have plenty of those. Maybe she'd go get a package.

She hadn't heard the bang. She'd felt it, though.

Inside her apartment, Nahla al-Ajuri, the mother of Leda, had been brewing a pot of tea when it happened, placing the kettle on a makeshift stove in her sink, one hastily constructed of tea candles, paper, and rags, when she heard a reverberating patter, followed by screams, and knew right away what it was.

Ninety minutes later, she was standing at the Bethlehem Morgue, identifying the girl they had shot, a face she didn't recognize, laid out on an aluminum tray. She knew right away what would happen, the revenge that would have to ensue. And were she another woman—like her sister, in fact, or Leda herself in later age, God bless her—she probably would have condoned it. At the time, though, she couldn't talk.

Now, mid-afternoon Saturday, twelve hours after the fact, she was sitting on the floor of her brother's apartment, listening to words from a henna-bearded leader, a cripple named Abu Srur. About three-dozen others piled on the floormats, most of them family or kin. Her husband was slumped along a chair in the corner, his face a bit brighter than ash.

"Excuse me, Sheikh." A young militant coughed, one of two bearing guns by the door. The other was inspecting the dates that were served: creamy *barheen*, which weren't ripe. The whole place felt humid and suffocating to her, yet she didn't have the strength to stand up.

Her brother's apartment, which was in the camp's western half, was newly tiled with pink limestone. He had taken a job with the Jews in Efrat, laying bricks for a shopping center. And it was ironic, she thought, or logical perhaps, that he would seek out his friends in the mosque. Her own gangly husband, with his pallor, rough chin, and damp, graying hair slicked to the corner—no gel, though—was disappointed, perhaps, but silent in place, because *she* had provided this service through family. Her husband's men—his brothers, their tribe—were as useless as their national slogans. So they turned to the Brothers. What more could she do? She didn't believe in their sayings. And the way they viewed women repulsed her at first. But at least they'd provide her with vengeance. And funds.

"Excuse me, Abu Shahida, some words of advice." The Sheikh was splayed on a floormat. Beneath the hems of his track pants, two oily bars were connected to the heels of his Asics. "I know this is hard for you and your wife, which is why I request that you heed. What I'm going to tell you are the words of the Prophet, Lord honor and grant him peace. In another time of war, 630 A.D., Abu Bakr was rounding his horses and kinsmen. As he approached the south summit of the Sarawat plains, he was surrounded by women of beauty. These faces. Lord have mercy on his soul, for blessed be he who calls forth the name of Right Vengeance, for this is the way and the light of before and in the words of the Prophet Mohammed, the blessed, the Lord shall have mercy and banish the souls of the infidel, heathen and scoundrel. For when He now speaks…"

The sermon dragged on. Nahla tried hard not to hear it. It was a recollection of the tale of the Prophet's First War, his conquest of Tai'f and Mecca, his "vengeance." She didn't even care what he thought "vengeance" meant. For all she knew, this freak was living. As for her daughter, her days were done, and nothing would bring the child back.

"Now I," said the cripple, "am Abu Srur. You have probably heard of my speeches. For justice. I do this for peace, but also for you, and to show that our children have value. You see this?" From the sleeve of his sweatshirt—which bore the word GAP—a jagged gray thumb was protruding. "This is the hand of the almighty God. It was bequeathed by the Soul of the Spirit, the Blessed. And He is here now. Watch as He speaks. I tell you, this hand commands vengeance. It does this."

She looked at his hand—its wobbly, white shape, and a few grains of rice wedged within it. His thumb was lined pink, like the paw of a cat. It pointed and talked to the ceiling.

"I come here for justice, but also for you. To show you the ways of our people, our body. For we are one body. Together we fight. We consecrate the names of the Prophet, the blessed. We shall seek vengeance and honor her soul and honor the name of His people, bless Allah, with an attack on the Jews at the al-Rabah Mosque"—Rachel's Tomb—"on the seventeenth day of Muharram."

Her brother was nodding. Other heads bobbed.

Nahla herself couldn't take it. "Wait," she protested, somewhat startled by her voice. Two-dozen heads sharply turned. "I don't want to do this."

"What?" said the Sheik.

"I don't want you to pursue our vengeance."

"What?"

The Sheik just ignored her and turned to Leuwii, her husband, who slouched in his chair. "What?"

"You heard her," Leuwii said. "That's what she thinks."

"What are you? The man or the wife?"

Her husband said nothing, glanced at the tiles. Then her brother said she was unsettled. Discussion ensued among family and friends, at least a good half of al-Aida.

"Enough," said the Sheik. "So what do you want? You want someone else to seek your revenge? That's fine."

"I will," she stammered.

"What?" Leuwii said.

Her brother nearly fell off his chair. "What?"

"I'll do it myself."

Then a chorus of laughs was interrupted by the Sheik's angered pleading. "How?"

"I want you to show me."

"What?" Leuwii said.

"I want them to teach me to do it."

"What?"

A militant grimaced next to the door. The other still chomped on his date. All the windows were curtained, though dozens pressed in, grabbing a meal where they could.

"This isn't a job for a woman," said Leuwii.

"What does she want?" asked the Sheikh.

Four hours later, she was down in her store, thumbing down a magazine's follower. She didn't even know how the bullets went in, but the militants graciously helped her. Both were quiet, small, eager men who were more than willing to lead her. For the past several hours, they'd shown her the gun, a massive, black, oily contraption. A "Dragunov." And her husband had pleaded, threatened divorce, but at the end of the day he'd relented. He'd said: "If you want to do this, this is your choice. And I'll honor it, as your husband."

"That's great."

The truth of the matter, Nahla thought, is, why shouldn't she pull the trigger? She'd raised the children, earned a degree, and worked ninety hours to sustain them. Her husband hadn't brought home a shekel in months; he hadn't even cooked them a dinner.

Behind her, the pharmacy's shutters were raised, and a pale, milky light sifted in. The place smelled like Leda: her sweatshirt, her gum, the spare yoga mat left in the corner, her tricycle.

"You need to bolt the chamber."

"What?" she asked.

He pulled back the gun's cocking lever. "If you don't do that first, the weapon won't fire. Now we need to practice your aiming."

It was a PSO-1 Scope, or so they had said, intended for

hunting small game. She didn't even know how to open its lid, but they said they would do it all for her. All she had to do was fire, if that was her aim, and make sure the chevron was centered. And she would only have time for one or two shots. Then they would have to take cover.

"And what if I miss them?"

"I'm sure you will. But at least you can send them a message."

"I don't want to miss them."

"You'll only shoot one, and I seriously doubt it'll happen," he told her.

"So then what happens?"

"We have to run and hope they don't shell the whole building."

"Do you think we could die?"

"That's possible," he said. This fighter was goateed and tan. He was wearing pressed blue jeans, bent forward to his arm, adjusting the sight on her counter. "Who knows?"

"Are you not afraid to die?"

"I am." He stood up. "All of us are. Of course."

He was surprisingly honest, much more than the Sheikh. And she thought he would make a good husband. "How old are you?" she asked.

"He's twenty," said his friend. "Both of us are ready to die."

"Well, that's nice."

She wasn't even sure how she'd gotten this far, peering out from the edge of a roof. The gun was assembled, mounted on blocks, as they knelt upon the flat gravel floor. They peered between carpets, out into dark, to the compound above, past the graves.

"It's seven hundred meters, possibly less." Her new friend

was adjusting the rifle. He was twisting the scope, eyeing its sight, while the other one lowered a camera. He was calling out numbers; both of them crawled, while she herself lay on a carpet and gasped. I'm not going to do this, she told herself, stuffing back hair in her veil. She'd gone out in sweat pants and a silver hijab—if only to lower suspicions.

"And what will I do after I shoot?"

"You immediately run down those steps." He pointed towards an unfinished slab near the edge, upon which some wood planks were set. "Are you ready?"

"I guess."

The militant coughed, while the other one chanted his verses. "There's no room for guessing. You will or you won't. If you don't want to, I'll pull the trigger."

"I'll do it."

"This'll be a first," the other fighter said.

"And hopefully it won't be the last."

As she sighted the roof of the compound ahead, which hove into view through the darkness, half-silvered, she could make out the tarp and the far, beady eyes of the soldiers who stood there on guard. At least two were standing. One held a phone and smoked beside a net-covered block. Another one leaned against the glass in his booth. He seemed to be reading and holding a flashlight up. "Which one should I shoot?"

"Whichever you want."

"How will I know when to shoot them?"

"I'll tell you."

"And then I start running?"

"First drop the gun. I'll pick it up, and I'll join you."

"Okay. And what about the wind, or the distance, or drop—" She could feel her heart kicking inside her, like Leda. And her pulse was throbbing, her veil steeped in sweat.

"Just aim for the head. They're close enough, none of that matters."

"And what if I miss?"

"You're not gonna miss."

"But you said—"

"Just do what I tell you."

"Okay."

"You can aim for the one who's inside the booth. But the other shot's probably cleaner."

The first fighter leaned in and angled the gun towards the end of the roof, near the smoker. "You see him?"

Nahla examined the face of this boy, this child who would die before morning.

"You ready?"

"I don't know," she mumbled.

"What don't you know?"

"I don't know if I'm ready to do this."

"Just give me the gun."

He reached for it then, and an explosion ripped out through al-Aida. She'd fired.

She watched a man fall beside a puff of red strings.

"Ya Allah," said the fighter. The gun barrel shook in her hand.

"So here's the plan," her brother told her, twelve hours later, inside his apartment in the al-Aida Refugee Camp. "You've got to kill another Jew. It doesn't matter how you do it. It doesn't matter if you die. The payment is twelve-thousand sheks."

That was it, Nahla realized. That was the worth of her life, excluding the cost of her funeral and the fees for rebuilding their house. Both would be deducted, of course.

Her brother was munching on a date as he said it, a gummy *barheen*, from the wake. He was wearing his Yankees cap backwards, as he always did, and watching *Arab Idol*, possibly distracting himself.

"What if I refuse?"

He didn't look up. He just spat his pit at the set. It clunked against the screen and bounced into a fake potted palm—a well-practiced shot. "No one refuses the Sheikh."

Suddenly, Muna dashed in from the store. "Abu Jabri said he can't help us anymore. But he gave me an ice cream and drink." Her brother's clueless daughter, still clad in her navy-striped school dress, was slurping a Fanta and holding a half-melted Magnum on a stick. She resembled her cousins in every single way—but for the crap that she ate.

"I'll do it," she told her brother, "on two conditions. First, Muna doesn't stay in this house. You'll let her live with her aunt in ad-Doha"—a neighboring village, outside the camp, where she wouldn't live in squalor and fear of bi-nightly arrests. "And two, all the proceeds will go to Leuwii." She hadn't spoken to her husband since the wake, nor did she intend to, though perhaps this would lessen the guilt.

"If you want to help him, that's your choice. The handlers will meet you at one. You'll pick up the vest when you get past the checkpoint, inside the monastery gardens. As for Muna, that's fine."

Her handlers, her brother told her, had found her a job, through covert channels, at a Jerusalem hotel, where Palestinians weren't normally employed. She'd have to dress up a bit, try to "look good." As if she hadn't come from a wake.

She would have considered it further, but she realized she didn't have a choice. She'd consorted with the fighters, had blood on her hands. At best they would give her up.

"Come here." She hugged her niece. Then she grabbed her thin, sticky hand. "You're gonna go stay with your aunt for a while."

"Why?"

"Cause ad-Doha is a much safer place."

"But they don't have any ice cream."

"Oh, they will," said Nahla. "Your father will see to that."

Her father didn't turn from the set. He wore a grave expression, possibly realizing—if he hadn't before—that his sister was braver than he.

After Muna dashed off, Nahla bathed, said a few prayers, and kissed her other family. Then, with the help of two militants, she recorded a video of herself draped in green flags, clutching a rifle, and professing support for their cause.

She thought about writing a note to Leuwii, but any feelings she had now were lost.

In the bathroom mirror, as she reapplied lipstick, she noticed her lips were too chapped. The militants had told her that that could be a telltale sign to security. But it was clearly from the *khamsin*. Outside, through the slatted gray window, a particled wind choked the camp, swarming through laundry, slabs of cement, and the chalky green leaves of a loquat, which she had once planted herself. Now all she wanted was to see the tree demolished. She could feel the hot wind in her throat. The going would be rough through the checkpoint, she realized, assuming traffic still crossed. Then she'd detonate herself outside the hotel, or wherever she encountered some guards.

In the kitchen, she smeared some olive oil on her lips and retrieved her sunglasses—an oversized tortoiseshell pair, like the kind that Umm Kulthum wore. Her life had been miserable, as well. Everyone's was, she supposed.

"Good luck," said her brother, bidding her adieu. "May God grant you peace and good health."

190

SHLOMO

The December administration of the Israeli Halakha Standards and Kosher Certification Board Exam, Level III: Advanced took place in a nondescript conference room on the third floor of the Jerusalem Gate Hotel. Twenty-five takers were in attendance, most of them progenies of well-regarded clans or has-been dynasties spanning the Pale and Carpathians. A few sprung from squalid development towns—Sderot, Netivot, Yeruham—or other rotting lands in the south. All were equally in-bred, and all were well-prepared for the test.

Shlomo Kaplan was not. He sat sweatily in back, gripping the desk of his writing chair, biting his lip, cupping his beard, deliberately avoiding eye contact with the furry-faced behemoth in front, a shiny-toothed *Litvak* named Yakov, who proctored in a glittering frock-coat. He was mumbling phrases inaudibly, lost in contemplative prayer, or otherwise trying to impress them. Shlomo should have paid him off. Across the aisle to his right sat Iddo, a smarmy Moroccan, grandson of the Sephardic Chief Rabbi, thick-lidded, round, and looking as if he might well have consumed his own weight in shakshuka that morning. He gave Shlomo a tomato-smeared grin.

> *Question 39: After the liver is broiled and the outer juices have stopped flowing, how many times must the liver be rinsed under a stream of cold water?*

Fuck this, Shlomo figured. He reached in his *rekel*, which was bunched below his desk, parted his tzitzit, and unsnapped the leather box of his tefillin. Then he pulled out a small strip of parchment on which he had scribbled some notes. Beside him, the Moroccan just leered. Shlomo knew it was written here somewhere between bugs and the boiling of kitchen utensils.

Three, he marked on the test. Then he whispered to the *shvartze* beside him: "God comes to us in multiple ways."

Shlomo's big break as a kosher inspector came a couple years later, when he discovered two or three shrimp shells inadvertently dropped into a package of cod. The order, which had been placed by some upstart caterer near Kiryat Yam, had fallen under the supervision of the municipal rabbinate, which had neglected its watch. Shlomo, as the Deputy Regional Inspector, was actually tipped off by a friend of his, a classmate from *kollel*, who owed him a ride.

There was hell to pay in Jerusalem. Three rabbis were fired—or not promoted, to be exact—and Shlomo's picture was displayed in the *Chief Rabbinate's Weekly*, which was circulated on all the important blocks in the capital and distributed as far west as Toronto. The article cited him as an "exemplary" inspector, one who is "G-d-fearing, properly trained, and responsible in all he undertakes." He even got to pose in a *shtreimel*, an enormous fur cap, which he didn't even own. Three weeks later, he was married to the Mir Yeshiva head's daughter and employed as a Sabbath supervisor at the new Laromme Hotel in Jerusalem. Things were looking up.

Then he committed a gaffe. As a side-project, and in effort to get his name out—he had hopes of becoming a district supervisor, if not more gainfully employed—he had founded a rent control committee in the Sanhedria neighborhood of Jerusalem, where landlords were gouging their tenants. Similar groups had been founded in Bnei Brak and other telescoping tenements. What he hadn't counted on was the owners being patrons of Shas, the largest rival party, and *Sephardim* to boot. Normally, one could negotiate with these people, and pretty much anyone wearing a hat. But when he showed up at the offices of Deri & Yishai, intending to outline his plans, and possibly squeeze them, he found none other than Iddo, his four-ton nemesis, sitting at the desk, picking an olive from his teeth.

"Multiple ways," Iddo said. Then he thumbed through the sheets of his prayerbook. "How's the new wife holding up?"

Twelve hours later, Shlomo was reassigned to the most isolated patch of the Negev, overseeing the kosher inspection for a senior citizens' home near Ofakim. To call the place desolate would have complimented the region. Actual scorpions crept along the sand, which had more the consistency of rock, and even in May, when he arrived, the thermometers simmered at 47°C. "I guess God wills it," said his wife, who detested him but didn't say a word, apart from that. She and their two kids settled comfortably into their pink-walled, swamp-cooled condo, which was in an eight-story building, ironically enough, despite being three kilometers from the next. Shlomo, for his part, only visited the center once or twice a week, just enough to watch people die.

Most afternoons, he played cards in the park and lingered around the yeshiva, dipping his toes in the bath or haggling with *Bukhari* merchants over the price of their babkas, which were obviously inflated, even for him. He took up smoking, as well.

Fortunately, things played out to his favor in Jerusalem. Iddo suffered a stroke at age thirty-six, which wasn't unexpected in his circles—they all ate a lot—but he hadn't even made it to the hospital in time to stabilize his brain. The result was that he had gone comatose—an awful, squishy state—and any other people would have pulled the plug. Shlomo visited him in the hospital once and felt a slight shred of compassion: the thin, charcoaled eyes, the scintillating mask, the cables affixed to his jugular, like some massive shrimp. Shlomo thought about pulling the cord himself. Then he stepped out for a smoke.

Twenty months later, his nemesis was dead, and Shlomo was called back to Jerusalem, where he attained a well-deserved sinecure as the Sabbath Inspector of the David Citadel Hotel. His wife, who had borne him two more, was elated, albeit unanxious to move. She also disliked moving back near her father, at whose home they were expected to gather each Friday night. That is, everyone in the clan except Shlomo, who made his rounds at the hotel.

One Friday evening around six, as a golden sun steamed through the clouds, igniting the cliffs of Talbiya and spraying warm light on his suite, Shlomo got up from the loveseat. He had been watching *Jeopardy*, sipping a good Cabernet (for which he had directed the import and levied a not-unreasonable tax), picking the jam from his toes, when it occurred to him that he deserved better than this. His father, a hapless shoe merchant from Netanya, had told him that nothing would come of this "life," this newfound devotion he attained at age seventeen, when he'd moved to a Haifa yeshiva and taken up the calling of God. Shlomo wasn't technically ordained as a rabbi, but he had always been spiritual, and he did His work. Hell, he married a hag and had children—four of them, from what he could tell—and prayed most weekends at the Wall. He was fairly compassionate. He never overtaxed the religious and always gave alms to the poor. And he had never actually cheated anybody—that is, asked for an outright bribe. At least not without reasonable grounds. He was diligent with his reports. He didn't aim to be a district supervisor any longer, but his wife deserved more than a two-bedroom flat on some derelict block in Sanhedria. And his Audi needed new tires.

He closed the drapes. He tightened his frock-coat. Then he picked up his half-emptied wineglass, wrapped it in a towel, dropped it on the floor, and stomped it. The shards were still settling in the bin when the deadbolt clamped in his door.

Downstairs, he made his usual trek through the lobby, where George, the Assistant GM, was berating a security guard for having patted down a foreign head of state. A red dusky light checkered the carpets, the wrought-iron tables, the porcelain trays—all of this secular crap. Outside, the wind loudly whipped at the pool. Must have been a *khamsin*. He could hear its hum through the glass.

As Shlomo barged through the swinging doors of the restaurant's kitchen, without warning, of course, he heard a thousand plates fall. Moses himself couldn't have exuded such power. In the center, beneath the hood of a vent and above a steel counter with plates, a goateed chef looked back at him in panic. "Rabbi," he peeped.

Shlomo just studied his thumb. He knew right away what had happened. The wind had blown out the stoves' central pilot light, but the sun had already set. Six hundred chicken breasts cooled on trays along the wall, and a half-dozen servers were scrambling, unsure of how they'd proceed.

"Go ahead, light it," Shlomo said to the chef, a *kibbutznik* named Ron, who wasn't even supposed to be working now.

"But what about—"

"Go ahead. Do it. See if I care." Shlomo eyed a young female server, an Arab, with copper-green eyes. He gave her a sumptuous wink. Then he approached Ron's counter, where a huge saucer of gravy was resting. He dipped his thumb in the pool, licked it, and turned to the five or six servers, all of whom were huddled by the door, waiting to hear his pronouncement. "I think it would be a shame to close you guys down now. What, with the delegation coming." The Mideast Quartet was dining that night in the ballroom, and what seemed like half the UN was expected to arrive for brunch.

The gravy tasted liquidy, dull. "Ron," Shlomo dried off his hand on his frock-coat, slowly fingered his beard. "Let me ask you a question."

Ron stared straight above the plates.

"How long have you been in this business?"

"Twenty-seven years."

"Any kids?"

"Just a couple."

"That's nice. Do you feel this place is a success?"

Ron didn't flinch. He had the look of death in his eyes. "I guess."

"Hmm." Shlomo turned to the young Arab server. "What's your name, sweetheart?"

She glowered at him, bravely.

"I'm sorry, I didn't catch that."

"Nahla." She grinned.

"What a beautiful name, Nahla. What does that mean?"

"Drink of water."

"I see." He turned to Ron, who was quivering beneath his white chef's hat. "You know, I'd like a drink of water."

"Okay."

Then Shlomo spun around to the hall, to the extent one can spin in a frock-coat. He brushed the door's slanted mezuzah and gave the young woman a passing tap on the back—like David seducing Bathsheba, he figured.

Outside, George was scrambling through the lobby, brushing past the legions of security guards and mustached UN personnel. "Rabbi," he pleaded. "I was going to tell you about the stove. There's nothing we can do. We couldn't ask a goy to light it, and the timers are already set."

"Just do what you wish," Shlomo said.

"But what about the license?"

"What about it?"

"How can we be sure it's okay?"

"God has his ways."

Shlomo didn't bother to come down for dinner that night. He didn't have to. He chose to eat in his suite. The chicken was cold, but definitely reheated, and it arrived on a long silver tray, along with a vintage Bordeaux and a chilled green bottle of Perrier. Beneath it was a manager's envelope stuffed with pink bills—banded two-hundreds—and an unstruck, newly-torn match.

Shlomo's suite was actually meant to accommodate his family—it featured two adjoining rooms—though he kept the doors closed in effort to ward off the ghosts: the ghosts of his father, now dead, his nemesis, Iddo, and his mentor, the *Litvak*, whom no one else liked but appropriately feared, since that was the only passable way.

He flipped through the bills, smelling their stack. Then he dumped them all out in the trash. Money meant nothing to him now, just part of his earthly abode. He wasn't sure why he was feeling this. But the sight of it rankled his chest.

Fuck his new tires and his wife. He grabbed the Bordeaux, uncorked it, and laid himself down on the bed.

At around three a.m., he heard a soft knock on his door. He stirred on his pillow, opened his eyes, and realized that his pay-per-view porn was still on. He reached for his kippah and rose, winding through the suite in his bathrobe. Peering through the peephole, he saw a young woman looking down, shielding her face with her palm. It was Nahla, of course. His drink.

"Good evening," said the woman, as Shlomo slowly opened his door.

He looked at her face, those soft Arab cheeks, the pouty, wet folds of her lips. She was wearing sunglasses, too, which she hadn't worn downstairs. But her nametag clearly said Nahla, and it was pinned to her uniform's vest. She also wore a matching blue skirt and white dress shirt with scarf, beneath which her massive breasts bulged. "May peace be upon you," he said.

Diffidently, she entered, looked about the suite, and studied the tall windows' glare. The curtains were drawn, and a wild orange light flitted in: the illumined stone walls of the Old City beyond, compounded with the sweltering dusk. It looked truly biblical, he realized. Like some heathenish plague, or a curse.

"Al-Quds," he said, using the Palestinian name.

"Jerusalem."

"Are you Muslim?"

She grinned, watching him retrieve two crystal flutes from a glass-covered, wall-mounted shelf.

"Then I guess you don't drink."

"There's a first time for everything." Smirking, she removed her black sunglasses and let down her long walnut hair.

As he bent to the fridge and pulled out a bottle of Clos Du Mesnil, '98—she was worth it, he figured, even if she was a bit overweight—he tried not to take his eyes off her, but he noticed she was watching the trash.

"Are those real?" she asked, referring to the discarded shekels.

"Nothing is real in my life." He untied the cork and it popped. Foam drizzled onto the carpet, along with his robe and his hands. His pajamas were silk, and the stain would be hard to get out. Not as hard as blood, though. This girl was a vision from God. "Do you want them?"

She eyed him fiercely, as if too enraged to respond.

"How old are you?" he asked her.

"Twenty-six."

"And you've never been with a man?"

"Is that what you are?"

"If you want to leave, that's fine. I'm not asking you to do anything you don't want." Still smiling, he held out a bubbling glass.

Slowly, she approached him and took it. She sipped it, coughed, and set the glass on the desk. He took her hand and pulled her into his chest. She smelled of perfume—some raw, earthly scent—and he could hear the soft tick of her heart.

"I'm scared," the woman whispered.

"You're scared?"

"Yes."

"Scared of what?" He could feel her whole body convulsing.

"About what I need to do for the cash."

He looked at her sullenly. Then he glanced about the suite—its crystal, silk, gold—like David's own palace of sin. "Nothing," he responded. "I just wanted you to give me a hug."

"What?"

"I'm old enough to be your father. I'm not going to do anything to you. And if you want to take the money, that's fine."

She was shaking madly, half-writhing in his arms.

"There, there," he said. "It's okay."

"No, it's not okay." She backed away. "Fuck you, you Jew."

"What's wrong?"

She eyed him darkly. "You forgot to inspect me," she said. Then she reached in her vest. "*Allahu Akbar.*"

"Shit."

The last thing that Shlomo Kaplan would hear—besides the sound of shrapnel impacting his head—was the sound of the wind as it rattled the glass, and an echoing, high, shrieking laugh. Whether it was the woman's, or Iddo's, or even his father's, Shlomo himself never knew.

1 IVAN

Two hundred ninety-six hours before his death, Corporal Ivan Belkin was sitting on the toilet in the barracks of the Rachel's Tomb Outpost, playing a game of Tetris on his phone, obscured by his Marlboro's smoke, when the half-attached knob of the door started jangling.

"The hell do you want?" Ivan said.

"Patrol's in twelve," said his friend, speaking in Russian.

Ivan flicked his cigarette, which sizzled in the shower's rank stall. Then he reached in his vestpack, which was slung around the sink, and pulled out a small silver flask. He took a long sip of his honey pepper vodka, leaned his head back, and sighed.

Outside, the sun burned a hole through the clouds and the tall cement beams of a base, the neighboring one up the street. Blinking, Ivan followed the procession of soldiers, each a shade darker, as they bounded up Derech Hevron. Then he closed his eyes and smelled the bright Bethlehem air: the scent of sweet diesel, Arab cologne, rotting roadkill, and smoldering trash.

"Ivan," yelled Shaul, his platoon leader, in front, "keep a watch to the rear and stay close."

The men treaded forward. They were heading for the graves down below, a small terraced hillside, adjacent to their base, that was layered with Ottoman tombs. Ivan was spinning. His eyes settled back in his head.

He heard a boom. He would later describe this as the turning point in his mortal existence. But when he heard it right then, it sent a shock wave inside him. Beside him, a whooshing explosion, like some bright, congealed force, flared up majestically, and in those squirming waves, he swore he saw the face of a god. Not a Jewish one, exactly, but some roiling figure, like a fluttering angel of death. Then Liav, who was the fourth man in line, walking about four or five paces ahead of him, turned to find a sparkling flash on his shoulder, as if something licked at his neck. He started swatting at it frantically. Before Ivan could react, let alone anyone else in the vicinity, he heard a sharp bang. Then another one, in fact. It was coming from up the road, beside a parked truck, where his commander had run with his rifle. He was bursting out rounds in quick fire.

Thirty minutes later, or what Ivan would take as thirty minutes—it was in fact four or five seconds—an Arab lay sprawled on the road's graveled edge, his chin at his nose, the thin sucking maw in his clavicle burbling what could only be described as a mulberry jam—this had been Ivan's favorite in Russia. His commander stood over the body, gasping like some great winded boxer while the others provided cover from the blocks. At some point during these last thirty minutes, Ivan found himself running to a large cement barrier, a chipped guardblock at which they would check Arab cars—none were now present, owing to a curfew—and, as he knelt on the pavement, two or three shots rang out from the hood of a Humvee ahead, where his platoon leader had run and, strangely enough, acted bravely. The rest of them froze.

Ivan, being the platoon medic, found himself obliged to act. Witnessing Liav on the pavement, about four meters down, he saw that the fire had sparked and receded. Liav was dead. No, he wasn't dead, Ivan told himself. He was only superficially burnt. The guy was still breathing. And whatever this thing was that had been hurled at him—a Molotov probably—contained fire and nothing else. Perhaps molten wax. Nothing that would disrupt his insides. Liav was still clutching his CAR-15. What was he hoping to do with that, Ivan wondered. Before he could resolve it, Ivan found himself running to the sandbagged caboose of their outpost, through its thick steel frame, and down to the barracks below, where he proceeded to remove his gray blanket, gather it up, consider folding it briefly—though that was beside the point now—and unhesitantly run, re-sling his gun, and pounce towards the checkpoint outside, where he proceeded to swaddle his friend with this bandage, which was undoubtedly reeking of sweat. Nevertheless, Liav seemed to appreciate the gesture, as if he were being bid goodnight. Beyond, his commander continued his firing. Or maybe he had just started it at that point. It was not immediately clear, and time had just enveloped itself in some ill-construed form, a sagging gray heap of bruised cotton reeking of semen and sweat, while above him, in this gray pewter day, with its evanescent sun and hewed clouds, dusk folded over the horizon like a lid sealing mulberry jam.

Ivan ran in haste now down to the foot of the road, where he attended the Arab who was sprawled like a kill, was a kill, in fact, the first they had seen on the line.

It was 1740, 11 March, on this, the thirtieth day of Adar.

In the black of the night, deep inside the bowels of the Rachel's Tomb Outpost, the door to the barracks slammed open. Ivan's two eyelids did not. He heard the flick of the light-switch, a flash of bright red, some stirring and groans from the duffels, chinked bed-frames, and the platoon sergeant's voice, huffing and loud, barking out orders in Hebrew: "Mission. At twenty-two forty-five, I want the following men out: Vasily, Boaz, Shibli, and Uri. And Yossi, you're coming. That's what it says. I don't want any shit, so get ready. Everyone's standing in ten with their gear, waters bottles filled in their packs. Get moving."

Ivan turned up and felt his warm cot, the sleeping bag tight on his shoulder. It was an immaculate feeling, so comfortable, warm: the knowledge that others were leaving. He figured he'd jerk off, maybe read a few books, go sit on the shitter for hours and ponder. Or maybe he'd sleep more. It was the first time this month that they'd slotted a patrol without the medic.

"And Ivan."

"*Pashol nachui*," Ivan said, meaning "fuck you" in Russian, and which the sergeant by now was aware of. Ivan looked up, slowly parting his eyes. He wondered if the sergeant had heard him. The door had banged shut, and the lights had gone up. It was blindly bright in the bunk-room, and cold out, and yet warm in his sleeping bag, so warm here inside. He wondered if he could possibly stay.

On the bunk bed below him, Boaz hissed at the lights. On his trunk lay his pomade, deodorant, colognes. He'd spruce himself up before leaving. And Ivan sometimes wondered if it occurred to the Israelis that this was the reason bugs bit them. They'd go out on missions with their hair gelled and greased, as if leaving home for a party. And it was admirable, really, the way that they served, the zest that they brought to these missions.

Ivan would leave this. He'd stay in his bunk. Another two years in the army, plus prison. Eventually they'd discharge him. He'd read in his cell, apply for a permit and visa. He'd go to

America, study computers, and get a good job in high-tech. And he'd send checks to this country in an envelope, stamped, and he'd make out a sum for the Captain and Colonel. He'd say he was sorry for leaving so soon, that he hoped they were enjoying the weather. He'd include pictures of his wife, his kids and new yacht, the cottage he'd built in the Hamptons. And he'd name his ship Aleph, for the men in his company. Then he'd take it out to sea and he'd sink it. He'd invest the return, cash a few checks, build them a playground and name it.

"Ivan, get ready," Boaz shot up. He had slept in full uniform and already laced up his boots. "It's time to get dressed for the mission."

"Right now?"

Boaz tore up the flap of his vest and squeezed in the ball of his poncho. "Yes."

This, Ivan thought, was the only defensible part of doing his national service. He liked fucking with Israelis, playing games with their minds. Boaz wasn't much of a challenge. "I'm staying."

"No," Boaz said. "You're part of this team, and that means you have to get ready."

He glanced down at Boaz, who raked back his hair and worked it into tall, pointed spikes. Earlier, he had washed it with a bar of Dial soap and rinsed off the foam with his thermos. Now he reached in his vestpack and pulled out a case, carefully unsealing its lid. He smeared his wide thumb along the base of his cheek, dragging a line of black pigment. Others came over and borrowed his war paint. Boaz kept packing his vest. Then he Velcroed the flap, buckled the straps, and told them he had to get going. "Ivan, get up."

"I will," Ivan said. "*Pashol na chui, chernojopey.*"

"The briefing's in four. You want me to fill up your bottles?"

"You do that." Rising, Ivan wiped off the crust from his

eyes. It was stunningly cold outside of his bag—at least ten degrees cooler than Bethlehem. It was the virtue of living six feet below ground, encased in the walls of a cellar. In the summer it was hot here, one moist cloud of sweat. In the winter, a perpetual freezing.

Even Yossi was awake on his bunk at the end, thumbing the pad of his phone. His black head was tucked in the hood of his bag, his face oddly brightened to emerald. Others were changing, digging for shirts. Boaz shouted that his helmet was missing. It was a complicated process, this going to war. But nobody here seemed to mind it, bizarrely.

And frankly there was nothing to keep Ivan here, except for that wrenching conviction: it was the knowledge that someday he'd look back on this place and ask himself what he had done.

He felt a sharp sting, like a rip in his gut. He would feel it each time before mission. His body was discerning. It knew where it headed. It would try to dissuade him with juices, their flowing. Of course, he ignored them. What else could he do? But the body, he thought, was quite prescient. It could see where it was going, the dangers it faced, and would issue stern warnings to conscience. And why he ignored it, why he rose from his bunk, is something he could never determine. What your body instructed is what you should do. Everything else was delusion.

Ten minutes later, the soldiers were seated in the Control Room upstairs by the maps. Ivan was scratching the back of his neck—a red bump had swelled by his helmet. He was hoping for head lice, an infectious disease, something to deem him inactive. Beside him, the others gazed blankly at Shaul, who was pointing to a board-mounted map. It was a topographic diagram, blue-numbered with grids and place-names all lettered in Hebrew—quite foreign. It might have been Bethlehem, the Urals, Sayans, the uncharted face of the moon.

As Shaul slid his hand across the crumpling sheet, he called out the names of the soldiers. They answered: where 3rd was stationed; the company's sector; where the response team would come in support, etc.

Ivan knew all of these answers in order. He would hear them each time before going. And he could feed back the expressions, the appropriate sayings, though he didn't really know what they meant. "The Green Line," he'd mutter, "is graves to the camp. The Red Line is graves to the outpost." The Red Line, he deduced, is where he could shoot without having to issue a warning. And the Green Line, he gathered, is where he could not, unless he confronted a weapon, like last week. He was never really clear on just when he could shoot or when he was expected to do that.

"All right," Shaul grumbled. "Here are the assignments. I don't want to say this again. Yossi, you're one. I want you beside me. You take the point with Aquila. Boaz, you're two. You've got the Madonna"—the radio—"and make sure you put her on mute. If you need a spare pack, get one from my room. I think your helmet is in there, as well. And grab a few stunners from the box on the floor, next to the epinephrine. Ivan knows where, so he'll help you. I don't think that we're gonna see any crowds tonight, but I want you to take a couple. You're the first fireteam leader. Vasily, you're three. You've got the Negev. You're the second fireteam team leader. Shibli, you're four. You've got the stretcher, and make sure the legs are all taped. Where's Ivan? Ivan, you're five. I want you in rear. Go help Boaz find the stunners. You hear me?"

"Yeah, Shaul." Ivan always said this with a comical ease, as if Shaul were his own older brother. He detested him, truly, but it got to the point where the two of them got on like family. Ivan knew it wasn't personal, the disdain Shaul had. Ivan was a constant goof-off.

Sometimes Ivan thought if they weren't in the army, Shaul and he would go drinking. But Shaul was aloof, and hard to know, and wholly at odds with the soldiers. Ivan also liked Dror—respected him, at least—especially when he made him do pushups.

"All right," Shaul said. "I'm number six. I'm the commander of this patrol. You will watch for my signals and follow. Like I said, Boaz is first fireteam leader. Vasily is leading the second. And Uri's upstairs. He's already in nest. Pinchas, you'll call to confirm him?"

At the end of the hall, beside the radio dials, Sgt. Pinchas wearily nodded.

"We'll leave through the back of the kitchen downstairs. Did somebody turn out the lights there?" No answer. "All right, everyone has got water—everyone except me?"

Ivan had honey pepper vodka.

"I assume we'll be leaving at ten minutes past. I'll call Company HQ and tell them. Again, when we get to the graves, no one makes noise. I don't want to hear a damn pin drop. You got that?"

Ivan looked up. Shaul looked back, his blue eyes alight on his clipboard. He had burning, blue eyes: wet, varnished with smoke. They echoed the rings in his pupils. And he had low, bristly eyebrows, a forehead that creased, a cleft chin that drooped to his shoulders, like a Russian's. He might have been a Russian. He was an Ashkenazi Jew. At some point they all came from Russia. And his features looked hardened, as if they hadn't seen war but merely the pain of his being. He could tell the Lieutenant had spent whole nights awake here, staring at the ceiling from his cot. He wasn't quite a soldier—too honest, not gruff. He had more the thick sheen of a commander, eyes blinking. And it was impossible to imagine that he'd killed with that gun were it not for his deeply-lined forehead and eyes. It was as if his own face were in conflict with itself, trying to break free of the body—or any visions it had witnessed, any sounds that it heard, as if a small gangly child were inside him, clawing. He had to be a Russian—to experience hell. Only a Russian could know this.

"Like I said, silence from the kitchen on out. I don't want the dogs there to hear us," said Shaul. "Anyone who's gotta piss should do it now. I don't know how long we'll be staying. If you need to bring gum or chew to stay awake, that's fine. Make sure nobody hears it. And nobody sleeps when we get to the graves. Ivan, you hear me? No dozing."

"Aye-aye."

"All right, everything clear?"

The five zombie-like figures all nodded. Then Shaul glanced towards the end of the hall, where Sgt. Pinchas was lifting two bottles. "You got them?"

"Yeah," Pinchas said. "I'll set them right here." On his desk stood two liters of Coke.

"Those are a present for when you get back. Be good, and you might get to drink them. All right, Pinchas, tell Dror to turn out the lights, and I want you to check Shibli's stretcher."

"I'm on it."

Shaul studied his group for any signs of dissent. "Uri is up and he's waiting. First Platoon's out. They're heading north. I don't think that we're going to see them." Then he checked his watch, a sleek Casio Frogman, and pulled back the banded cloth cover. Ivan peered down at his own fleshy wrist, the gray thing that passed for a timer. Three after.

"All right, anyone who needs water, go fill up now. Shit, piss, do what you have to. We're leaving in ten from the basement's back door. See Pinchas if you have any problems. Dismissed."

The others stood up. Ivan did not. "Shaul," he said. "There's a problem."

"What is it?"

"My cigarettes. I only got four. Someone took the pack from my duffel."

Shaul squinted.

"And I can't go on mission without having a smoke. But then I've only got three till my next leave. So I was thinking that maybe if you have one or two—"

"Go fuck yourself, Ivan. Then shower."

Outside of Rachel's Tomb that night, the sky had gelled into a lavender abyss. Thin mists of clouds were ranged to the west beyond the sloped face of the hill. Beyond them, al-Aida lay steaming in some endless black chasm of rows.

Meanwhile, inside the walled compound, two soldiers went seeking supplies. They stopped at the brink of the commanders' quarters, parting the drapes with their hands.

There was always something peculiar about the confines, no matter how many times they'd gone in. This time, Ivan found himself gazing at the dome-vaulted ceiling, which was girded with arches and Arabesque panels, like the tomb of some pasha or bey. At the end, he saw Shaul's bed layered with ash, a carton of Pall Malls, a few steamed-up bags of what might have been bread, a frayed orange softback called *Out of Place*, and a dented guitar case, which was stickered with the face of Lou Reed.

"It smells like somebody died here," said Boaz.

"It's probably Shaul himself."

They could hear him outside, beyond the walled drapes, haranguing his soldiers with Pinchas.

"You see my helmet?" Boaz asked him.

Tracing a scent, Ivan nodded to the corner. "On the floor... by Penis's bed."

"Halle-fucking-lujah," Boaz said, retrieving the mesh-covered bundle.

Hesitantly, Ivan approached Shaul's bed, where he set about filching some cigarettes. When that didn't happen—all the packets were empty—he arrived at what looked like a wallet tucked in the sleeping bag's fold. This gave him pause. Ivan was not a thief—by conventional standards. And yet he was inordinately curious to see what this wallet contained.

No, this is wrong, Ivan figured, and he returned the wallet to its place on the bed, not really sure what impelled him. Then a quick image struck him—almost like an afterthought, in fact, or something he'd glimpsed on the bed. Indeed, it had come from the wallet.

"What about grenades?" Boaz asked him.

"I don't know. Somewhere under Dror's bed."

Boaz tromped over to a rope-handled crate and loudly unclasped its hinges. "*Privyet.*"

Ivan ignored him. He kept studying this wallet, this mystery splayed on the bed. He had definitely seen a small picture inside it—a picture, he thought, of a girl.

"You know, I should probably take a few extra," said Boaz. "Since I'm the first fireteam leader."

Ivan looked up for a second and briefly considered his partner. Then he opened the wallet, and what he saw in its bill-flap amazed him. Poking out from the fold, beneath a few bills, was a stained, faded shot of a woman—a passport photo, it seemed.

Ivan often wondered about Shaul, if the man got around. It seemed like he had lots of orgies. A player. But Shaul wasn't a player. He was strung out and gaunt. And yet there were eyes in this picture: deep brown ones. They looked Middle Eastern, though thinner than a Jew's, and her eyelids were shaded with kohl, like Cleopatra. She seemed almost Asian—or Arab, in fact. And the border said "PhotoRamallah."

Shaul came in through the curtains. He stopped. "What the fuck are you doing?"

Ivan stepped back. His hands were touching the sleeping bag. "Just looking."

"Just looking?"

"Yeah."

"Looking for what?"

"Grenades, like you said."

"I got em over here," mumbled Boaz.

Shaul shot a look towards the depth of the room, where Boaz still knelt by the box.

"I only found frags," he continued. "I didn't see stunners or gas."

Ivan said nothing. His hands didn't move. The wallet was squarely between them.

Promptly Shaul came over, picked up the wallet, and cast him a searing glance. His icy eyes flickered. His nostrils flared. Then he slowly turned round to face Boaz, his gun barrel flanking his arm. "You don't need 'em," Shaul muttered, sticking the wallet in his pants.

Ivan's hands were clasped behind him. He slowly backed up from the bed. Beside him, Shaul said nothing, appraising each man in turn.

"And what about the pack for the set?" Boaz asked.

"You don't need it," Shaul grumbled. "The battery's working just fine."

"But you said—"

"Go."

As the men stumbled out through the curtains and down towards the light of the hall, Shaul called out in a hoarse, grainy voice: "Oh, and one more thing, Ivan. If I catch you in here again with my stuff, you'll finish your tour up at Yadin."

That Saturday, inside the Rachel's Tomb barracks, Ivan slept for what seemed a full week. Then, around 1700, his phone started buzzing on his trunk. There was only one person who called him, and he knew he should have shut it off.

"Vanechka, what are you doing sleeping? It's almost dark."

"Just trying to take a nap."

Despite her firm tone, Ivan's mother, Ludmilla Petrovna, sounded mildly relieved that he was still confined to his base. Recounting the day's latest news, she explained that a broad-based military operation, known as "Defensive Shield," was sweeping over the Territories. It was an operation that had her support—like most Russian émigrés, she was firmly patriotic. Yet she was concerned for the well-being of her son, who, as it were, remained her only blood relative, the heir to her estate—which comprised half a Lomonosov tea set, three schlocky Matryoshkas, and the full Prague Recordings of Richter—and her deepest source of pride, despite her propensity to nag him.

"It isn't Stalingrad, Mom."

"Be careful. I love you."

"Goodbye." At that point, he hung up and tried to fall sleep, but there was all sorts of commotion upstairs. About two-dozen reservists were stamping through the halls, along with a host of M.P.'s. What the hell they were doing here, Ivan didn't know, but he had heard a review was underway. He figured he would probably be questioned at some point. He figured he'd say she was armed. Or he thought she was, anyways. How was he supposed to know who she was?

He roused himself briefly, forced down some cholent. At 1800, he was summoned to guard.

For four hours, he paced along the roof, silent as always,

stealthily sipping his flask. He watched the Jeeps flicker and arc down Hevron Street; the reservists had finally left. To the north, a gibbous moon slid through the clouds and ignited the slabs of the graves. They looked furry and molded, like some mammoth, white, vine-covered jaw.

Fuck them, Ivan thought, if they tried to accuse him. He was just doing his job.

At 2200, he returned to sleep in the barracks. Then at 0150, he was re-awoken and dispatched once again to the roof. This time, he was joined by Yossi.

"Long fucking day, ain't it?" Ivan said as they climbed the north steps, emerging in the lamp-lighted darkness.

Yossi didn't seem to have heard.

"You want the booth or outside?" Ivan asked him, hoping for the booth, where he could sleep or read.

"The Sergeant said I've got the booth."

"I'll give you the rest of my cigarettes." Ivan held out the packet of Marlboros, which he didn't care to note contained two.

Stupidly, Yossi accepted it.

"I didn't know you smoked."

Yossi grinned brightly. "Fuck you."

It was probably the longest exchange, Ivan realized, that the two of them had ever shared.

"You think we'll get rapped for what happened this morning?"

Yossi stared out at him blankly. "What?"

"You know, shooting a defenseless child?"

"I ain't seen nothing," Yossi replied.

Brothers in blood they now were.

Inside the roof's northern lookout, Ivan leaned back on his stool, observing the night through the armored glass plating and savoring the last of his Nemiroff, which ran like fire down his throat. To the east, beyond the stacks of Beit Sahour and its endless white slather of roofs, two neon-green minarets pinballed the moon, and Herodium tilted its bore. To the west, Yossi kept pacing beside the parapet wall, his pants at his knees, his rifle slung back, his dangling chinstrap traced by al-Aida's orange-phosphorous glow.

Ivan thought about offering his partner a swig, but the guy would probably fall off the roof. Instead, Ivan emptied his flask. Then he dug out his flashlight and a Russian translation of Wells's *War of the Worlds*, a book he'd read twice here already, and of which he hadn't grown tired.

He continued reading as Yossi paced by him, trailed by a fluttering cloud. He wondered if Shaul would check on them here.

No, Ivan realized. He was downstairs, long ago asleep, lost in the world of his dreams. And who knew what those entailed for Shaul: flying carpets, veiled women, dead girls?

"Hey," Yossi asked, knocking on his glass, startling him briefly. "You want the last one of these cigarettes?"

His words were too good to be true. Ivan rose to get it, and as he stepped out, he was met by a thunderous bang.

2 IVAN

They were sitting on a bench in the weight room. Boaz was smoking. Ivan was stroking his forehead, wiping away the sweat beads that had formed beneath the stretched leather band of his helmet. They had been on guard duty together for most of the last twenty-four hours, and now, Monday morning, Ivan wondered how he managed to sweat his way through thirty-eight-degree temperatures, near frostbite conditions, and the paralytic brain freeze that seems to accompany standing in place for four straight hours at a time, staring at a wall, pondering life's greater mysteries.

Surprisingly, none of those mysteries seemed to involve the shooting of his platoonmate that weekend, nor the deaths that preceded it. Instead, Ivan focused squarely on Boaz, who suckled a Noblesse beside him, despite the prohibition on base. It wasn't immediately clear to Ivan whether Boaz was aware of this rule—that smoking was illegal at Company HQ, and army bases generally—Shaul's being the exception, because Shaul was Shaul—or Boaz was in fact aware of it and visibly flaunted his disregard by stubbing out his smoke on the weight bench, which he did then by extending his cig to the cushion. The burning tip

217

melted the fabric, hissing bizarrely and producing a colorful array of foam patterns, almost like fractals, thought Ivan, and to which Boaz paid little mind.

Either way, smoking on an army base was immediate grounds for detention, particularly in light of all the heightened restrictions this weekend, though in the case of Aleph Company, with all its attrition and soldiers gone clinic, the best they could hope for was three days of kitchen duty, which Boaz must have wanted. On some level, Ivan had to respect him for doing it, smoking in the weight room; it possessed a certain beauty, if not outright defiance, and he hadn't thought the guy had it in him. In fact, Ivan wasn't entirely convinced that Boaz had anything inside him, aside from raw sexual yearnings and an insatiable craving for *Loof*.

The weight room, which spanned a full, doublewide trailer and more frequently served as a briefing room, consisted of a dozen racked dumbbells, a vinyl-sheeted floor, and an enormous steel NordicTrack machine, which ominously loomed in the corner. The machine had two worn rubber ski-tracks, and it was doubtful that anyone had ever used it, much less the rest of this equipment. As far as Ivan knew, the weight room had been donated by a couple of American sponsors, as indicated by a small, greasy plaque near the door. How the facility ended up at this base was a mystery to everyone, not least of all Ivan, who hadn't used exercise equipment since enlisting in the army, and barely before then. He liked the rubber ski tracks, however. They reminded him a bit of cross-country skiing in St. Petersburg, which he used to do back when his father was still alive.

Next to the machine sat an oily white treadmill, which had long, sloping bars and a rusted, salmon belt. It had a vaguely scientific feel to it, almost like an oversized gerbil wheel, and Ivan wondered if that thing had been tested on soldiers—whether they were guinea pigs here, and if so, who was funding this experiment. A couple times, the platoon sergeant had told them to run on it. He said they were getting fat since arriving on the line, since all they ever did here was jerk each other off and eat sandwiches. Sometimes they guarded. Ivan wasn't entirely clear what the platoon sergeant had meant by that remark, but he did see him running on it once—the last time he was dispatched to HQ—and Ivan found it to be a curious display: Sgt. Dror was running, jogging in sweatpants, patting his wet, glinting head. His CAR-15 was slung around the machine's rubber arms, and he didn't seem to care that the other soldiers were watching him. There was always something profoundly strange about a soldier who exercised while serving on the line, as if the sheer stress of combat weren't enough, and perhaps he was trying to maintain his appearance, keep up the physique, but none of the soldiers had girlfriends any longer, including Sgt. Dror, and Ivan occasionally wondered if he, like the others, wasn't maintaining his image for the sake of other men. The only females they saw here were counselors, and they didn't really count, as it were, because Orly wasn't hetero, and the others were beastly.

He pictured the Captain—whom he could hear talking outside along the pavement—wearing a white lab coat, smiling, slowly grouping his chin-hairs. Ivan detested the Captain. He detested every form of officer, right down to the lieutenants, though Shaul was a possible exception to this rule, because he wasn't really qualified to lead other men. As far as Ivan knew, the only reason Shaul had sought his commission was that it involved seizing Arabs, and he had a particular fondness for doing that. The other officers, however, were assholes, almost without exception. And he figured that was probably true of any standing army, probably any reigning government, for that matter. Anyone who thought he was predisposed to lead other men was inherently an asshole. It seemed to be a requirement for such positions, if not the fact of giving orders. Nevertheless, Ivan thought that he should have led them, if only because it would make for a more entertaining sitcom—sort of like Shaul's show, but darker.

Ivan noticed that since the shooting this weekend, extra sandbags had been placed in the trailer's slat windows, lending a particular mugginess to the room, even more so than usual, as if the concentrated blend of rotting iron and stale sweat were not enough. The air here was visibly roiling. Above him, the lone ceiling bulb occasionally flickered, which must have been an everyday occurrence for the residents of Bethlehem, but it scared him immensely, as if he were living in a bunker. This wasn't World War II. He was not now in Gaza or camped along the banks of the Sinai. Despite the fact that his company had seen a bit of action, it didn't feel like a war yet. There were no mortars raining down, and he suspected that if it ever came to that, he would shoot off his head first, as he generally considered doing.

They had been in the trailer for all of twenty minutes, though possibly several hours—time was not really quantifiable while serving—and Ivan wondered how much longer they'd be waiting for the Captain. Ivan also noticed that the tiling by his boots took on a particular luster, as if soldiers had scrubbed it for weeks, and he still vaguely hoped that would be his assignment.

Yesterday morning, he had assured his mother that things were going fine, that he was coming home shortly. He even thought about telling her of the funeral that day, assuming she didn't know—news traveled exponentially fast through the halls of the Rishon LeZion apartment blocks, most of which were Russian, and sort of like fractals—but he didn't want to deal with her sobbing, and then he'd have to talk to his "stepfather," or, as Ivan preferred to think of him, the man that she married.

Leaning back, Ivan also noticed a thin poster-board next

to the wall. It was probably awaiting a top-level briefing, and it displayed a glazed map, which looked rather stunning in comparison to those plastered along the boards down at Rachel's Tomb. This one was annotated, and it showed the skilled trade of a *jobnik*, someone who'd devoted at least six or seven hours this week—likely his entire week's output—to diagramming the spots throughout Bethlehem where attacks had been staged. Curving blue and pink arrows sprang from text bubbles, which remarked on events such as

20 MARCH. 0030. SHOOTING/SNIPER ATTACK. 1 SOLDIER KILLED. RACHEL'S TOMB OUTPOST, BETHLEHEM. *ATTACKER(S) UNKNOWN, NOT APPREHENDED.*

Just down the road from that, another bubble stated:

11 MARCH. 1700. INCENDIARY ATTACK. 1 SOLDIER WOUNDED. RACHEL'S TOMB CHECKPOINT, BETHLEHEM. *1 ATTACKER KILLED, 1 NOT APPREHENDED.*

Ivan was slightly amazed at how regularly they must have updated this map, since the latest shooting, Yossi's, had occurred less than twenty-nine hours ago. Someone had even taken the time to apply a thin coat of laminate. Ivan wondered where they got that in Bethlehem, and he couldn't quite reconcile it with the lack of toilet paper on base, not to mention the scarcity of body armor. Nevertheless, he was impressed that the *jobniks* had gone to work on these figures, as if someone actually cared what went on here, aside from his own mother, and that the lesser-page write-ups that the newspapers gave them—"Soldier Killed in an Undescribed

Incident," said the latest *Yedioth* heading—weren't an accurate testament to this country's indifference.

The other attacks around the base and along Route 60 included minor scuffles or incidents involving former units, mainly from the previous year, when the Paratroops worked here. Of notable absence from the map was the incident last Friday in which he may or may not have shot and killed a six-year-old Arab girl, possibly younger—though Ivan pondered that one less now and thought it was vindicated on some level by the execution of Yossi. It was also somewhat discomforting, he realized, to see a map without his victim on it, as if she had suddenly ceased to exit and lived solely in the void of his memory, possibly that of others' in the Battalion.

Boaz had a festering jock itch. It was slowly destroying him. It was eating away at his leg skin, and he was afraid it would reach to his lower sack. He had talked to the doctors, and they had given him lotion, but then a blister had started leaking, and he didn't want to touch it. Sometimes, while standing at guard, he would rub a little bit of gun solvent on it, which he kept in his vestpack, but that didn't help much, and it still smelled like brine.

At the funeral yesterday, he tried to imagine what would happen if Orly snuck off with him behind the graves; he figured she'd have to go down on him quickly in darkness; but then it got overcast, and he figured he wouldn't have to worry. Even so, she stood the whole time with the officers, Shaul especially, and Boaz thought she must have been avoiding his presence. Maybe she was jealous of his girlfriend or unsure of just how she'd approach him. She had heard him talking on the phone once, saying *I love you* to Ruti.

Boaz looked at Ivan, who always had that puzzled stare, as

if the army were too much for him to bear. He looked perpetually unhappy. Sort of like a rat, Boaz figured, if it wasn't given biscuits.

Boaz liked the food at Company HQ, and he was happy to have come here, since the only thing they ever had down at Rachel's was Ramen packs, and those were getting stale. Here, they had *Krembos* and a fridge-full of icicled *Choco*. They even had hot showers, which was what he desperately needed, though he was afraid of running water on the folds.

Since the shooting this weekend and the death of his platoonmate, Boaz was feeling more and more confused. It seemed as if the army didn't care about him any, and all they wanted to do was use him as a shield against the Arabs, protecting all the settlers and penguins. He wondered where they got off thinking they could do that—especially for the sake of the settlers, whom he didn't even like.

Sometimes, when Boaz was guarding, he told himself that the only ones he was protecting were his fellow platoonmates. He didn't care about Ruti. Possibly his parents, but they were not threatened, and neither was she much. And as for the settlers who came here: who gave a shit, really, if a couple got shot? It was probably good for their movement, and it's what they all wanted. All Boaz really wanted was to be at a club with his girlfriend. Or better yet, Orly. Sometimes, while riding on the buses, he would think about Orly and how he was protecting her on base. She would see him with his jacket and gun, his huge M203, and she must have thought how handsome he looked, how firm and in-charge, and she must have wetted herself thinking about him.

Whenever he was making love to Ruti—which he always did quickly, cause that's how she liked it, or rather insisted on doing it, otherwise, he had a tendency to crush her—he would imagine himself taking Orly at the guardbox. Sometimes he would picture only the guardbox itself, since he had come to associate it so much with jerking off and fantasies of Orly that he didn't even need to see Orly, let alone his own girlfriend. There was something so ingrained and sexual about that guardbox—as if the very stool were erotic, with its cracked, vinyl folds—that the thought of it gave him an instant erection, and he'd immediately shoot his load. Of course, all of that changed when Yossi got killed there.

He didn't think much about Yossi. Tried not to, in any case. Last night, it was hard during guarding. And he almost cried at the funeral, in spite of seeing Orly. But he'd worn his black shades there, and he took it hard like a soldier. Sometimes he thought about writing Orly a letter, professing his love to her, and he thought he should do it now, since she would obviously miss him more and bear in mind his discomfort. As for Ruti, she was easy, and the girl didn't say much. Usually, she just nagged him or complained about the smells from his crotch.

Boaz was looking forward to getting back in the action. Earlier, when walking over to this base with his compadre, he told him, "I hope we get to shoot somebody soon." Ivan just watched him.

Twenty minutes later, Ivan looked up as the company's First Sergeant came barging through the slat-door. CAR-15 and cellphone in hand, he turned to appraise them, sniffed at the air, examined them warily, and said, "You two are taking a *Sufa* up to Regional. Go get the radiator fixed, and while you're there, stock up on medical supplies. Catheters, chest seals, whatever you need, and a stretcher, if the old one's not clean." The First Sergeant seemed a bit unnerved by this last part. He sucked in his breath and looked up.

"We're going alone then?" asked Boaz.

"No, you'll pick up Pinchas. He's at the mess. He'll drive.

Just make sure you get the *Sufa* back by noon. We need it for al-Aida tomorrow night."

"What's tomorrow night?"

"You'll find out soon. Any other questions?"

"Yeah, any chance we'll be getting a leave soon?" asked Ivan.

"No chance," said the First Sergeant.

"One more thing," said Boaz, who rose. "I was just wondering, but maybe it's too early to ask…"

The First Sergeant was studying his phone. "Go on."

"Well, I was just wondering if there's been any talk about who might get Yossi's M4."

The First Sergeant looked up, more perplexed by this than anything.

"I mean, I've always been a pretty good shot, and you know this one time, my dad and I, we were out hunting—"

The First Sergeant glanced at him sullenly. "Boaz?"

"Yes?"

"Are you by any chance insane?"

Boaz stared at his boots. "I'm sorry, commander. It's just, you know, we've been under a lot of stress lately—"

"It's truck number four. The keys are inside. Now go get your sergeant. And if I see either of you smoking again, I'll have you both detained. Dismissed." The First Sergeant turned and exited the trailer, descending its aluminum steps.

Beside the bench, Ivan turned to face Boaz. "This is bullshit," he said.

"I know. They're gonna give Shibli that gun."

"No, that we're fucking stuck here. You know the others are going home now, right?"

"What?"

"You heard me. Uri's going home"—they had seen him with

a bucket by the showers—"and Vasily got off. Hell, even Shaul's at home. He took off last night from Mount Herzl."

"That fucker," said Boaz.

"Don't tell me. I know."

Ivan, when he considered it, didn't actually want to go home. There was little he could say to his mother. And what would he do on his leave besides sit and jerk off, shovel Pringles with his fingers, and play *Doom* on his desktop till dawn? It was better than dying, yes, but there was something almost strangely engrossing about this weekend and the deaths he had seen. He didn't really have friends he could talk to about them, at least none who were serving. Maybe he could speak to his mother or the Israeli she married. But what would he tell them? *I killed. Now I'm fine?*

Outside the trailer, along the base's sleek pavement, stood a long row of company Jeeps. There must have been a dozen of them idling. Older reservists were scrubbing down windows, and they were joined by policemen. At the gates of the base, which were surrounded by reddened, steel lookouts and blank, little guards, Ivan noticed the Captain strolling out, followed by the groveling First Sergeant.

"What a cunt," Boaz muttered.

"Yeah, but he's not the one who assigned us to stay. It was Shaul who did that."

"I know."

"Why do you suppose Shaul hates us so much?"

"Probably cause we found him with that picture of the Arab."

"Who gives a shit," said Ivan, "if he's fucking some veil?"

"Most of the Company." Boaz took a slurp of a *Choco* he'd stolen. Then he tossed it over the base wall. "I don't give a shit. It's not like I care what he does on his furlough. All that matters is he's back at home, and we're stuck on base."

Passing under a canopy of camouflage tarps, Ivan noticed the cloud-covered sky, which had a glassy veneer, as if the sun were about to peek out and start mocking them brightly. At least it would be warm during guarding, which they'd get to do enough of this week. "So where's Sgt. Penis?"

Boaz was gazing out at the base's north end, which was brimming with kit bags and Jeeps. "Over there somewhere. Probably waiting to jerk off the Captain."

"And we're supposed to go get him?"

"I guess."

"Which one of those is ours?"

Boaz had that puzzled look in his eyes—the kind that a soldier will get in the midst of great battle, the kind that officers often worry about, write of, and inordinately deal with in training, because it is the same peevish expression, the same look of outrage, that ignites conflagrations, bestows tragedies upon humans and makes warriors out of privates. Boaz wasn't smiling. He was staring straight into the back of a cabin. There were reservists inside it. They were rinsing off the bucket seats. "I think he said four."

The *Sufa* consisted of a floating front axle and a reinforced frame, powered by a six-cylinder, in-line diesel engine fitted with a Vortox-2 stage cleaner at 180 horsepower. It also had gun-slots. It was basically a Jeep with a modified wheelbase and a great deal of armor appended, though light in comparison to an armored fighting vehicle.

The transmission was auto, which disappointed Ivan—he had learned to drive stick back in Russia at age seven. But it had good off-roading capabilities, especially for a vehicle of its dimension: about four meters in length, two more in width, and a couple thousand kilos of mass from the coachwork. It did have some issues with handling, and, as any armored unit knows, is particularly vulnerable to landmines. But they wouldn't be seeing any of those today in Bethlehem.

Ivan had never actually driven a vehicle in the army. None of the men had. This was a privilege normally reserved for officers and reservists, if not the disgruntled staff sergeants. But for a newly enlisted man, let alone a corporal, to get hold of an armored *Sufa* is sort of like an ape getting hold of the cosmonaut station. Ivan was shitfaced.

He slowly descended the parking lot's steps, his arm around Boaz, ignoring the passing soldiers and the glances from sergeants. His green eyes kept flitting, darting around nervously and settling finally on the thin, speckled headband of the sentry at the gates. He would have to make maneuvers. This would not be a problem for Ivan, however, who was well-equipped to deal with such encounters. While he might have lacked the physical wherewithal of most army combatants, and certainly the mindset, he more than made up for it with a particular dexterity of vision.

In this case, as he peered through the windows of Armored *Sufa* No. 4, it briefly occurred to him that while disciplinary consequences would invariably follow his infraction, this might very well be his last opportunity in life to take full command of a small, armored vehicle. While his motivation was uncertain, it can be said with some degree of assurance that the pending raid on al-Aida, as well as revenge on his lieutenant, must have figured into the equation. Ironically, and in spite of Ivan's best estimate, the same logic was applied in Boaz's weening, and the latter insisted he drive.

There wasn't much deliberation between the two soldiers, nor consideration of the matter, as Boaz settled into the driver's seat. He compressed his rear buttstock and nestled the gun in the doorslot. Then he reached for the ignition and turned to face Ivan. Ivan wasn't watching him, however. He was staring straight out at a sergeant who passed them. Ivan thought about asking him to inspect both their guns, as was properly required before exiting the base. But it was fairly clear at this point to both the young corporals that playing by the rules was not a modus operandi.

"Does this thing come with a parking brake?" Boaz asked Ivan.

"Yeah," Ivan said. "I think we just saw him."

Thus, on the morning of March 21st, after approximately eleven months of guarding, washing plates in the kitchen, scrubbing grime off the walls using only a miniature screwdriver, sleeping in a pillbox, eating meat from a tin can, slicing the meat using only the lid from said tin can, fighting off jock itch, showering once a week (occasionally less), trekking through sand or cold, freezing rain up to sixty kilometers at a time with a machine gun and pack, howling and snapping, doing pushups on the rocks using only bare knuckles (twelve by Ivan's count, two by the platoon sergeant's), hiking, earning a blissful reprieve in a medic's course, returning, doing sprints without a weapon, passing out along the dry mud floor of an obstacle course and then barfing on the sergeant (a feat which Ivan took pride in), scooping up a dead cat using only bare hands (a task which the platoon sergeant had singled Ivan out for, possibly in retaliation for the barfing, after one had frozen solid beneath the walls of a trailer; Ivan thought it would kill him, lifting that thing; it didn't, it turned out, but hardened him emotionally to a level of which he would only later become aware and probably explained his own indifference to the shootings this weekend, if not the purpose of such methods in training), shooting at the

Arabs, watching them perish, scooping his friend off the floor of the roof, inserting a 14-gauge catheter into him and then watching as he was whisked away silent on a gurney without handles, watching as sunlight breathed down above the Jerusalem corridor like faint wisps of light and eerily nacred, stopping for a second to stand guard in the heat and peer up at the sun, examining its purpose and asking himself blithely what it was he was doing here in serving and more or less succumbing to every utterance of bullshit, which is what the army taught him, Ivan got to take full and unaccompanied leave of a small, armored vehicle.

Boaz revved the engine. "One last time. Do you think we should go get the Sergeant?"

Ivan didn't hear him.

Exiting Company HQ presented numerous obstacles in this case, though not ones for which the young corporals were unprepared. If the army taught them anything, aside from how to scrape grime and shovel dead cats, it was how to navigate bureaucracy. Aleph Company HQ was in its own special way the very emblem of that bureaucracy: two iron-slatted gates demarcated the southernmost exit and faced down the alley towards Rachel's, beside which stood berms and stone walls. To the right of these gates rose some high, melded beams and a long, crooked row of white columns— all of which were designed to either prevent intrusions or frustrate escapes; both served the same purpose. There were also some trailers around them and a thousand leering men.

Naturally, when anyone exited Company HQ, soldiers took notice, as their chief preoccupation in the army was not defending the base with which they were charged, but rather noting the comings and goings of lesser-ranking soldiers, determining who was getting leave when and who was getting punished. As with any standing group of primates, politics played a key role in determining the group's social interactions, at least until more pressing concerns arose, such as those of sheer survival. Ivan had fireworks with him. Where he got those in the army would become a point of some contention at the hearing. Nor would it be lost upon the lesser-ranking soldiers, who would ultimately commend him for his efforts. Ivan had a couple of sparklers in his pack, which he'd stolen from the Arabs, along with a thinly fused cherry bomb. Using these on an army base required a careful dispensation, as well as a basic working knowledge of acoustics. Any form of explosion, let alone a loud one, can provoke disastrous consequences, at least among the frightened, and when the earth shook that morning, ricocheted by bombs—or their more dastardly specter—the Armored *Sufa*, a.k.a. Truck No. 4, slowly wheeled out to the southern gates. The stated reason for its departure was another matter and required a bit of solemn explanation.

"We're going to get our captain."

"You're what?" asked the sentry.

"We're going to get our captain," Ivan told him. "He told us to wait down at Rachel's. Didn't you hear the shooting? Come on."

The sentry who watched them, undistracted by the bombing, had a slightly boorish demeanor with a roughly-shaven chin. He was in his mid-to-late twenties, American, perhaps, and he occasionally served as a driver. "So let me get this straight. You guys want to exit the base, you're not with a sergeant, you don't have permission, and you're driving a *Sufa*?"

"That's right."

"Well then, get going."

Ivan had seen this soldier beforehand. He had once caught him drinking out back behind the trailers with Shaul. Despite the fact that he was an American and probably foreign to this army, he understood it perfectly. Ivan thanked him profusely by offering a grim nod—that same grave form of communication often imparted between men of common understanding and regardless of any age or nation or rank. Boaz said nothing.

As the truck lumbered off with Boaz at the helm and Ivan beside him, the two soldiers noticed the men of their company running about wildly, like dogs set apace or some unexplained hell unsheathed in its torment. Men were taking up position behind the chafed blocks, hands on the pavement, gun barrels drawn. This base was in chaos. Boaz hit the headlights.

The next obstacle lay at the foot of the drive, where men from their platoon were stationed at the Rachel's Tomb checkpoint. Ivan could see a couple of sentries at the blocks, along with a couple of Russians. One wore a giant, purple cape of a backpack, and they were waiting for the bus that would get them, allowing them to depart on furloughs. Ivan hated these soldiers. He hated nearly all of the men in his unit—Boaz included. In fact, he hated people. But he also had a certain respect for them, as soldiers often garner upon seeing initial combat. He didn't know why these other soldiers were leaving, but when they saw him pulling up, assisted by Boaz and unescorted by sergeants, they deduced right away what had happened. They cast appraising glances—suspicious ones, rightly—which they'd grown quite used to throwing at his stead. At the foot of the drive stood the platoon sergeant, Dror, though he didn't seem to notice them pass. He was fumbling with the clip of his rifle.

"*Na kaleni, cyka*," Ivan yelled to the Russians, meaning "On your knees, bitch." The Jeep whistled on.

Ivan thought he should have been more discreet in his bidding, but the men would respect it, and they knew where he was headed. Even if he and Boaz lacked a single, concrete destination in mind, there were few if any soldiers who would have doubted the motive for such occasions, let alone its necessity.

Boaz checked the rearview. "Do you think they'll go tell the sergeant what happened?"

"Not if they plan to return."

As the Jeep ground through Bethlehem, a crumbling, limestone affair, much like their compound, replete with arched buildings, cupolaed roofs, and an assortment of strange vatic shrines, Ivan asked Boaz: "Do you think we should go get the radiator fixed?"

"Not really. I think I want a shawarma."

There aren't a lot of places to get shawarma in Bethlehem. The West Bank is rife with such vendors. But because the Old City is mainly a tourist attraction, chock-full of craft shops and wares, it's actually more difficult than one would expect to find an adequate sandwich, particularly during curfew. Worse yet, the liquor stores were closed, and this bothered Ivan greatly. Had he been planning for this occasion, he would have grabbed Shaul's flask—or the jug he called "water." As it were, Ivan was glad that Boaz wasn't drinking, since the guy couldn't drive.

They hit a few dividers—red plastic Jerseys—and tumbled out on the shoulder. They had driven this route at least six or seven times with their sergeants, delivering food to the checkpoints and the accompanying pillboxes. Usually they'd go with their feet out the back, hanging off the Hummers, and they didn't pay much attention to navigational decisions. Ivan regretted this sorely. "Do you know where you're going?"

"Not really. But I think there's this falafel place ahead."

There was birdshit on the windshield, gargantuan globs of it, which the reservists must have missed. The morning sun was electric, almost gaudy in reflection, like the spark of a pearl. It cast a faint haze through the gratings—there were black iron cages on the window, intended to repel Arab rocks. The glass itself was a polycarbonate plating, said to withstand the rounds of automatic weapons, though Ivan doubted this seriously and wasn't planning on testing it.

In the backseat of the vehicle, alongside the central column and the molded steel shelves, sat a heavy, wooden crate stenciled DANGER. Lying right next to it in a gray folded blanket was a hefty-looking shoulder-fired weapon. It was actually an American grenade launcher, vintage type, with a rotating cylinder and glazed walnut stock. It looked like a Tommy Gun. Ivan had never actually seen anyone use it in the army, though the Captain was reputed to carry it around on patrols. The sheer sight of that thing would strike fear in the heart of every twelve-year-old Arab, and it was rumored to have taken off a head once, having been fired at close range with teargas or flares. The truth is this gun was less effective than the squad-issued M-203, which Boaz had affixed to his M16 Long. His fired the same round, a swooping 40 mm that could be fitted with chaff, gas, or buckshot, not to mention the HE rounds. Ivan only guessed at what the wooden crate was now hiding.

As they scuttled down Derech Hevron, slowing by the buildings of the al-Azza Refugee Camp, a derelict alley where Arabs lay wasted or holed up behind shutters, Ivan was actually surprised at how quiet the streets looked. He thought he saw the reflection of legs in a window—someone was running behind them. And it occurred to him, as it often did on missions, that the Arabs were more terrified than he, although this never seemed to offer him much in the way of lasting consolation.

Neither of them knew in which direction they headed, though Ivan judged south, since they passed by a boarded-up hotel where the Sergeant ran sorties. A couple minutes later, as they sped past some ruins and a puzzle-piece shape of a home, Ivan remembered a quick way of determining direction. He tilted his watch to the sun.

"The fuck are you doing?" asked Boaz.

"Figuring out the direction."

"To what?"

"The city's main enclave. You know, to get food."

"I think it's due north."

"Are you sure you're heading north?"

"Not really," said Boaz.

"That's why I'm checking."

For the briefest of moments, Boaz must have sensed Ivan's terror: that neither had even the faintest idea where they were located, let alone any recognizable coordinates. They still had the radio with them, which occasionally summoned them. Neither one paid it much heed.

There was no question that six or seven thousand of the local populace would have opted to kill them had they been given the chance. This wasn't lost on Boaz, who kept flexing and wrinkling his brow. It even made sense now to Ivan why discipline was so rigorously enforced in the army, and why the base at which they were stationed came equipped with thick coils of razor wire, T-walls and beams, and a dozen armed sentries with Kevlar. He knew what the Arabs would do. Several faces peered out from among the wrecked buildings—these colossal, rich ruins, as if peopled by spirits or the wailing gray phantoms of Troy. Ivan did not detect any faces, but he could feel their eyes watching. And he knew they'd abide.

Ivan panicked for a second then slid back the cloth on his watch. "Which way's the sun?"

"I don't know. I think it's behind us. What the fuck are you doing?"

"I remember this from training. Yossi taught me. If you

point the hour on your watch to the sun, then half-way between that and the twelve is the direction for north."

"What?"

"It's complicated," said Ivan. He held up his Rolex—a fake one he'd purchased in Tel Aviv, resold at face value, and had to buy back on account of ill will. "Here, see." He showed it to Boaz. "That means that we're heading south."

"Okay," he said, cutting a U-turn.

The vehicle rode on two tires.

Being behind the wheel of a vehicle, alone in this city, Boaz felt like a commander. He felt that this position assumed a certain amount of integrity on his behalf, as if, while not actually delegated the assignment, responsibility had suddenly been bestowed upon him. He was alone in this wasteland, surrounded by Arabs and accompanied by a pale, skinny, underfed Russian. It was his duty to protect them, and that he would do.

Ever since the funeral yesterday, in which he'd helped carry the coffin, Boaz felt there was something strangely uplifting about Yossi's death; that the army took on a certain importance in their lives by the fact that it could claim them. Until then, Boaz didn't see what all the fuss was about on missions—their insistence on "safety," the routine procedures—and he could see that those procedures existed for his protection, much like this vehicle. He was thankful for the greater workings of the state, the machinations of industry, for even if they'd put him here, they were also trying to protect him. Someone had installed all this wiring and tubes, the glass-fitted cage and plate armor. They'd even taken the time to install a few stereo speakers. The radio wasn't working, but he'd brought along his Discman. Determined to find it, he leaned his head forward and combed through his backpouch, bracing the wheel with his chin.

"Are you crazy?" Ivan shouted. "Keep your hands on the wheel."

Boaz leaned over, and Ivan clutched the wheel.

From outside their truck, the faint outlines of a gray, moving cylinder were visible across the Bethlehem ridge, rocking and skidding. Headlights shot up, followed by dust motes. Behind them, shorn hedge nettles swirled, and a rock badger matted their tires.

Ivan thought they would die. "What the fuck are you doing?"

Boaz wasn't listening. He'd managed to obtain the leather pouch of his Discman, which he proudly held up. "It's a Case-Logic 48, fully water-resistant, twin-sleeved—"

"That's nice. Would you keep your eyes on the motherfucking road?"

Boaz glanced out at a couple of *Sufim* that passed them. They were ordinary trucks from Battalion. A warrant officer grimaced in one.

"What do you want to hear now?" Boaz asked, flicking on the overhead mic.

"You think the thing works?"

"I know it works, man. I tested it Friday. I was driving here with Dror."

"Did he give you instructions on handling?"

"I've always loved John Lennon."

Ten minutes later, "Instant Karma!" was blaring from the overhead mic. Ivan was lighting a joint.

"Where the hell'd you get that?" Boaz asked.

"Stole it from Shaul's bag."

"You motherfucker. No wonder he hates you."

"That's not all." Reaching in his vestpack, Ivan removed the small photo whose border said PhotoRamallah.

"Is that what I think it is?"

"Yeah," Ivan said. "But maybe we should go ask our friend."

Minutes later, having wound through Beit Sahour and circled back to Hevron, they were parked at the Bethlehem Checkpoint, where they were awaiting the oncoming guards. The topic of discussion was Shaul.

"It's disgusting," said Boaz.

"I think it's pretty funny myself."

"What's that?"

"That here he's banging an Arab, and then there he is shooting them."

"Makes perfect sense to me," Boaz said.

A couple troopers approached the left side of their vehicle. One appeared Russian, and they wore the pleated grays of the Border Police.

"Was up little niggas?" Ivan said to them in Russian.

Neither one smiled. "What you iz doing?" one asked.

"We're just heading up to Central."

"Okay," said the Russian. He was rail-thin in glasses. "You guys hear what's going on in the north?"

"What's in the north?"

"An invasion," said the trooper. He was darker than a Russian, probably Bukharian. "Army's headed into Ramallah. Some kind of reprisal. If you guys are going north, you might want to watch where you go." This was mostly in Russian, and Boaz didn't hear it. He was looking out at the city: a white cluster of buildings perched high along the cliffs above Gilo.

"Well, we're supposed to go up to Central Command and get a few papers."

"I'll bet," said the trooper, sniffing their cabin, which was littered with *Choco* packs, shell casings, gum, a faded, stained *Maxim*, spilled sunflower seeds, and a revolver-type, double action 40 mm gun.

"Be careful," said the trooper, and he nodded to his friend, who pulled back the link on the fencing.

"What did he say?" Boaz asked Ivan. "Something about an invasion in Ramallah?"

"He said we should go there and see."

"I was thinkin' we'd hit up the beach."

"I think I got a better idea."

Exactly what prompted the two soldiers to exit their base is probably open to speculation. But what encouraged them to drive through the war zone, beyond the banked streets of Jerusalem and up to Ramallah's south end, God only wonders. They didn't even stop for a shawarma.

They wound through Anata, a sprawled mountain village of squat cement homes. Dead dogs feathered the road. Ahead, diesel trucks clamored for position at the checkpoint. They streamed past the men checking papers. Boaz flashed sirens.

Inside the town of A-Ram, the streets looked deserted. Above them sprung huge mountain villas, like castles on hills, none of them finished or limed.

Beyond lay the slums of Amari. The soldiers hung tight to their weapons, which they'd recently cocked, but they didn't see signs of invasion. There were dozens of tanks in the city, all thundering loud, but they must have been north of the square.

The men didn't talk much.

"It looks like a war."

"I don't know," Ivan said.

They saw ambulances scream through the city. White

pockets of gunsmoke. Cameramen running. Tourists, perhaps. A vested man lugging a parakeet cage. Above, the sun frizzled out through the northeastern sky, glinting off stacked, flattened cars.

"Where the fuck are we?"

"Don't know," Ivan said. "I guess this is central Ramallah." Bricks clinkered down on top of their roof, and glass bottles crashed on the pavement. "Boaz, get going."

The *Sufa* truck rumbled and pounded exhaust, breathing its smoke on the natives. Wild children abounded, like ants rudely poked from a rock. Boaz tried hard not to hit them.

Ivan turned up the overhead speaker, which was blaring "Give Peace a Chance."

The *Sufa* truck ambled. It stopped along the outskirts of town beside a hilled, wooded garden where other trucks idled with soldiers. A couple tanks had moved into a lookout position. Inside the park was a fenced-off brick building, where artillerists guarded some Arabs. There were Medivacs posted. Humvees with discs. It must have been a temporary encampment, or possibly a jail. There were almond trees lilting.

"Let's go," Ivan told him.

"Where to?"

Ahead of them, a soldier was leading a preteen.

"I don't know. But I have a feeling Shaul is here."

They were winding along dirt mountain roads. A few rocks pestered them scatteredly. They headed east to Baytin. Beyond the blackened plum groves and desolate ruins of some ageless, vine-covered house, a faint rainbow emerged on the plane. Ivan studied it warily. Then he passed the joint and flipped through Boaz's discs. "Is this all you got?"

"What do you mean?"

"The CDs in here, they're all blanks," Ivan said.

The lit joint crackled sharply against Boaz's lips. "They aren't blanks," he murmured.

"What?"

"They're filled up with movies."

"What kind of movies?"

"The good kind of movies." Beside him, two spinning smoke rings, like discs of their own, wafted up to the sun.

How they would go about entering a television station and securing transmission of the film would later be disputed at the hearings. It is undoubted that there were heavy fortifications in the city—army troops bunkered—and gaining safe passage among the boulders and ruins, the large flaming tires and the throngs of riled Arabs, would require considerable heed.

Ivan unraveled a map. While he couldn't be said to have any special ability in navigating men, he did understand topography. He also knew that the most pivotal point on any army map is always its highest location.

They could see the tower, like some great scepter, stenciling the skies of al-Bireh. There were no distinct clouds out that morning, but had there been, they would have rivaled the height of its antennas. Beyond it, white chopper blades flitted, and the sun swam in waves like a gull.

The building itself lay north of the city, and it faced down the slopes of the Jordan. They knew that it had already been taken over that week, since it represented the highest point inside of Ramallah, and probably the Central West Bank.

Down at its base, between the sprawled cypress limbs and the knotted oak clusters, they could make out green camouflage netting. Some older reservists, probably married men with children, had spent the better part of their week ringing up a barbed wire fence. Shattered glass had been strewn along the edges of the lot, and mine-flares were visibly laid.

Ivan directed them. "Roll down your window," he told Boaz as they approached the west gates, where two reservists waved them down to a roadblock. Both appeared weary-eyed, dazed, and late forty-ish. Neither had shaved in a week, as was their time-honored right.

"Don't say anything," said Ivan. "It'll be quicker that way."

A scraggly sergeant major looked up from his booth. He was carrying a skein of rolled copper.

Boaz slowed next to him. "Hi."

The bearded oaf nodded, flashing his teeth, and the metal gates lifted beside them.

"That's the ignorance of age," said Ivan.

"That was probably my dad."

Inside the lot, they were struck by the sheer number of vehicles. There were armored cars, tanks, and mine-clearing trucks. These were parked among Volvos and Camries.

"Do you have a specific plan?" Boaz asked him.

"I have a couple ideas."

They parked beside another *Sufa*, which was unarmored and had a white donut-like device fastened to its hatch, presumably some sort of receiver. Boaz said it belonged to a major.

"I'm gonna need to borrow a film," Ivan said. "Preferably the worst you can find."

After ten minutes of talking to various Russians, mostly men they had served with in training and all of whom had subsequently dropped, Ivan was able to determine who was stationed on this base, what it was they were doing, and who could assist in their cause. As it turned out, Michael Arcadiev, a.k.a. Misha, was present this morning, and he would be conducting affairs.

"Which Misha? You mean the one who was in our squad?" Boaz asked.

"Uh-huh."

"I thought he was in jail."

"According to the law, he still is. And make sure you lock up our ride."

Having left behind the bulk of their armaments, they approached the tall building, which was fronted with a stone colonnade. Above it rose a brutalist tower, like some prison erected by Greeks. Fastened along one of the portico's plinths was a shiny brass plaque that said MINISTRY OF CULTURE in English. Boaz wasn't sure what that meant. "You think they got any food in this shindig?"

"I doubt it," said Ivan.

"Maybe we should order a pizza." They had done that one time at a pillbox.

Between two columns, a rose-haired M.P. with an ankle-length skirt and a Galil on her back was guarding a man in a chair. His face was covered in flannelette, his hands tightly bound, though he didn't seem to mind his estate.

Inside the lobby, several men carried planks. They wore handguns alongside their toolbelts—civilians. By the elevator shafts, a party of Ethiopian corporals was sliding a fridge, debating which route they should take. Someone suggested the stairs. Beyond them, pink light skittered down through the half-shattered panes, and a water fountain bubbled out soot.

Boaz looked out at the wreckage. Ivan kept dialing his phone. "*Blyad*."

"So where is he?" asked Boaz as Ivan hung up.

"Well, that's the problem. No one is entirely sure."

Finally, Ivan received a short text: "4-basement. Knock twice. Come alone."

The men took the stairs. There was dogshit everywhere. Some of it might have been human. The smell was near-fatal.

The staircase led down past three lower levels and stopped at a high voltage door.

"What is this?" Boaz asked.

"I don't know. But make sure you stay at my side." Ivan knocked twice. No one answered. He fastened the clip on his gun. Then he pushed on the door, and the giant hinge bellowed and creaked. Inside, they heard a soft whimpering. There were lights overhead—small, grainy, green ones, as if strung on lit Christmas tree branches. The space inside was indeterminate, glowing.

As his eyes readjusted, Ivan thought it looked like any cubicled office, except there were copper wires dangling from ceiling to floor and metal shelves toppled on desks. A few cubicles leaned in the center, and electrical cages ran along the walls to the back. Before them lay coffee cups, tuna cans, coats, a chess set without any pieces, a Glock, and a couple of soldiers sprawled on the floor, unconscious and reeking of drink.

Towards the back, they heard tapping, which slowly drew closer. A small figure emerged with a cane. He was wearing khaki fatigues and a linen neck scarf and carrying a bamboo rod.

"My brothers," Misha rasped.

The men hadn't seen him since August, when Misha claimed to have injured his knee during training on some kind of run with the stretcher, which Ivan found ironic, because Misha wasn't even carrying the stretcher at the time; he was riding atop it, as Misha always did. But he spent the next month-and-a-half undergoing some kind of treatment before he withdrew from their squad. He shook Boaz's hand and gave Ivan a cologne-scented hug.

Boaz asked him how his recovery was going.

"It's fine." Misha smiled. He wore a felt red beret, which was rakishly cocked and might well have been Soviet-era. "It's so nice to see you. Tell me, what can I do for my pals?"

"Well," Ivan said. "We thought we might see a few movies this morning."

"Yes, let's see what we can do here. Come in."

As they stumbled towards the back, stepping over pillows and Styrofoam cots, Ivan noticed the walled iron cages. There were glass dials inside them, generators, tubes, an Arab boy wrapped in a blanket, leaning, perpendicular columns, pink insular foam, brass padlocks and cartons of fruit.

Behind Ivan, Boaz kept grabbing his crotch. He spat out a wad, and he sighed.

"You know, I kind of miss our old days there, back in the sand, in the shit," Misha said. Ivan wasn't sure if he was kidding. "How's everyone in Aleph?"

"They're fine," Ivan said.

"You should tell them I miss them."

"Okay."

Behind them, Boaz still studied the cage, where the Arab was licking a peach.

"How's it going down at Rachel's?"

"It's shit," Ivan said.

"Yeah, I heard about Yossi. That's awful," Misha said. "And I'm sorry I couldn't get to the funeral yesterday. I've been having a few gripes with the law."

Ivan wondered if he slept in this dungeon. Unlikely. During training, Misha was rumored to spend whole nights off of base while other men slept there or guarded. Nobody knew where he went. His father had a compound outside Caesarea and was said to keep a condo in Paris. He also owned sports teams and was alleged to run guns, for which he'd been indicted in Europe.

Misha stopped before a bright corner office. "Please, come in."

245

Inside, hanging on the wall in a gilded glass frame was a portrait of the Palestinian leader, markered with horns and red fangs. On the floor there were speakers, loose cables and cords, television sets and equipment. Beside them, a young corporal sat typing, hunched before a console with bays. He didn't look up as they entered.

"So," Misha said as he stooped beside the soldier, placing his hands on his crown. "You said you wanted to see a movie this morning. I think we can have that arranged. Is there anything in particular you'd like?"

"We had a few titles in mind," said Ivan, extending the case with the discs. "Boaz, isn't that right?"

Boaz flipped through the sleeves and pulled out a disc that was marked.

"What is it?" Misha asked.

"Oh, just something our Lieutenant will like."

The writing was squiggly and hard to make out. It said, Seeds of Peace, barely, in English, though Ivan wasn't sure what this meant. "You think you'll be able to show this?"

"The only question," said Misha, "is where." He handed the disc to his younger assistant and flashed a bright, gold-plated grin.

Twenty minutes later, the soldiers were seated in a conference room on the top floor. They could see the Kinneret, the Dead Sea, and the coast, all shrouded in a somnolent fog. Inside, Misha presided from the head of a lacquered oak table while dozens looked on from their chairs. Most men were smoking. All appeared new, mainly from ex-Soviet republics. Their shoulders bore the tags of the Intelligence Corps. Maybe half of them served in the army.

Ivan sat down in a Plexiglass chair with adjustable handles

and settings. On the floor lay some packets of Camels and chew, Chimay Rouge bottles, and kvass. About three-dozen weapons were stacked against the wall, including a beautifully-inlaid, birchwood-stocked, antique Mosin-Nagant.

"So," Misha announced, "I want to thank you all for coming today. It's such a pleasure to have you with us. Most of you I know already, but I'd like to make a few introductions." He was speaking in Russian, though Boaz didn't seem to mind. Someone had passed him a joint and a bag of lime *Bissli*, and he gladly leaned back in his chair.

"Okay," Misha said, having introduced his friends and packed a corncob pipe. "As some of you know, we'll be watching a movie, a little gift for our neighbors outside." He dipped his beret, struck a wood match, and exhaled a slow, lingering cloud. "I'd also like to thank the Palestinian Ministry, some of whom are seated downstairs, along with our resourceful technical crew. Where would we be without them?" Outside in the hall, a dozen men ran, most wearing headsets and shouting. "As far as I know, we'll be screening this live. We're aiming for the whole Middle East." Then he pointed to the wall, where a tiny pink bulb was projecting. "When that thing goes on, it means we're on air. We're tracking down three different stations."

A white screen descended near the front of the room. Around them, the shades had been drawn. A projector above started scattering lights, a crackling spectrum of colors. Then the conference room dimmed, minus the screen and the flickering glow of a pipe.

"What's he saying?" Boaz asked Ivan.

"Truthfully, I'm not really sure."

Then a news program appeared on the wall-mounted screen. It was al-Jazeera, or some Arab channel. Two headscarves were talking live in Qattar. Misha looked on at them, puzzled.

The news showed some pictures of Humvees and tanks, armored Jeeps rolling into Ramallah. Then there were scenes of a mob in a street. They were hoisting up legs through a window. "What the hell is this?" Misha yapped in his phone.

"Two soldiers got killed here last evening," said someone.

"I am aware of what happened. Would somebody please change the channel?"

Earnestly, Ivan studied the screen, trying to make out what had happened. Two reservists, it seemed, had come here from Beit El, gotten stranded with their Jeep and then lynched. Beside him, Boaz didn't say a word, as if he didn't quite get what had happened.

"It's disgusting," said Misha. "These people are beasts. Why we don't bomb the whole town, I d—"

Then the news flicked off. The screen went blank. "Okay," said Misha. "We're rolling." On the wall in the corner, the bulb glimmered red, and a dozen men watched the projection.

A test screen went on, followed by codes and some kind of industry warning. Ivan wasn't sure what he was looking at next. The screen showed more crackling dots.

Then it sounded like water. He could make out a pipe and the shiny, white tiles of a shower. A small, tan arm extended across the screen and reached for a brass-plated handle. The camera was blurry. It slowly panned out, and the back of a girl was in focus.

A couple guys hooted or clapped in delight. Boaz kept puffing his joint.

They couldn't see the face of the girl on the screen, but her butt cheeks were tawny and dimpled. She was stroking her hair with her hands at her side as the water rushed down from her shoulders.

"*Cyka*," said Ivan. "This thing is on air?"

"Don't know," Misha said. "Maybe you could go ask the

neighbors."

Outside, they heard shooting, but it wasn't too loud—just itinerant cracks from the square. The whole building seemed silent and glaringly still. Misha leaned in to the table. He whispered, "We'll see what happens."

Nobody moved. Above them, the porno continued. The screen showed a picture of a full-bosomed girl staring straight at the camera. She seemed to be lost in contemplative gaze, as if she knew they were watching.

"She isn't—" asked Misha.

"She is," Boaz said. Then the girl began singing aloud. She was chanting an Egyptian or Lebanese tune. Umm Kulthum, maybe, or Fairuz. She looked at the camera with dark, solid eyes and her hands firmly fixed on her hips. Then abruptly she turned and looked to the side, where a soldier was waiting in *Bet* pants.

"You're kidding," said Ivan.

The men started howling and pounding their fists, clanking cups on the table.

"You've got to be joking." Ivan was shocked. He studied this man in the shower. It wasn't his Lieutenant, but it might as well have been. He was bare-chested, blue-eyed, and stringy.

"*Ween-ha hawiyye?*" the young soldier asked—"Where's your I.D. card?" in Arabic.

"Oh my, oh my," she responded in Hebrew. "I forgot it. What can I do?"

"*Iftaa hablusa. Enah laazem bodek.*" In English: "Lift up your dress. I'll have to do an inspection."

"By God," she exclaimed. "That's forbidden."

He traipsed through the shower and reached for her hand. Then the two of them kissed in the water. She undid his buckle, loosened his belt, and slid down his pants to his knees. He was barefoot, erect, and massively endowed. A grim silence fell over the table.

Around Ivan dozens, possibly more, sat gazing straight up at the screen. The room had grown darker, smoky and hot, as he slowly leaned back in discomfort. He wasn't sure what he witnessed, if this broadcast was real, if they were live and on-tape in Ramallah, or if anyone else could see this outside, or what he might say to his mother.

Above him the screen showed two dripping figures massaging and locking their chests. He was grabbing her thighs, her stomach and hips, probing her depths with his fingers.

Misha leaned back and puffed on his pipe. "Well, it looks like she ain't got it on her."

Ivan got up then and walked through the room as the other men watched from the table. He picked up his weapon and went for a walk, stepping over ash heaps and bottles. Outside in the hall, the air filtered through, and soldiers stood gazing at stations. They all showed the same thing: two bodies awash, floating and fucking and feeling.

Soon Boaz came out and tromped down the hall, joining him at the exit. "What are you doing?"

"I'm going downstairs."

"You don't want to stay?"

"No, not really."

"You didn't like what we showed?"

"I did," Ivan said. "I'm just a little freaked by that lynching."

"What lynching?"

Downstairs in the lobby, hazed light trickled in, illuminating cracks in the panes. The pavement outside was shattered and wet, and someone had turned on the hoses. A few steaming *Merkavim* were barreling west, blinking and covered with tarps.

"Do you want to go back now?"

"I guess," Boaz said. "Assuming our truck is still here."

They backed through the lot and across the scraped trees, over the plains of Ramallah. They stopped along the way at the Qalandia Checkpoint, passing by troop trucks and columns. And as they scudded through the rain, the wet, passing beamed lights, the large trailer trucks, tractors, and Humvees, who did they see, but a man on the road, walking all alone with a duffel.

"Who is that?" asked Boaz.

"That isn't Shaul?"

"Holy shit. That's our commander. That's him."

"*Blyad.*"

"Well, I'll be damned. What's he doing out here?"

"And what's with the foam on his shirt?"

For the men of Aleph Co., the invasion of the al-Aida Refugee Camp was but one in a series of mishaps, inevitable perhaps, much like their consignments in life. How many of them were drafted or had chosen to enlist is equally hard to say. Certainly, of the 64 recruits who remained in their company, all of them had chosen to fight in some form or another, even Ivan, as he crouched beside his bunk in the barracks of the Rachel's Tomb base.

It was three in the morning on Tuesday, the air a wet soup with the sneezing and congestion of men. Others were stirring, though he was the only one full-awake. He was hugging his chest now, padding his arms, desperately trying not to sleep. *I'm not going,* he told himself. *There's no fucking way.*

He stumbled to the bathroom, took out the last of his joint, and examined his face in the flecked, rusting web of the mirror. *I am no different than any of these men. But this is my life, and my breath.* He snapped his lighter, ignited the roach, then stuffed the thing out in the sink. He knew he couldn't smoke here. At least not that. And he didn't want to fall back asleep.

He kept on pacing down the dark aisle, examining men in their crypts. Yossi's was empty. His pillow remained, and a dusty worn sheet, and his watch.

"Look, Ivan, we're going."

"I know."

"You ready?" Uri asked him.

"I guess."

They boarded the *Bardehlas*. It was an armored green truck with the hull of a tank and a hatch that slanted down like a drawbridge. They had waited by the blocks, sipping cups of black Turkish. Now the engine was ready.

Ivan went first, followed by Uri. Boaz was already in there. He had been arguing with Shaul from inside of the truck, something about not wearing a seatbelt. What Shaul didn't say, and Ivan well knew, is there was a reason they didn't have seatbelts: if the vehicle flipped, or worse yet, blew, they had seconds to get out of the rear hull.

A guy that Ivan knew—they had emigrated together, and their mothers had been friends in St. Petersburg—had died down in Gaza early last June after driving over one of the landmines. They identified him by the shape of his teeth. Arabs ran off with his helmet.

Ivan unlooped the gun from his neck and sealed up the flap on his vest. Then he walked up the plank and lowered his head beneath the black rubber pads of the portal. It was hot in the *Bardehlas*, too hot to breathe, even with air from the open hatch streaming.

As Ivan plopped himself down on the hard-cushioned bench, clanking his kneepad with Boaz's, he thought about fleeing or shooting his foot. Then Shaul announced from the front:

"Everyone down. We're moving in two, so get ready."

Smoke billowed out from the back of the truck, dissolving in plumes by the spotlights. The walls began beeping and raising their hatch, collecting the rails of the platform: two greased, metal bars that collapsed into coils. He could feel the slow sweat on his shoulder. It was hot in the truck now. Too dark to see. But he could hear all the soldiers around him: the breath from their faces, their dark, muted stares, the clicking of heels and thin helmets, tapping. And he could smell their rank bodies, their fungus and lice and the fear in their veins and their filtered Time Lights.

Past the slow-raising hatch, he could see a small pack of men standing round with tefillin. They were bobbing in prayer shawls, shutting their eyes, their gilt prayerbooks cupped like grenades to their chests. Then the metal door bolted and locked into place, blocking out night and the engines. Turning bolts clicked and clamped in the door. Lights flickered on in the ceiling.

"We're moving," Shaul told them. "Everyone down. Make sure you grab something solid."

"How long we out?" somebody asked.

"Don't know," Shaul grumbled. "Probably the rest of our lives."

The engine blocks rumbled their sputtering noise. Through the walls, it sounded like digging. Static bleeped up from the front of the truck. Beside Ivan, Boaz was singing:

As long as a soul yearns deep in the heart,
And an eye is cast eastward to Zion,
Our hope is not lost, 2,000 years' hope,
For we shall be freemen in Zion.

It was the national anthem that Boaz was singing. They had heard it this week at the graves. For three days it had echoed inside Ivan's head, and now in this truck while departing.

Twenty minutes later, he was gripping the steel bench, his water bottles sloshing behind him. The truck was in full gear, grinding its noise. Ivan reached for the strap in the ceiling. He could barely make out the eight figures around him, whose shapes gently merged with the walls. And the walls were smooth metal: a cream-colored green, which vibrated slowly around him. Above him, rubber tubes ran the full length of the ceiling, pumping the compartment with oxygen. Then a red light went on in the caged bulb above, illuminating helmets and shoulders, and thinly coiled wires that jutted from bars, tacked with clear hooks to the ceiling. Inside the rear corner: two dangling chains that hitched up the slots for the stretchers. But the stretchers weren't on them. They were on Shibli's back, or tucked underneath with the .50.

Beside him, Boaz kept blaring his anthem, even louder than he had "Instant Karma!" The other guys murmured or told him to stop. His manpack kept clanking behind him. And Boaz kept moving his hands back and forth, pushing the cream-colored ceiling. It looked a bit brighter now beside the red bulb, like the smooth-polished walls of a coffin, or test-tube.

"Ivan," said Boaz, halting his singing. "You got any Acamol? My fucking head's about to come off."

Ivan went to work finding the pills in his pouch. "You want anything else?" he snickered.

"Ivan, shut up," Shaul called back. "I don't want to hear any talking." Shaul was reading a map in the front, calling out signals to Battalion HQ. "Another thing, Boaz, enough of that crap. If you're gonna sing a song, at least you could pick something decent."

Boaz looked down at his boots on the ground. He kept

shuffling his hands and his feet. He turned to face Ivan with bright, steady eyes, and he continued singing his anthem.

To his left, Uri kept chanting his prayers, a little bit softer than Boaz. Earlier Boaz had asked him what it was. Uri said that it came from the Bible. It was from the Book of Ezekiel, a mystical verse, where the prophet was raising an army. It was the army of Israel, at the end of all days, when he was casting up the dead from their graves.

And as I spoke then, there was a noise, and I could behold all these bones and their shaking. And these bones came together, one to the next, I could see all the sinews upon them, and flesh, and there was fresh skin on all of these bones, but no voices or breath from within them.

Ivan hunched forward and reached in his vestpack, parting his saline and tubes. He dug his hand in the pocket and pulled out a cross, sliding it up by its chain. Then he leaned down and kissed the cool cross, feeling its smear on his lips. It was a small silver trinket his father once gave him. He checked to see nobody saw it.

Ten minutes later, it was black in the truck. Ivan was gripping the rope-cord above. His rifle kept bouncing up between his legs and clacking the shears in his vestpack. Then his helmet shot up. His head hit the wall. "Sorry," someone yelled from the front. They must have hit a bump or curve in the street. Ivan felt like he was riding a boat now—like that dinghy he'd taken with his father on the lake when they went fishing up north beside Finland. Ivan had only been ten at the time, and his hands, he remembered, got chafed. And he remembered riding back in the small, jerking boat while his father was drinking a beer. The sun had long set, and the moon hit the waves, and he remembered the scrape of the oars, and what his father had said as he tied up the cleat: "Vanya, the tumor is spreading."

Two years later, his father was dead, and Ivan took off with his mother. Her family was Jewish. She'd never been, but it was enough to get permission and flights. So they arrived in Rishon, and she worked as a baker, even though she'd once been a chemist. And she didn't mind it. Their family was safe, and she'd found a new man, whom she loved.

Even Ivan didn't mind it. He liked being here. He liked the sharp rise in his stomach. He liked the way the metal bars glistened with oil as they pulled up the plank to the *Bardehlas*, beeping.

It was almost like a giant beer can he was in. He could smell all the liquors around him. Shaul had been drinking before they got on. Ivan saw him outside with the driver. The driver, he knew, was an American Jew. He said he had come for the service. He and Shaul had been talking out back. The American, Ivan knew, was a writer. He had seen the man earlier, outside with his flask, jotting things down in his notebook. Ivan asked him what he was doing. "Nothing," he'd replied. "I'm defending the nation of Israel."

Inside the front seat now, Shaul was speaking. He could hear him talking into his phone. "No," Shaul was saying. "I don't give a shit. There's no reason to make me a sculpture."

Ivan didn't know what his commander was saying, if his girlfriend was some kind of artist. Earlier, he had overheard him talking again when they were about to depart for the mission. Shaul was talking to the driver. Shaul said he was mad, that he couldn't even talk to his parents. When Ivan had heard that, he looked at his hands, and he thought about the boat and his father.

Now he thought of his mother, the way she made bread. How she kneaded it down with her knuckles, smudging the warm dough and watching it rise, the gaseous blue light in the oven.

Above his own helmet, Ivan saw light—the sizzling flame of the light bulb. On its checkered red glass, a tiny black bug was zapping its way through the caging. A beetle, he thought, or some spindly black roach, an insect that was trapped on the mission. It was destined to serve here and fight in this war and melt in this place with the soldiers.

He didn't hear shooting, no distant whine, no crash or soft thud of the mortars. He didn't hear bomb bits, no blasting white shells, no screams or dark cries from the city. But Ivan heard laughing. It was coming from the front. The driver was clutching the gearshift. Tears streamed down from the side of his face. Shaul put a hand on his shoulder.

ACKNOWLEDGEMENTS

Portions of this novel first appeared in different forms in *Tampa Review*, *Shenandoah*, *Anamesa*, *The Loudest Voice Anthology* (Figueroa, 2010), and *Birmingham Arts Journal*. The excerpted news article, "Palestinians Complain Israelis Broadcasting Porn from Captured TV Stations," is adapted from an article of that title by Agence France-Presse.

Many thanks to those who provided input on this manuscript, including Cris Mazza, Aimee Bender, T. C. Boyle, Dana Johnson, Joseph Boone, David Treuer, Alexis Landau, Bryan Hurt, Stephan Clark, Jessica Piazza, Dan Gross, Michael Busk, Suraj Shankar, Thomas Winningham, Dan Green, and Sergei Tsimberov, along with friends and colleagues at the Universities of Illinois-Chicago, Southern California, and Minnesota Duluth; Kim Kolbe, Danielle Isaiah, and the staff of New Issues; Dana Krivogorsky, Evan Brier, and Krista Twu; Jenny Bernstein and Jim Lindstrom; my parents, Nancy and Gene Bernstein; my children, Sarah, Naomi, and Abram; and most of all my wife, Dina, who made this book possible.

J. A. Bernstein is the author of a forthcoming story collection, *Stick-Light* (Eyewear) and a forthcoming chapbook, *Desert Castles* (Southern Indiana Review), which won the Wilhelmus Award. His work has appeared in *Boston Review*, *Kenyon Review* Online, *Chicago Quarterly Review*, and other journals. His honors include the Hackney Novel Prize, a Fulbright Scholarship, and the Gunyon Prize at *Crab Orchard Review*. A Chicago-native, he teaches in the Center for Writers at the University of Southern Mississippi.

writingwar.com